THE FINAL TABOO

A new novel
by
Dan Wasserman

To my late grandmother Marion, who after she moved into the retirement home, often said, "You kids have no idea what goes on in this place!"

"Sex among the elderly...It goes on until we die."

William Masters from *The Life and Times of William Masters and Virginia Johnson*, 2010

ta·boo

adjective \tə-ˈbü, ta-\
: banned on grounds of morality or taste <the subject is *taboo*>

Source: http://www.merriam-webster.com/dictionary/taboo *The Final Taboo* is a work of fiction. Names, characters, places and incidents are the products of the author's imagination or are used fictitiously. Any resemblance to actual events, locales or persons, living or dead, is entirely coincidental.

Prologue

Paul and Mei Ling Chen were hustled from their magnificent home at gunpoint into a waiting limo with extremely dark tinted glass. The car immediately made its way east to Bayview Avenue, turned right and then executed a sharp left on Stouffville Road, eventually heading south on Highway 404. They exited at 16th Avenue, making it to Buttonville Airport in a mere fifteen minutes. On arrival they were waived through the simple security checkpoint ultimately pulling up to the largest executive jet on the tarmac. The plane's door was open and its air-stairs had already descended down to the pavement.

The thug facing Mei Ling in the jump-seat waived his Glock, indicating they were both to get out and enter the aircraft. As soon as the couple was standing beside the car, the other hit-man leaned over and cut the plasti-cuffs from both of their wrists. Not a word was spoken the whole time.

Once aboard, the door immediately closed and the engines were started. Paul checked the pantry as he walked towards one of the ultra-plush seats and saw that it was well stocked with sandwiches and sodas. Any liquor that had once been in the bar had been completely removed.

They settled into the extremely cozy seats and strapped themselves in. At this point the pilot's voice came over the intercom and said, "Folks this is going to be a very long trip with no stops. I suggest you make yourselves as comfortable as possible. You will not see any of us from up front, and we have been instructed not to be in contact again until immediately before landing. There is food in the pantry, which you will have to serve yourselves since there is no wait staff aboard."

With that Mei Ling leaned over and said to Chen, "Husband, this is our goodbye."

And with that a single tear rolled down her cheek.

BOOK ONE – THE EARLY YEARS

Joseph's Story

Chapter 1

May, 1995

Joseph was ecstatic. High school was finally over and he had the whole summer ahead of him before college started.

He was still recovering from his experience in Italy. Never before in his life had he been personally responsible for the potential demise of another human being. How close he came to causing a person's death not only gave him pause, but made him reflect on his father.

He'd always idolized the man in spite of his mercurial temper and rabid abhorrence of Joseph's using any form of drug. Some of this was because he suspected his dad had a long history supplying recreational medicinals to people of all ages. As well, he wondered how many times the man he loved had actually killed people. There was ample evidence of this, and the ease with which he had suggested his son harm someone was chilling.

The fact that a girl he hardly knew was never going to walk again, solely because of what he did to her in the Cinque Terre at the behest of his father, was reason enough to hate the man. But that wasn't Joseph's nature and in spite of everything, he still adored the man.

Anyhow, today was not the time for such dark thoughts. Fun loomed for the next eight weeks and he was determined to make the most of it.

Upon hearing the front door close, Louie, his father's most trusted employee and oldest friend, glided silently into the living room.

"Joseph, please come in here and sit down," the old man said.

"Hi Louie, I didn't see you over there."

Casting a glance towards the man, Joseph thought he looked somewhat haggard and definitely upset. "Louie, what's wrong?"

At that point tears started flowing heavily down Louie's nearly gaunt cheeks and he said in a broken voice, "I have some very bad news to tell you."

Joseph recoiled saying, "What's wrong? What's happened?"

"Your parents are gone," he blurted out.

"Gone where?"

"Just gone. You're old enough to understand."

"But I don't understand. They were both here this morning before I left for class. We actually had breakfast together and they wished me a great last day of high school!"

"That was then. This is now."

"What do you mean?"

"Around noon, some very bad men showed up. Your father had done business with them in the past and he let them in. What he didn't realize was the three of them had guns and drew them as soon as they were inside. They called me out of my office and told me to stay put. However, they put plastic handcuffs on your parents and took them away. The leader's parting words were "Louie, Chen's uncle told us to tell you that they will not be returning. You are to take care of the young Chen and see no harm comes to him. Money and the house will be left for his upbringing, but his parents will not be back.

"Joseph, by now they are dead. I do not know how they died, but be assured they ARE dead. I am so sorry."

Joseph was in shock.

How could this happen? He knew his father had some unsavory contacts. He also knew the man did things that may not have been legal. But, he was still his father.

Also, what did this have to do with his mother?

This was too much to take in all at once. How was he to cope? What did Louie mean by having money to take care of him?

Chen was almost eighteen and soon would no longer be a minor. But, he was still a kid in many ways. Yes, college loomed but his emotions were little more than a mix of child-like responses to hormone-infused stimuli. He broke down completely.

After a while both of them started to compose themselves and it was Joseph who first shifted gears.

"I take it there will be no funeral," was his opening remark.

"Yes, and I'm sorry, but we can't even report them missing," Louie replied.

"So what do we tell our neighbors, dad's business acquaintances, our friends, everyone?"

"Let's start with they went on an unexpected trip. After an appropriate amount of time, maybe a month or so, we can see if there's a natural disaster where in we can claim they perished. Or, if their bodies show up during that time, we can respond to the condition in which they are found. The last thing we can do is involve the police."

"But, I thought dad had friends on the force."

"I wouldn't exactly call them friends. They could help out in certain circumstances. And, they were well paid. But in this case they would be put into a compromising position and that would be bad for all of us.

"As you may know, your parents set me up as your legal guardian a long time ago. Since you only have mere months to your eighteenth birthday that is basically irrelevant. But, the critical period is the next couple of months and during that time you're still a minor. At this point that is probably a good thing since I can take care of issues as they come up and deflect things you would still be ill equipped to handle."

"Louie, I have always considered you more of a relative than my dad's right hand man. But, I have to ask you a question. What happens to dad's business interests now that he's gone?"

"You were always perceptive and that is an excellent question. The honest answer is there are no interests."

"Dad was very wealthy, how can there be no interests?"

"His wealth was dependent on those who invested in his ventures. Those are the same people who took your parents. On their removal, everything reverts back to the investors. Whether it is through legal channels or just by fiat, they now own everything."

"That can't be!"

"Yes, as I said, except for the house and a trust fund that was set up for your benefit, nothing else exists. Or, if it technically exists, it won't in very short order."

"You can't be serious."

"As the expression goes, I'm as serious as a heart attack.

"However, one thing your dad insisted on was that in addition to the trust fund, which will cover your living expenses, your education until the age of thirty, and many incidentals, it also covers me."

"Can I ask how much money that represents?"

"Since you are almost eighteen and the age where the first dispersal would be made, I can tell you it is well in the seven figures, almost eight. However, the more important point is that there is no requirement to prove your parents are deceased to access the funds. They only have to be unaccounted for, for a period of four weeks. And, in the meantime I have a separate bank account in my name that will cover all our immediate needs. The only change will be that I will permanently move into the guest area in the basement."

"Louie, would you mind if I called you Uncle Louie? I have no other relatives in this country and as I said I've always considered you to be my blood."

"I would be honored."

The two of them embraced until the emotion passed.

Chapter 2

August 1995

The summer flew by quickly and in spite of the deep pain at its beginning, both Joseph and Louie started to feel the weight actually dissipate around the time Joseph left for college, towards the end of August.

By then Louie was able to use his vast resources to create a story, which somehow was augmented by physical proof, that the Chens had been lost in the massive floods that hit China during July. Specific dates of their departure from Canada, flight manifests, hotel receipts, and various other flotsam were found to support that they had taken an extensive trip to mainland China. There they were caught in one of the floods that plagued the country over the summer and perished along with countless others.

Why they had traveled on such short notice was never discussed. But the evidence provided sufficient proof for Joseph and Louie to be able to hold a small memorial service. This included a number of past business acquaintances plus their neighbors. Sadly, there were no relatives in attendance.

The physical material Louie was somehow able to come by also served to cover the real facts behind their disappearance. Surprisingly, it even helped the two men to emotionally cope with their loss.

Another outcome of his parents' apparent deaths was Joseph becoming a model nephew and student. Although he definitely went out with friends, much of his summer was spent reading the classics. He never appreciated the depth of his father's library, which was stocked with original editions of every major author of the late nineteenth and early twentieth centuries. For eight weeks he plowed through more than two-thirds of the editions and vowed that he would finish the rest by Christmas, using the copies he knew would be readily available in the school library.

Joseph was enrolled in a pre-medical program at the University of Virginia in Charlottesville, Virginia. He knew it was at least a ten hour drive from his home in Canada. Plus, he would have to add additional time to cover the issuance of a student visa when he crossed the border.

Louie engaged the same American immigration lawyer to facilitate Joseph's entry into the US that Paul Chen used to use when he was running his entertainment empire and constantly traveling to Los Angeles. Since all the documents were in order, Joseph entered the customs office at the Peace Bridge in Buffalo, NY, and left without incident, sporting a fresh F-1 visa stamp in his passport within fifteen minutes after his arrival.

From here he would take the I-90 west branch of the New York State Thruway towards Erie, PA, head down the I-79 towards the Pennsylvania Turnpike, also known as the I-76, head east until the Somerset exit and then zigzag until reaching route US-250. From that point it's a straight shot right into Charlottesville, VA.

Since universities were at the leading edge of Internet usage even at this early date, Joseph was able to register for all his classes, set up his dorm accommodations, select a meal plan and even scout out fraternities, entirely online.

He was dedicated to making the most of his undergraduate years and to put behind him the waywardness of

13

the recent past. Moreover, he figured he was just as smart as his dad and was determined not to repeat any mistakes his father made...wittingly or unwittingly.

The fact his father was drummed out of the most prestigious academic institution in Canada, at no fault of his own, but with his whole future ahead of him was never discussed within the family. That history was only known by Joseph because his mother, Mei Ling Chen, told him in strictest confidence what had happened. However, the outcome of that tragic episode is what set Paul Chen on his life's course in crime. It was only in later years that he became a respectable businessman running a billion dollar conglomerate. Yes, there were illegal aspects to his wealth, which led to his ultimate downfall, but as far as Joseph was concerned, all that was in the past and his future would never be clouded by these types of occurrences.

-o-o-o-

The first two years in college passed without incident and Joseph maintained an academic record that would have made his parents proud.

However, near the mid-point of his third year he too was nearly expelled from the school. This would have been devastating and he could picture his father flying off the handle had he known about it.

The incident started out innocently enough. He and two fraternity brothers decided to take up the offer to attend a party hosted by another frat that tended to cater more to the jock segment of the student population. After many years of drought, the basketball team that year had shown much promise and at

14

that point, was leading their division. Everyone was looking ahead to March Madness where UVA could be a top contender.

What they didn't count on was that the jock frat boys had invited a couple of sororities to a party to watch one of the out-of-town basketball games on their big screen TV. Booze, sex, some soft drugs and loud music in addition to the game on the tube was the typical mix. However, in this case the majority of those who showed up were freshmen. This meant virtually all of the attendees were well under the legal drinking age of twenty-one.

By midnight the party had gotten beyond out of hand and the police showed up. The officers were in a foul mood since they had to work while a group of spoiled brat students were able to watch the game of the season. And, they were galled that they missed seeing the school's arch rivals going down to a flaming defeat. Not only did this improve the home team's chances of getting to the "dance," but the juveniles had drunk themselves silly.

As a matter of course, the campus cops asked for I.D. and it didn't take long to see that much of the crowd were underage and well intoxicated. This led to a full roundup of all present including Joseph and his two pals.

Although Joseph was now of legal age, and definitely not drunk, that didn't matter to the cops. All they wanted was to extract a measure of revenge even if it meant charging everyone who could drink with serving liquor to a minor.

Everything was slipping in the wrong direction until Joseph's current roommate showed up at the police station. He was in his second year of law school and immediately asked if sobriety tests had been taken of the students picked up in the raid. When told no, he demanded that although the results may not be admissible in a court of law, the police would still have to be able to identify those who were inebriated versus those who weren't.

This left the officers little choice but to test everyone. However, to make his point the roommate threatened to call his father, a well-known criminal attorney back in San Francisco, if the police didn't act quickly. That would separate those who were intoxicated from the rest although the police still faced the conundrum of determining who served alcohol to whom. Unless that could be cleared up, the burgeoning lawyer claimed they should forget charging anyone with serving minors.

It took about an hour to test all those being held and more than half were released. This included Joseph who didn't even register on the breathalyzer. The same was true for his two friends, meaning they all got to sleep at home that night. However, charges were brought against the frat brothers who were not only still inebriated, but also responsible for serving the liquor to at least ten young women who were still drunk. Although the police couldn't prove they were the ones who had actually served them liquor, their punishment for hosting the party plus being drunk and disorderly ranged from sanctions to one expulsion.

Joseph, especially since he was a foreign student, dodged a major bullet.

After this episode, Joseph vowed to finish his final year of undergrad studies stone cold sober. Not only did he refuse to drink alcohol but he also wouldn't attend any student-led event where he thought liquor was likely to be sold, until the day he graduated.

Chapter 3

May 1998

Where did the four years go?

It seemed like only yesterday Joseph was driving by himself into Charlottesville for the first time. The car was loaded to the gunnels and he had butterflies in his stomach. Unlike most of his senior year classmates from high school who had at least one friend accompanying them to college, Joseph was entirely on his own. Now, he was closing this significant chapter in his life.

From the time he arrived at UVA, except for the one incident, he had dedicated himself to his studies. Yes, there were Cavalier football games in the fall, Thanksgiving and Christmas vacations back home with Uncle Louie, and spring break in Fort Lauderdale providing many memories over the period. But for Joseph, the main thing was achieving his goal. Simply put, he wanted to be able to enter a top-flight American medical school upon graduation.

Like many of his peers, Joseph wrote the MCATs in his junior year and did extremely well. He believed this was partly due to his teetotaling ways after the run-in with the college police.

It was no surprise that with such outstanding results, he was invited to a number of interviews from some of the most well respected medical schools in the USA.

Throughout each interview Joseph was circumspect, knowledgeable, and professional in demeanor. He felt they all went well, but harbored a fear he would not be accepted. So, he studied harder and worked towards ensuring a GPA of at least 4.0 by graduation. As well, he made sure he had practical experience. This included part-time jobs with the local paramedics and as a lab assistant for some of the professors who also taught in the UVA medical program.

His most harrowing experience as a volunteer paramedic was an ambulance run one Saturday afternoon. There was a construction boom taking place in town and a worker had fallen from the top level of a four storey scaffold. Everyone figured they were going to arrive to find the victim dead-on-arrival or DOA, but were pleasantly surprised to find the man very much alive.

He was impaled by a re-bar only one floor below the one from which he fell and was flat on his back three stories above the ground.

This wasn't the typical accident scene Joseph had encountered in the past. But it was the professionalism of the team that really impressed Joseph. And, what blew him away was they made sure to include him in every step of the process..

First the team secured the site around the fallen worker and brought up their gas-powered grinding saw to cut through the steel rod. Here they had to make sure the metal was cut quickly and kept as cool as possible. Joseph was charged with holding the exposed bloody length of re-bar as steady as possible while another EMS slowly poured bottle after bottle of water under the man. Finally the EMS responsible for cutting powered up the saw, worked it under the injured man as two others slightly elevated him and in one motion cut through the bar.

Once the man was free they had to lower him to the ground. For this they had called in a ladder truck that had a winch and emergency basket assembly. Since the basket was designed to hold a patient and caregiver, Joseph was assigned to ride down the three levels with the man to ensure the immobilization of the protruding steel as much as possible.

It only took a few minutes to get the patient from the site of the fall onto a gurney, which was then loaded into the ambulance. Through all this Joseph kept a cool exterior while holding the rod as steady as possible.

On arrival at the hospital, Joseph accompanied his medical charge into the emergency room. Once they had reconfirmed the man's vitals taken during the short trip from the scene, the lead trauma doctor ordered the man to the first available O.R. However, he crashed before leaving the E.R. and it was decided, once they revived him, to remove the offending steel bar right there.

Since there was no time to properly gown-up and except for releasing the bar while the patient was repeatedly being hit with the defibrillator paddles, Joseph kept a firm hold on the metal. When the time came to actually release it, Joseph was tasked with pulling up on the shaft with as smooth a motion as possible. He did this as if he'd be doing it all his life and was awarded the bar as his reward for his remarkable contribution.

The man's wounds were quickly assessed and treated, so that not only did he live, but he was released from the hospital with an excellent prognosis less than seventy-two hours after the incident.

-o-o-o-

When April finally arrived, so did the medical school acceptance letters. Joseph applied to six schools in total and was welcomed at all of them. The decision came down to staying in Charlottesville for another four years, going to Johns Hopkins, which was still quite close geographically being in nearby Baltimore, or traversing all the way to UCLA in California.

The other three were also from excellent schools, all with world-wide reputations. But, Joseph had to balance the familiar with the unknown.

He had already proved to himself that he was capable of surviving on his own. In fact, he excelled. But, medical school meant kicking it up much more than a notch. Now, he'd have to work as part of a team and compete for the crumbs the interns, residents, and attendings would grant to the grunts. In short order, Joseph heard from a number of his classmates who had been accepted and where they would be going that fall. A few were planning to stay at UVA, but most were moving elsewhere.

Joseph was unsure of how to proceed and at the last moment booked a flight back to Toronto. He needed to talk to somebody he trusted to provide honest advice and who better than Uncle Louie?

Louie met him at the arrival level of the International Airport. After Joseph cleared Canadian customs, he crushed the old man in a giant bear hug.

As time went on, the two of them became as close as if Louie was his real uncle instead of his past legal guardian and the executor of his parents' estate. He was a trusted friend and confidant.

"Uncle Louie, it's great to see you!" he exclaimed on entering the Lexus GS sedan.

"I agree, but you'll have to explain the urgency and why you felt it necessary to fly all the way back here for a weekend when we could have just as easily talked on the phone," said Louie.

"Uncle, it's really easy. I'm seeking your advice on what is proving to be a difficult decision. Which medical school I should attend?"

"I agree you have something of an embarrassment of riches by being accepted by all six to which you applied."

"That's the problem. It would be easy if I'd only had a single one, or even two that accepted me. But all six and the fact they range from coast-to-coast makes it really difficult.

"I don't know if I should just stay put in Charlottesville. That would be simple to do. I know the town; I know many of the professors I'd have as faculty, since a number of them taught both undergrads like me as well as in the medical program. I would also have a few friends with me that have already committed to UVA. But, is that the best school of the six and would I find I'm not challenged enough?"

"Those are all good questions. I have to say that I'm proud of you, not only for the multiple choices you now have (obviously because you have dedicated yourself to your studies), but primarily since you're treating this with the level of seriousness it deserves.

Let me ask you the simple question, where do you think you would like to go?"

"If I'm totally dispassionate, and also ready to re-establish myself in a completely different environment, I would choose UCLA."

"Then why don't you?"

"Uncle, I would be at least five-hours away by air and three time zones different than yours. Other than a brief trip to Los Angeles for my interview last year, I have spent less than seventy-two hours in the state of California in the past eight years. I'm also afraid of ghosts."

"You don't really mean that, do you?"

"Not in the physical sense. But in the vernacular, I know my father did a lot of business there and made some powerful enemies."

"He also made a lot of money for some people and had many as his friends. Frankly, I wouldn't let his past stand in your way. If you really want to go to medical school at UCLA, you should treat it the same in your deliberations as you would any of the other five."

"Thank you, uncle. You make things so much clearer."

"It is my pleasure. As for your school tuition and other costs, you have sufficient funds to cover attending any of those where you have been accepted. And, I mean everything, including not only tuition, but books, accommodation, transportation (both locally and for flights home should you choose the West Coast), along with any incidentals. Your trust fund has done well while you've been at school plus you've been extremely frugal at UVA."

"That's comforting and I sort of suspected that to be the case. In fact, I hadn't even considered the financial implications and it's good to know they won't be a problem."

At that point they were pulling into the driveway at the home Joseph had hardly seen over the past four years. After dropping his bags in his bedroom, Joseph met Louie on the back porch facing the lake.

This was his father's favorite spot in the whole house. The deck was attached to a five thousand square foot structure backing onto a lake that was mostly private and facing to the north. Paul Chen would take his morning coffee there, serenely watching the mist rise from the surface on most spring and summer mornings. Even in the winter, Paul would often bundle up to sit with a steaming mug of coffee, a worn duvet as a blanket, and his morning newspaper while facing the ice and snow drifts blown up by the prevailing winds.

Joseph wandered out and saw Louie sitting in his dad's old chair. What he hadn't realized was how much the deck had weathered over the years and that it badly needed a sanding plus new varnish at a minimum. It was much colder north of Toronto than the midlands of Virginia, so the two of them were wrapped in warm blankets as they again entered into the continuing deep conversation.

Louie said, "I've been thinking about what you said and as you know I am not one to make snap decisions. But, with all due respect I think you should go to UCLA."

"Why?"

"Simply put, that is where you want to go. And, the core reason for why you want to go is probably something you've subconsciously been thinking about for a long time. Perhaps since you submitted your application and definitely after your interview."

"What about the other schools?"

"I purposely asked you on the drive over here where you really wanted to go. You didn't hesitate. You didn't justify. You didn't ask about funds. You said 'UCLA.'

23

"To me that was pretty indicative of an intelligent mind working out a complex problem. No, you didn't openly state why you wanted to go there. But, that isn't the issue."

"Uncle, you were always clear-thinking and I thank you."

"No nephew, you are the clear thinker."

Chapter 4

December 2001

Except for the nearly seventy-two hours Joseph spent in L.A. for his medical school interview at UCLA, it was almost three years since he'd spent any real time in the area.

His uncle Louie had convinced him to sell his old car and fly out. He said, "You deserve a new car, possibly a convertible, and I'll ship your belongings to you so you don't have to worry about them. Unlike your undergrad years, this is more of a fresh start than an extension of your basic education."

In preparation, Joseph checked out various car dealerships on the Internet. He also used the Web to set up his accommodations. As such, on arrival at LAX, he was met by a salesman from Beverly Hills BMW holding a sign with his name on it. The salesman had purposely driven the exact model Joseph had described in their e-mail exchanges to the airport, and asked him if he wanted to drive it back to the dealership. Naturally, the answer was 'yes' and recalling the route from memory Joseph whisked the two of them to the showroom on Wilshire Boulevard.

Once there, Joseph signed the papers for the new 325 Cabriolet he'd just driven and shortly after pointed the silver beast west towards his new digs in Westwood. He'd found a small furnished bungalow for rent on Wellworth Avenue near Selby, which made it easy to walk to the UCLA medical school on most days. This meant he had the ideal car for his California down-time, whenever that happened, but could keep his exercise up by not driving to school.

According to Louie, his limited possessions would arrive in three days, so for the time being, all Joseph had was what he'd carried on-board the airplane.

School didn't start for a week giving Joseph some time to acclimate himself and enjoy the summer in La-La Land. Naturally, this included the beach, the tourist sites, and when he felt like it, cruising the Pacific Coast Highway with the top down on his new toy.

With the heavy demands of medical school rotations what he did over the three years leading up to September 11, 2001 was a blur. Classes followed by studying, followed by time in the hospital, followed by more studying left little opportunity for romance although sex was freely available. It seemed that the pressure faced by all the students was released by casual encounters.

None of these came close to the one he'd experienced years before in Italy, but neither had any of his assignations while at UVA. In the meantime, the last thing Joseph was seeking was a long term relationship since anyone he was likely to meet was just as prone to move to another city for their internship, or residency, as he was. So, whenever he had even a little down-time, his natural inclination was to head to the beach.

The sands at Santa Monica were a mere fifteen minutes away by car, but he had access to every other famous beach, stretching from Santa Barbara down to La Jolla, readily available.

That didn't mean Joseph wasn't attracted to the beauties that still flocked to L.A. for the weather, movies, or school. Many were Asian or Eurasian like Joseph and their exquisite features captivated him. Only, none of them would be able to claim him. His career came first.

Then tragedy hit.

It wasn't personal although it felt that way. America had been violated and although all four planes hit targets on the East coast, the impact was felt across the country. And, even though he was still on a foreign student visa, the fact he'd lived in the US for the past seven years meant that in many ways he felt more American than Canadian.

Immediately upon hearing the news, all the third year students were put on high alert at the UCLA Medical Center for possible local terror events and mass casualties. However, even though it turned out that Los Angeles was never a target, the impact of what had happened in New York and Washington, DC hit him hard. This was especially poignant when he thought about all the friends he had made attending UVA and who were still close to one of the "ground zeros"

Add to that the fact all aircraft across the whole continent were grounded within a little over an hour of the last tragic crash in Pennsylvania meant the skies were clear and the air suddenly still. It was an unreal time. However, that night was one that begged human comfort and Joseph was not immune.

Sitting quietly in a staff room at the hospital nursing his twelfth mug of coffee that day, Juliette Lui entered and said, "Hey Joseph, want some company?"

She too was a third year student and since arriving at UCLA they'd hardly spoken more than a couple of sentences to each other. However, they definitely knew they both existed and so did the rest of their class. It was often whispered, "If those two ever got together they'd make the most beautiful babies in the world!"

Joseph silently pointed to the coffeepot with its wicked brew and continued to stare glumly at the floor. His funk was deep and focused.

Having poured herself a mug, then adding one teaspoon of sugar and a small amount of milk, Juliette shuffled over to the couch where Joseph was sitting. Instead of moving to the extreme opposite end, she crowded his space by plopping down right next to him.

After quietly sipping for a few moments they each glanced sideways and then slowly lowered the mugs to the floor. Before he realized it Juliette was in his arms and they were passionately kissing. Joseph raised his hand to her breast and she moaned.

"This place is just too public," he gasped. "Why don't we go to one of the ready rooms?"

With this, the two of them left their mugs where they'd casually placed them on the floor and headed down the hall. Finding the first room already occupied, they stole into the second and quickly tore off each other's clothes. Lab coat, followed by scrub top, scrub bottoms and then underwear hit the floor. Immediately they fiercely embraced and Joseph carefully lowered Juliette to the cot. He was already erect and lifting her legs entered her.

Their coupling was aggressive, passionate, and over far too quickly. They then climbed into the bed and cuddled closely. Not a word was spoken. Nearly instantly, Joseph was erect again, pressing into Juliette's perfectly contoured behind. She felt him and reached behind softly stroking his penis. Then, she turned over, spread her legs and said, "Let's do it more slowly this time."

And, they did.

"I've waited three years for this to happen and it took a national tragedy for us to finally make love, let alone acknowledge each other," she said.

"I've noticed you since the first day of class and was always too afraid to approach you in fear of rejection."

"I guess we both waited too long."

-o-o-o-

From that day forward, during any down-time the two of them had that coincided, they were inseparable. They ate, studied and often slept together. At the beginning of their last year at UCLA Joseph suggested Juliette move in with him. He had the place to himself and since she already had a key, plus her lease was ending sooner than his, he felt it only made sense.

She agreed, but with some reservations. The big issue was whether this relationship could go anywhere. They were assigned to different off-site rotations for most of the remaining year. The good news is they were both specializing in oncology at their respective hospitals, which meant they'd be able to really challenge each other during their study sessions. But, it also meant the only time they would have together would be when their actual schedules aligned. That was actually a plus when it came to the two of them living together. The negative was their knowing that a separation of mere miles in L.A. would be nothing compared to the possible separation of over a thousand miles when it came to where they were each matched for their residencies.

For this rotation Juliette was working at Centinela Hospital in Ingelwood, CA, just east of Los Angeles International Airport or LAX. Joseph, though, was in the same program at the world famous Cedars Sinai Hospital in Beverly Hills. That meant their cases would likely be different with Juliette seeing mostly hard working blue-collar patients surviving off their health insurance benefits, while Joseph would likely have his share of encounters with the rich and famous, especially those in the entertainment business.

After the first few weeks at their new assignments, the differences between caseloads became extremely marked. They had hardly seen each other over the period and tonight they were both going to start a thirty-six hour break – together.

To celebrate, Joseph had made reservations at the Hamlet Garden for eight o'clock. Not only did he like the restaurant, but it was an easy walk from the house. Typically, he felt they could both benefit from the exercise since they had been driving to their respective hospitals, plus it called for a wonderful evening with temperatures in the mid-seventies.

The restaurant was at the corner of Glendon Avenue and Lindbrook Drive in Westwood Village. It was known for its wonderful guacamole and freshly prepared food. This was the upscale star in the Hamburger Hamlet chain, although the kitchen in that facility was far from pedestrian or fast food. Everything they turned out was comparable to other eateries that charged twice the price.

This was a chance for the two of them to recount their experiences to-date and compare cases. Juliette arrived home first. She showered and changed into a colorful dress. Just as she was putting the final touches to her makeup, Joseph walked in. "I'll hop into a quick shower and grab a shave," was his greeting. No kiss, no "hello," just words issued at sixty miles an hour.

Fifteen minutes later he emerged nicely cleaned up, sporting a pair of tan slacks, a button-down blue oxford shirt, and penny loafers without sox.

"Shall we go?" he asked.

Juliette put down her copy of the *New England Medical Journal* on the coffee table, stood up quickly, gave Joseph a peck on the cheek while taking his arm and said "Lead on my knight in shining armor. I'm hungry!"

It took about twenty minutes to walk to the restaurant and they were right on-time for their reservation. The hostess showed them to their table in a cozy corner and they immediately ordered two glasses of chardonnay with a side order of guacamole even before she laid down their menus.

"Would you like to hear our specials?" the hostess asked and with their agreement, she read off the list. Then she left to place their drink and appetizer order. Upon her departure the two of them started to talk at once. After a couple of seconds they both laughed and Joseph said, "You go first. But, I must say you look spectacular!"

Juliette replied, "You don't look so bad yourself."

She went on, "I actually want to talk about the head of the department. When the five of us students met him in his office the first day I couldn't help but notice the MD degree on his wall was from the University of Toronto. He also told us he has had a couple of bouts of cancer, the first nearly six years ago. In fact it was pancreatic, yet he's still alive. In fact not only is he still here, the man is a whirl-wind!"

Juliette went on about this amazing doctor for ten full minutes without interruption. In that time their drinks were delivered and silently the waiter had made a bowl of delicious mashed avocado, tomato, onion, a drizzle of olive oil, a pinch of fresh cilantro and a squeeze of lime at their tableside. In fact, the wine glasses were well-misted by the time she actually seemed to take her first breath.

At that point they clinked their glasses, toasted each other and Joseph said, "My turn now?"

Juliette blushed and said, "Of course darling. Sorry I monopolized the conversation, but it seems like we haven't said more than two words to one another each day for weeks."

"You're right, we haven't. So, please don't take any offence. You just seemed to have everything bottled up inside and it seemed to explode," Joseph said with a smile.

That was one thing she really liked about him. He had a wonderful smile and a lovely dimple.

"All I was going to say is it sounds like you've got a great role model as your chief."

"That couldn't be all you were going to say. You too have tons to tell me and I want to hear it. We've had so little time together, let's spend some of it here talking then we can make passionate love later when we get back to the house."

"Sounds like a deal to me!

"Well, before you ask," he said, "yes I have met some celebrities. I have also met somebody who knew my dad. And, contrary to my earlier concerns about any ill feelings that may exist down here about him, this guy didn't seem to harbor any."

"Why would anyone have ill feelings towards your father?"

"That's another whole story and some day I promise to tell you. But tonight, let's concentrate on good things."

"OK, tell me about your celebrities."

With that Joseph launched into his own monologue. He not only talked about the cases but also name-dropped some of the biggest Hollywood stars, who now advancing in age, also needed treatment for various cancers. Most were relatively minor in nature like non-melanoma skin lesions, but others, sadly, were being treated for truly life threatening conditions.

He also told her about some of the more important behind-the-scenes movie people he'd met, including Waldo Stone.

Waldo was the man he mentioned who'd met his dad. For most of his career he had been at Columbia Tri-Star where he retired a number of years ago as the Senior Vice President of Production. It turns out his nick-name was "The Film Doctor," since it fell to him to take a poorly produced production and turn it into an award winning candidate. As well, he'd worked on many of the James Bond movies plus the Muppet films. But, for Joseph, it was finding somebody in L.A. who had known his dad that was so amazing.

They didn't leave the restaurant until nearly eleven and feeling more than tipsy decided to take a taxi home. The ride was short and after some serious necking in the car, they were well warmed up for the lovemaking they'd put off for so long.

-o-o-o-

There was an enormous elephant creeping into the room.

33

March was here and the critical medical resident match date was fast approaching. It was just before the Ides, which not only corresponded to the death of Julius Caesar, but was the latest date for which the medical students would receive their all-important letter confirming where they would be doing their residency program.

Two months earlier Juliette and Joseph submitted their ranked order preferences to the National Resident Matching Program and made a pact not to tell each other either the specialty or hospitals they'd selected.

Now it was deeply affecting their relationship.

The chances were miniscule that come July they would be able to live in the same city, let alone undertake their next stage of training at the same hospital.

Joseph arrived home first on that fateful Thursday in March 2002 and with trepidation opened the mailbox. Yes, both envelopes were there and by tomorrow all the results would be posted online at www.nrmp.org. He knew Juliette would be arriving soon, so in spite of his anxiousness he decided it would be best if they both opened their envelopes together. Fifteen minutes later she breathlessly rushed through the door.

Her first words were, "Are they here?"

"Yes, and I waited for you to open mine."

"OK, let's do this," was her succinct reply.

The each grabbed a kitchen knife, slit the top of their respective envelopes, extracted the folded pages and looked at the results. Joseph's eyes lit up and he said, "So, where are you going to be?"

Juliette replied, "Johns Hopkins in gerontology, you?"

Joseph was stunned. He didn't reply.

"Joseph, what's wrong?" Juliette said in a hushed voice. "Why aren't you saying anything?"

He stepped forward, embraced her in a bear hug, and said "Let's get married!"

"Married, what are you talking about?"

"We're going to be in exactly the same program at the same hospital, so what are we waiting for?"

Juliette shrieked in joy.

Chapter 5

2005

Joseph loved Baltimore's inner harbor. It reminded him of the Toronto waterfront, but with fewer condominiums blocking the view of the water. Juliette liked it too, although growing up in San Francisco, she thought anything around a shoreline was great.

They were married in July, less than eight weeks after their graduation from UCLA in a small civil wedding in Los Angeles. Juliette's parents flew down and her older sister drove in from one of the LA valleys with her family. Joseph had only Louie in attendance who, now that he was becoming frail, said he doubted he could stand another five hour flight. But, he was willing to visit them in Baltimore, since it was only a little over an hour from Toronto.

The reception was held in a private room at the Kate Mantilini Restaurant in Beverly Hills on Wilshire Boulevard near Doheney Drive. Joseph had frequented it often over the past year, while working at Cedars Sinai. When senior staff wanted to impress somebody, this was the restaurant of choice. It was close to the hospital and also a well-known watering hole for celebrities. As such, a couple of the older more famous patients he treated had asked him to dinner there as a personal thank you after their release.

Their honeymoon was spent in the splendor of Sedona, Arizona. Being summer, they hit the Interstates with the top down and let their cares drift in the wind. After a few days filling up on gourmet fair and enjoying the red rocks, they headed east to Baltimore. Again, except for the odd spot of rain, the top was safely stowed in the down position.

Money wasn't an object for the young couple, although time was. They were both looking forward to starting their residencies but still needed to rent a home, buy two new cars (they decided not to keep their current one), and get acclimated with Baltimore.

Like the UCLA Medical Center, the famous hospital where they were now both going to become specialists had its own cachet. In spite of the fact that Joseph decided not to take his medical degree at that particular school when he had the chance after his undergraduate years, medical residency was a whole different matter.

Unlike Joseph, Juliette had never considered attending Johns Hopkins for her MD degree. She only applied to "UC" schools since her financial situation was much different than his. Not only was she dependent on the lower in-state tuition rates, but the ancillary costs of accommodation and travel were cost prohibitive. Now that they were married, especially with Joseph's financial resources, everything had changed.

Within days of arrival they purchased a brand new two-storey home near Pikesville, MD, one of the northwestern suburbs just off the Baltimore beltway. Even in the worst traffic, travel to the hospital downtown would rarely be more than twenty minutes door-to-door. And, they figured the house value would likely increase over the course of their years in the area since Baltimore was part of the Greater-DC technology corridor that some referred to as "Silicon Valley East."

37

The two of them settled into their routines relatively quickly. The only real downside was again their schedules were opposite each other and any time spent together had to be treasured, wherever they happened to be. If it was their own bedroom, great! If it was a ready room at the hospital, so be it. They wouldn't be the first couple to have sex under those circumstances and, unlike most of the others, they were actually married.

Time off that actually corresponded to both of their schedules happened at best once each month. For these miraculous occasions, they had decided in advance they would take advantage by taking local excursions.

Being located in Baltimore meant that within a two-hour driving radius they could explore every major Civil War battleground from Gettysburg to Richmond, VA. Going north they could see the Philadelphia sites associated with the war for American independence. And, they could always visit the numerous Smithsonian museums in Washington for free along with the many other DC tourist sites like Arlington National Cemetery, the Capitol, and Jefferson Memorial.

When they didn't want to travel they had the Baltimore Inner Harbor with all it offered just steps from the hospital. With their study load, plus limited personal time, they maximized every available second for the four years they were in the area.

Both of them appreciated the education they were getting from the excellent facilities afforded them by Johns Hopkins. They realized that much of what they learned was at the leading edge of geriatric studies. Everyone knew the American population was aging. They also understood this put enormous pressure on the cost of care. As people age their medical demands increase exponentially while their ability to pay often decreases proportionately. However, health-based expectations often outstrip the financial resources and even medical capabilities. Learning to balance these while dealing with sensitive patients was a major part of what the two young doctors had to absorb.

As well, the sheer volume of conditions, diseases, cancers, and psychological issues presented by this segment of the population taxed all the residents in the program. Moreover, this was a relatively new area of study and the two of them had to think ahead about where they would ultimately practice, and if there were other programs they should undertake to further their specialized knowledge on behalf of their future careers.

Both of them came to geriatrics as a result of their oncology rotations, realizing that as people age their likelihood of cancer either ending or at least impairing their lives increased proportionately.

-o-o-o-

In spite of their enormous study and case loads, Joseph somehow was able to add another dimension to his knowledge base. Being a Canadian he had studied both the Civil War and War of Independence from a distance. Since they were now living so close to so many of the important locations pertinent to both seminal events in American history, he made it his business to become as knowledgeable about them as humanly possible.

Juliette often chided him about his compulsiveness, but this only served to drive him harder. And, amazingly, he still out-scored her on every exam or quiz they received in the hospital.

She was not nearly as interested in these extracurricular activities as her husband, so the two of them came to an accommodation. For every two excursions Joseph planned, Juliette would get to pick the third. After all, she was born in California and like many Americans felt learning about these battles in school, backed up by a couple of field visits, was more than enough information about the topic.

However, it was only when they visited Gettysburg for the third time, it sunk in how futile the whole campaign was. The terrain was a mix of open field and rolling hills with large boulders and sharp drop-offs. The townsfolk at that time considered the whole affair an amusement, where they could sit on the sidelines and cheer on their troops as they died.

The soldiers were swathed in heavy wool uniforms with even heavier packs often weighing nearly two-thirds of their body weight. To reach Gettysburg they had marched for over a week in eighty-plus degree weather to reach the battleground. Then, they had to climb, run, charge, or march again while facing cannon shells and minie balls, both types of munition causing untold mutilation when they didn't outright kill.

If not killed immediately, there were massive deformities often resulting in amputations, which is why the battlefield doctor's most invaluable tool was invariably the bone saw. Joseph made sure the two of them visited the National Museum of Civil War Medicine in Frederick, MD. He felt that collection expanded both his general medical knowledge and his understanding the war itself.

-o-o-o-

One of their excursions that happened to have been picked by Juliette, was at the beginning of their final year of residency. En route to a late season Baltimore Orioles baseball game Joseph said, "Honey, I've been doing some research about our future options."

She didn't respond immediately since Joseph was following the amazingly coordinated hand-waving signals of the various young people directing them to a parking spot in the crammed lot next to the stadium. Once out of the car, they joined the crowd making their way into Camden Yards. The Orioles were playing the Toronto Blue Jays and as they passed a hat vendor, Juliette stopped to buy Joseph a Jays' cap while she couldn't resist buying one of the San Francisco Giants hats for herself. No matter how she tried, the Giants were and always would be her team.

They picked up hot dogs and beer on the way to their seats and settled in. Since they missed batting practice and the first pitch was only five minutes away, they concentrated on their food until the singing of the national anthem.

It was one of those games that by the end of the fourth inning, Joseph had removed his Jays cap and was now moodily watching the Orioles wipe his team's face in the dirt. With the home team up seven runs over his beloved Jays, there was no reason to keep cheering for a lost cause.

At the seventh inning stretch Juliette said, "That's a leading statement."

Being totally out of context and hours later, it took a few moments for Joseph to realize what she may be referring to. When he caught on, he said, "Yeah, I know we've both applied to a number of hospitals, but there's something else I think we may want to consider."

"What's that?"

"The PhD program at the University of Haifa."

"What, go to Israel?"

"Why not? It would give us the opportunity to not only tack on a PhD to our credentials, but we'll gain a phenomenal amount of additional training in the social aspects of aging. I'm confident that alone will help us in dealing with these types of patients as our careers progress."

"I'm not saying it's a bad idea. But, it is somewhat sudden."

"Not really. I've been thinking about this for some time and believe there are two key benefits. The first is obvious. This adds a significant dimension to our training that would expand our knowledge base into an area that is going to become ever more important as time goes on. We already know much of our patient load isn't related specifically to disease and being able to handle the broader social aspects seniors are facing would make us better doctors.

"As for the second, neither of us has ever been there and it would be great to live overseas for a few years. We're still young and could start a family on our return."

"How would we pay for it?"

"Juliette, you know that is not a problem. I have my trust fund, neither of us is carrying any student debt at this point, and there is no doubt we can sell our house for a tidy profit. Naturally, we'll rent something over there and one thing I haven't told you is

I've already started to source professional references for the two of us as part of the approval process for the program."

"Joseph, everything you've said is fine with me except for the fact you've gone behind my back."

"Honey, the first enquiry I made was just about ten days ago. Considering we haven't said more than 'hello' to each other in the past two weeks, mostly as one of us was either coming or leaving the hospital, this is the first chance I've had to actually talk to you about anything."

"You are forgiven," she said and then leaned over to kiss his cheek.

By this time the game was a foregone conclusion and they decided to leave and head home for some bedroom calisthenics.

Marilyn & Milt's Story

Chapter 6

1965

Nothing was better than taking Daddy's brand new Pontiac Bonneville convertible, putting the top down, heading for McDonalds, and blasting the Supremes through the optional back seat speaker. Marilyn knew that with this car she could out-drag almost any other vehicle on the road and, often at stop lights, made it a point to burn a definitive strip of rubber. She was a free spirit and the 1960's were proving to be the ideal decade to be a radical Jewish daughter growing up in Skokie, IL to a couple of Holocaust survivors who were now living the American dream.

Not long after the Nazi's annexed her father's homeland, he was about to enter the top university in Czechoslovakia to study law. Although the family was very much aware of the *Anschluss* that took place in 1938 that appropriated their country into the greater Germany, up to that point they'd felt relatively safe. But, on the first day of studies, when her dad entered his indoctrination class, he was told to go home and never return. At that point they frantically started to make plans to get out of Europe, but they were too late. In mere days the family was rounded up. Only her father and a great uncle who later immigrated to Israel in 1948 survived the slaughter.

As for her mother, she came from Hungary and it wasn't until 1942 that her family was sent to the camps. Nobody from her side lived through the war and it was in a DP camp that her mother met her father, fell in love, and married. Marilyn was actually born in 1947 on the ship bringing her parents to the United States.

Although her parents never spoke about their war experiences, she knew her father learned his craft in the death camps at the hands of the Germans.

He became a baker in the US. But, not just any baker, he was the largest artisan baker in the Chicago area. How that happened is that early on in the camps he realized being assigned to the bakery was an opportunity in two ways. The first was immediate...by having access to flour meant he would never starve. As for the second, feeding thousands even their meager rations meant he had to learn how to mass produce a commodity.

In the concentration camps the paramount demand was to know how to be able to serve multitudes from the minimal resources available.. However, once he was building his own business in America, knowing how to make the most profitable yet best tasting baked goods on a continuous basis, was what set him apart.

By the mid-fifties, he had contracts with many of the local bakery shops to be their primary supplier for fresh breads. Cookies, cakes, and other pastries he left up to them to bake for themselves. This gave him huge economies of scale and it wasn't long before the emerging food chains also wanted to stock his branded products.

This was the time when supermarket chains made their greatest advances in the North American suburban markets. For Marilyn's father it was a huge opportunity since by him specializing he could service both the conglomerates and even the smaller local bakeries.

Another opportunity that arose was that the already large Jewish population in the Greater-Chicago area was growing quickly with additional waves of immigrants. That meant the demand for his products at family lifecycle functions was likewise increasing. Since he grew up knowing the Jewish dietary laws, it wasn't difficult to set up a separate fully kosher division just to service the Bar and Bat Mitzvahs, weddings and even funerals. This too added to his success. So, once he could afford it, Marilyn's father made it a point to buy a brand new top-of-the-line American-made convertible every two years.

Life wasn't easy for her parents while they were building the business, but it was much better than their early years under German domination. Plus, living in Skokie with so many of Marilyn's friends also being the children of survivors meant their nuclear families were similar. The large majority did not have grandparents, few had aunts or uncles, and social gatherings were most likely to be composed of familial groups who originated from the same town in Europe as one of her parents. And like her, with only a younger brother meant families were usually composed of two or three siblings in a household.

That night, another reason Marilyn was so happy was because once she turned eighteen, she was able to get a doctor's appointment without her parents' permission. Last week she had visited Dr. Levine who gave her a prescription for the brand new invention: birth control pills. In her purse was the little round dispenser that now had ten blank spots where that many days ago there were little white pills.

Dr. Levine told her to wait a full week before having "relations." But, when she pushed, he said that after a few days she should be safe. Since it was actually longer that that, tonight she was going to put this great emancipator to the test. Bobby

46

was to meet her at McDonalds and after a Big Mac or two she was going to see just how juicy his own Big Mac was.

At nine-thirty they both drove out of the fast food emporium and ditched Bobby's three year old Ford. They left it in the closest Jewel supermarket parking lot, just a mile up Skokie Blvd. at Golf Road, since the store had already closed. He then got into her car and they drove east towards the beach. After Golf changed to Emerson, they continued on it until it met Ridge. From there it was a straight shot up to the Baha'i Temple across from the shore. Their only question was whether to park in the Temple's parking lot on its most secluded side or use the beach-side lot. They decided the Temple was just fine.

Once there Marilyn put up the convertible top and the two of them hopped into the back seat. After some passionate kisses, they quickly stripped down and the rest came naturally.

Marilyn was glad her dad ordered the premium vinyl seats. Not only were they comfortable, Bobby's Big Mac was really juicy and unlike cloth seats this made the clean up quite easy.

For the first time she could enjoy sex without any fear of becoming pregnant. Bobby wasn't her first conquest and she knew that going to college in the fall with Dr. Levine's prescription in-hand would ensure she could maximize her fun.

The only down-side was her parents refusal to let her go more than a one-day drive away from Chicago. Studying maps in her junior year at high school, she determined the farthest away she could get was the University of Buffalo in Buffalo, NY. Based on this geographical limitation, that was precisely where she applied and was accepted into their Bachelor of Arts program.

Chapter 7

1969

Marilyn decided she didn't want to go back to Chicago to work during the summer break between her junior and senior year so she landed an assistant file clerk job in a downtown Buffalo law office. She was well liked and made friends easily especially amongst her peers. The practice also hired a law student going into his last year. He was concentrating in a new field of study: environmental law.

Brian was his given name, but everyone called him Buddy. He was definitely cute, but she rarely said anything to him that wasn't related to the job.

She also befriended Martha, also known as Matty. Matty had graduated from UB the prior year and, being only a year older, they considered each other contemporaries. By the end of the first week of the summer break, the two of them were inseparable. They went everywhere together and during their down-time they often double-dated.

Moreover, they were both on the pill and considered themselves to be women of the new era. If they wanted to bed a boy, or preferably a man, they did so. However, sex was only a pastime. They were just as interested in music, art, and Canadian beer. With Fort Erie, Ontario just across the border, getting hold of the good stuff was but a short ride away. Naturally, they were equal opportunity "party girls."

Just before the middle of August, Matty showed up one morning all excited. "Marilyn, did you hear about Woodstock?" she asked breathlessly.

"No, I can't say that I have," was her reply.

"Well, it's going to take place at the end of this week and run the whole weekend. There's going to be every band imaginable playing and I guarantee it will be lots of fun. What do you think we jump in my car and spend the weekend at Woodstock?"

"I'm trying to save some money for the coming term. How much is this going to cost?"

"If we split on the gas and Thruway tolls, plus we both eat like birds, and since the admission is only $24 at the gate, we can probably get away with less than a hundred bucks each."

"Who is playing?"

"Well, if you can believe it, Joan Baez, Santana, Grateful Dead, The Who, and even Jimi Hendrix. They've lined up over thirty bands and all of them are beyond cool!"

"I'm sold, let's go! What time can we hit the road?"

"Let's see, if we can blow out of here by four on Friday and take off Monday as one of our vacation days, I know we'll probably miss some of the opening acts, but we can drive back here without any pressure."

"Great, I can't wait!"

-o-o-o-

Even leaving at exactly four that Friday afternoon, they didn't park the car until three in the morning on Saturday. Then they had to make their way through an obstacle course of every imaginable vehicle. By far the most common was the Volkswagen micro-bus, but it was apparent getting out of that mass of steel and rubber on Monday was going to be another challenge. The backlog they'd just pushed through getting into the parking area was a two-hour bump-and-grind. It was obvious from the

49

hundreds of cars abandoned on the roadside, the delay to park properly was just too much for those folks.

Whether some of these cars ran out of gas or burned out their clutches, or their drivers just gave up and decided to walk, was a mystery the girls didn't want to contemplate. All they knew is that these vehicles were going to add further pressure to everyone trying to get home on Monday.

So, they ignored the mess and made their way to the fence with their twenty-four dollars in-hand.

When they got there, nobody was present to take their money. So, they just carried their bedrolls and meager belongings with them and followed the myriad of other people working their way towards the stage. That was the beacon clearly seen and heard by all.

Santana had just wrapped up and John Sebastian was about to start. The ladies were so psyched that once they found a clear patch of ground facing the stage, they unceremoniously dropped their stuff and set themselves expectantly on a semi-soft hummock. Within minutes the first bongs started to make their way around the newly arrived. These were then followed by 40-ounce bottles of cheap liquor and even the odd can of beer. The girls forgot to pick up any personal stimulants before leaving Buffalo and by the time they got to Albany, every convenience store or rest stop they visited was completely sold out. That was their first indication this was no backwater sideshow event.

By daybreak they had heard a few more of the awesome bands, smoked some wicked weed but both passed on acid, cocaine, heroin, along with a few other intoxicants they didn't recognize. They infrequently made their way to the handful of concession stands for coffee and anything else nourishing they could find. On their way they were greeted by people sporting peace signs and in various stages of disrobement.

Saturday morning was a blur and by early afternoon the sun was streaming down on the masses. As the temperature soared, more clothing fell off. Before long many attendees had stripped to their birthday suits. With the presence of drugs and alcohol actively removing any remaining inhibitions, augmented by the free love attitude of the sixties, it wasn't long before trysts started. No matter where you looked, it didn't take much to spy one couple or another locked in a passionate embrace often rapidly escalating to noisy intercourse.

The two girls were not immune and by three o'clock that afternoon their tops were off and their panties waiting to also be removed. However, neither of them actually engaged in anything more than a kiss with some passing dude.

Around one Sunday morning, in the middle of Credence Clearwater Revival's performance, Marilyn found her eyes drooping. She didn't want to miss anything so decided to make her way back to one of the coffee concessions and get a couple of cups of the hot black liquid to perk her up. By this time most of what was being served was either burned or watered down, but either way it contained the caffeine she craved.

Marilyn carefully maneuvered around the sleeping and fucking couples on her way back to Matty. Although she was sound asleep when Marilyn returned, Marilyn felt it would be cruel to wake her friend up and decided she might as well drink both cups no matter how bad it tasted.

On taking the first sip of the terrible coffee, not only was Marilyn upset she had bought the two cups, but immediately wanted to spill both of them out. However, that meant she'd have no way to keep herself awake for the upcoming bands. So, she started to ask some of the other people sitting around her if they had any sugar to mollify the bitter taste. One of them winked and said "sure." He then gave her two cubes and she dropped them both into the cup she was currently drinking.

It took about five minutes, but suddenly she thought the edges of her vision had started to pulse with all the colors of the visible spectrum. Then the music appeared to take on a shape. This was followed by the face of the guy who had given her the sugar looming large in front of her eyes virtually leering into her mind.

She couldn't quite make out what he was saying, but he looked really nice to him. The next thing she knew, or thought perhaps later recalled, was stroking his penis. Then there were two penises, or was it four? This went on for some time and it all felt good. In fact, it felt better than good. There were the colors, the music, and some warm body parts making her feel better than she could ever remember.

At some point she felt a penis enter her. Who it belonged to she didn't know or really care, but after a while it started to feel not so good. In fact, the colors started to swirl faster and faster until they all blended together and before long turned shades of black. Not grey, but black.

That was the last thing she remembered until she felt an annoying dripping on her face. Groggily Marilyn awoke to find the enormous field nearly clear and the stage partially dismantled.

52

Matty was nowhere to be seen and the only clear sounds were of the roadies yelling instructions to each other. Looking behind her towards the parking area, she saw it too was almost empty.

She also realized she was naked and immediately comprehended three things; first it was now Monday and she had no actual recollection at all of what took place on Sunday. Second, it must have rained at some point since she had conked out, so the run-off dripping from the trees must have been what woke her up. And third, she had no visible way to get back to Buffalo.

The good news was that her body actually sheltered her clothes from the rain. So except for being dirty and damp they were wearable. However, her purse was gone along with all her money. But, on putting on her jeans and adjusting the pockets, she felt the twenty-four dollars that she didn't have to pay at the gate on arrival. This would more than cover a bus ticket to Buffalo as long as she could thumb a ride into the town of Woodstock. Knowing this spurred her into running as fast as she could to try to flag down one of the last departing cars.

-o-o-o-

Tuesday morning Marilyn received a warm greeting from everyone at work but Matty. They all wanted to know about her experiences at what was now being billed as the greatest rock event in history. Matty couldn't have cared less. She had already told her tales of hearing all the great bands, the freely available drugs and wild orgies.

However, after a couple of days Marilyn noticed a thawing in Matty's demeanor and later that morning they agreed to go to lunch for the first time in almost a week.

53

"What the hell got into that stupid mind of yours?" were the first words out of Matty's mouth once they were seated.

"Frankly, I haven't a clue. The last thing I remember clearly is asking those cute guys sitting next to us if anyone had some sugar for the terrible coffee I had just bought.

"You were sound asleep and I decided not to wake you. So, I went down to the concession trucks on my own and got a couple of cups to keep awake. The coffee was disgusting and I seriously thought of spilling it out. It was probably made hours before I bought it and warmed so many times it was beyond burned. Stupid me I needed to put something in it just to get it past my throat. Which is why I asked if the guys had some sugar.

"What I now think is the sugar cubes were spiked with acid. The first part of the trip was awesome, but it deteriorated into a horror show and then I passed out. At least I believe I blacked out. Who knows? The next thing I knew for sure was it now was Monday morning. There water was dripping into my eyes and you were gone along with just about everyone else. On top of that I had the sum total of twenty-four dollars in my pocket courtesy of the unexpected free admission."

"Shit, you really were screwed."

"The problem is I don't know who, how, or how many times that's true."

After that their discussion flowed on to other topics of interest. It was just like old times.

Later that afternoon in the second mail delivery of the day, the latest batch of magazines for the firm's reception area arrived. It was Matty's job to replace the old ones with any new ones and in the bundle was *Life Magazine.*

The cover article was dedicated to Woodstock and since she was there Matty flipped through to see what the authors had captured of that momentous event. Sitting in the secretarial pool the gasp she made was heard by almost everyone in proximity, not the least of which was Marilyn.

Grabbing the magazine and leaning over Marilyn's shoulder Matty whispered "come with me to the ladies room, right now!"

Marilyn dutifully followed and once inside Matty looked under all the stalls to make sure there was nobody else present. She then blocked the door with her hip to keep unwanted ears outside. Next Matty flipped to the photo of a naked couple in a tight embrace and thrust it in front of Marilyn.

"Oh my God!" Marilyn screamed.

"You're damned right! You are s.c.r.e.w.e.d," said Matty.

"That must have happened on Sunday. The day is a total blank in my mind."

"There are millions of people who get this magazine every week. I bet your folks do. What are you going to do?"

Since there was no doubt it was Marilyn, even though the caption didn't identify who was in the picture, she knew her mother would recognize her immediately.

"I'm going to write my parents. I will need to rebuild their trust and become the daughter they wanted, not the whore they are going to think I am."

"That's a start," said Matty.

That night Marilyn wrote her parents. At the end of the summer she entered her last year, determined to make something

55

of herself in college. As well, she thought it was time to earn her "MRS" as well as her B.A., and set out to find a suitable mate.

Fate behaves in strange ways and a couple of weeks after classes started she bumped into Buddy from the firm at a Jewish Students Association mixer. Although already a graduate and in his final year of law school, he still made it a point to attend the odd event.

He spotted Marilyn immediately as she walked in and made it a point to talk to her. Buddy was a perfect gentleman and spent almost the whole evening talking like they had been close for years while in the office the two of them hardly said a few words to each other over the whole summer.

At the end of the evening he asked her out for the following weekend. This was followed by a series of dates that went on for some time and, just before Thanksgiving, when Marilyn was to return home to be with her family, he said he would like to fly her to Florida at the Christmas break to meet his parents.

Marilyn was thrilled both because this looked like a relationship that could turn into something permanent, plus it was a chance to escape some of the winter.

After dropping her bags in her room back in Chicago, she told her parents who were still very frosty to their daughter. On hearing the news her mother went wild with excitement. After that, "We're going to have a wedding!" was all she could say the four days Marilyn was in the house.

The trip turned out to be a total success, even if she and Buddy had to sleep in separate bedrooms. Somehow, the two of them found a couple of hours each night to steal into the other's room. However, there was no proposal. On the other hand, while there they shared lots of sex, sun and booze. Plus, both of them had a good time enjoying the Lauderdale beaches once Marilyn realized her mother had jumped the gun.

But, for spring break the two of them drove to Chicago to meet Marilyn's parents and at Friday night dinner, Buddy proposed. He also had made arrangements to interview with some of the local law firms and, with his grades, he knew he would have his pick of the crop. By the time they left to go back to Buffalo, Buddy had a firm offer from the practice that handled Standard Oil. Over the years the firm had grown to be able to properly serve this huge client and one recent realization was that they would need depth in their nascent environmental law practice. Buddy was a natural.

Buddy and Marilyn graduated a day apart and were married in Chicago at the end of August. The couple honeymooned in Maui for a week, returning very much in love.

Chapter 8

1978

Buddy was ahead of the curve, deciding to become an
environmental attorney when he graduated law school. As
expected, his primary client was Standard Oil of Indiana, which
had built the Standard Oil building at the corner of South
Michigan Avenue and 9th Street, affectionately known as "Big
Stan." At the time it was the tallest building in Chicago and
retained the title for a year until the Sears Tower was completed.

His office was on the 44th floor and since his promotion,
he now had a clear view of Lake Michigan.

When he started with Inglenook, Shapiro, and Kent they
had just been mandated by their largest client to build a unit to
protect them from what they saw as their greatest impending
challenge. It was obvious that the court cases against Dow
Chemical for both napalm and "agent orange," which were widely
used in Viet Nam, could easily spill over to the petroleum
manufacturers in America.

One might wonder why Standard Oil who primarily
produced gasoline, motor oil and jet fuel would be concerned
about law suits against Dow which had supplied the Department
of Defense war-related chemicals. The issue was that returning
veterans were claiming these chemicals impacted the
environment and that they were directly exposed to them. The
question then became what effect would there be state-side,
where the chemicals were produced, and how their non-
commercial byproducts could possibly adversely affect the
domestic population. This sent chills through the management of
Standard.

Rather than being reactive, the client wanted to be proactive and ready to respond immediately should the hammer fall.

Over the eight years since graduating, Buddy had advanced through initially studying new case law and pending environmental litigation and to attending trials that would likely impact his client in the future. Then, in July the *Niagara Falls Gazette* broke the story about an American tragedy beyond comprehension – the Love Canal. Buddy knew this was going to impact his client even if they were almost 450 miles from the epicenter of the calamity. The Canal was front page news and Hooker Chemical, a division of Occidental Petroleum, one of their fellow oil exploration colleagues, was in the cross-hairs.

The day after the story appeared Marcus Shapiro called Buddy into his office.

"I know you've been doing some great work here, but up to now it's been more research oriented than the type of action you may have thought you'd be seeing," was how Shapiro started the conversation. "That is about to change."

"Yes sir, I read the *Sun-Times* article this morning and the Niagara Falls thing is looking pretty bleak for Hooker."

"That's not the half of it. I spent the past eighteen hours holed up with the senior management team at Standard trying to get a handle on this. They aren't concerned about being implicated in this particular event, but they too have sites across the country, which are disasters waiting to happen. And, we're all convinced that over the next decade this will make its way to the Supreme Court."

"Sir, I think you're right."

"Buddy, stop this sir stuff, I'm Marcus and from now on I want you to address me as such."

"OK, Marcus. What did you want to discuss other than current events?"

"That's the spirit!

"What I want is to give you the bottom line about what our biggest client has decided. They are going to pay us a monthly retainer of one million dollars. With that I want you to put together a team of lawyers who will be dedicated to one thing. That is, checking out every possible site in the USA where Standard could be sued for any possible breach of existing environmental laws. And, I want you to personally bird-dog this Hooker thing all the way to its end."

"That's a tall order."

"It goes farther than that. The team you put together needs to be able to work with the engineers our client is assigning who will also be dedicated only to this one endeavor. The company's plan is to eradicate and remediate each and every one of these potential catastrophes as quietly as possible. But, they need legal guidance to both prioritize the order in which these are done and to quell any resulting local backlash."

"This sounds like the kind of work I can really sink my teeth into!"

"Oh, by the way, I am doubling your salary and giving you a $50,000 bonus effective immediately."

"Wow Marcus, thanks."

"You're more than welcome. Keep this up and you'll make partner in a couple of years. Also, I want you to take the rest of the day off. Take your pretty wife out to dinner on the firm. Pick a nice spot on Rush Street and we'll cover the baby sitter too. Tomorrow will come fast enough and I'm going to have personnel start to line up candidates for your review in the morning. Now scoot!"

-o-o-o-

"Honey, what are you doing home so early? Is there something wrong?"

"Marilyn, you aren't going to believe this. Shapiro promoted me today and we're going to celebrate!"

"To partner?"

"No, that's still a couple of years off."

"Shit, Lorraine's husband made partner at his firm last month," was her disheartened reply.

"Honey, I'm making more than that jerk Lawrence."

"How can you say that?"

"Look at this check and you'll know for sure."

"Holy crap, that's fifty thousand dollars! What did you do?"

"It's not what I've done, it's what I'm about to do. Shapiro has made me the official lead of our new environmental law practice. He wants me to hire a hand-picked team that will both follow the Hooker Chemical thing that I read to you from this morning's paper. I'm to lead the team that will work with our biggest client to identify and help them eradicate every possible infringing dump site they have anywhere across the country.

"Oh, and in addition to the fifty thousand bonus, my salary just doubled!"

"You gotta be kidding me," she said with both admiration and some doubt.

61

"I'm not. In fact, Shapiro told me to take you out to dinner to anywhere on Rush Street, on the company. And, he's covering the cost of a sitter too."

"I'm calling Amy right now to see if her daughter is free tonight since Lindsay seems to really like her."

"Great, I'm going to make a couple of calls on my business line in the study. I want to get hold of some of my law school buddies since I need to staff up. Even though Marcus wants me to take the day off, I want to get things started."

"Why don't you call your friend Steve from U.B.?"

"Chances are he's in the thick of it on the side of the government."

"So what, you're still old friends"

"You're right. I'll give him a buzz."

With that Buddy went into the room he used as an office when at home, and after dialing long distance said, "Mr. Glazer's office please."

"May I ask who's calling please?" said what sounded like an even more officious receptionist than they had at ISK.

"It's Buddy Stone, a friend of his from law school."

"One moment and I will connect you."

After a couple of clicks he heard, "Buddy, how the hell are you?"

"I'm great Steve, how's it going for you?"

"Well, as you probably guessed, I'm up to my neck in alligators on this Hooker thing."

"That's why I'm calling. I'm heading up the environmental law department for ISK, and we're staffing up. Any chance you'd be interested in moving to the windy city?"

"Come on Buddy, you know me. If you're on one side of the case, I'll always be on the other."

"That's what I thought. So, let me ask you the other question since I know you're waiting for that shoe to drop."

"Yes, I can think of a couple of folks who may be suitable for you before you grovel."

"Steve, that's what I always liked about you. You are so prescient you are really able to read my mind," he said facetiously.

"Don't get all mushy on me. Give me a couple of days and I'll FAX you some names."

"That would be great!"

The conversation continued for another few minutes as the typical pleasantries were exchanged and wagers placed on a couple of upcoming sporting events.

-o-o-o-

Buddy and Marilyn had a five year old daughter who was the love of their life while also the bane of their existence. They indulged her continuously even though she was a terror. Having even a single baby sitter with whom she got along was a godsend.

Marilyn had settled into married life in the Chicago suburbs and once Lindsay arrived in January, 1973 she decided one child was enough. To make sure this was final she had her tubes tied.

Her typical routine included the Tuesday bridge group, the Wednesday evening mahjong ladies, the country club in the summer and annual trips to Florida every winter to see Buddy's parents, the Stones.

These were normally timed to coincide with Lindsay's birthday in the middle of the month plus it gave Buddy two full weeks of down-time he sorely needed by that time each year.

The night of the promotion they feted on the firm's money knowing not only would their net worth increase, but that Buddy's available family time was going to plummet. It was a trade-off and both of them were mature enough to face it, at least at the conceptual level.

Over the next few years, as the case against Hooker grew and the angst in Standard Oil paralleled the increasing legal machinations the law firm had to put in place to proactively defend their client, Buddy spent less and less time with his family. And, many nights even when he wasn't traveling, he still didn't come home. Eventually, the couple purchased a little pied-a-terre in downtown Chicago so Buddy had a place to crash, shower and store some fresh clothes on those nights.

Marilyn didn't like this arrangement and her libido was always greater than his. They had an OK sex life although she craved more. However, whenever she thought about straying, her mind was drawn back to the confrontation with her parents so many years ago.

She was beyond embarrassed. Her parents had already seen the Woodstock photo-spread in *Life Magazine* and as she suspected her mother instantly recognized Marilyn as the girl in the nude embrace with a strange man. The dismayed look on her parents' faces as she came into their house after sitting for twelve straight hours on a bus from Buffalo was heartbreaking. They had tolerated all her antics as a teenager and suspected less than honorable activities at college. But to have their daughter's naked image splashed across all the living rooms of America was beyond belief.

"How could you do this?" her father said with tears in his eyes.

"Papa, I honestly don't know."

There was no way she could tell them she was stoned into oblivion at the time. They wouldn't understand, nor would they care. This was a slight to them personally.

Over the years the rift had slowly closed. They were ecstatic with Buddy as her husband and beyond joy with Lindsay. But, for Marilyn, they were the conscience on her shoulder ensuring Buddy's wife remained an honorable woman.

Chapter 9

1982

Buddy found his work rewarding. Yes, he missed his family but was dedicated to making sure he never missed attending his daughter's birthday party in Florida. In fact, for the past few years he had flown his in-laws down from Chicago to be with his parents so they could all enjoy Lindsay's special day together. It wasn't that Marilyn's parents couldn't afford to travel to Florida on their own, but Buddy felt it was his duty, plus a way to make up to his family for the amount of time he was absent.

Lately he had been spending an inordinate number of days in Washington, D.C.

There were hearings to attend as well as visits to the Supreme Court. He also started to meet with prominent politicians, which, now being a full partner at ISK, meant certain doors started to really open for him.

His client was extremely happy with the work Buddy was doing and the firm supported him in every way they could. However, this January in 1982 he absolutely had to be in D.C. for a special hearing taking place behind closed doors. The venue was a little known meeting room in the Hart Senate Office Building on Constitution Avenue at Second Street, NE. The building hadn't officially been opened as yet, but the meeting was so important the participants wanted a place that anybody outside their limited circle would consider beyond unlikely, if the discussion was ever leaked.

Buddy spent two days in Washington preparing for the meeting while the rest of the family had already flown down to Florida. His bag was packed and he was prepared to grab the first flight available once the meeting wrapped up. The good news was it started on time and concluded just before noon. Under normal circumstances this should have given Buddy plenty of time to make it to National Airport, located just the other side of the Potomac River. However, the weather conditions were terrible. Sleet mixed with snow started around ten that morning and hadn't let up.

Undaunted, he grabbed a cab and tried to patiently ignore the slow crawl through downtown and across the Roosevelt Bridge. The cabby said the fastest way in this weather was to stay on Constitution and then grab the George Washington Parkway once they were across the river. He thought that would move quickly southbound, since most of the traffic at that time of day normally was headed either to the north or west further into the Virginia suburbs.

It turned out the driver was right and Buddy paid him a nice tip before making his way into the airport chaos. He barged his way to the Florida Air desk and on facing the agent said, "Any chance of getting on a flight today to Lauderdale?"

"Sir, flight ninety has been delayed by weather and is still on the ground. I can put you on stand-by for it so keep your fingers crossed."

"That sounds good to me," he replied.

For the next couple of hours he waited as stoically as he could. Since this was before the advent of constant communication by cell phone, e-mail, or texting, he called from a nearby pay phone to let the family know he was on stand-by and would call again with the flight number and arrival time, once he was confirmed. Alternatively, if the flight left without him, he said he'd also call so they would know when to ultimately expect him.

Finally, the flight was called along with the first batch of stand-by passengers. His name wasn't in that group and he cursed his luck. Then, when three of those passengers didn't show up to claim their boarding passes, they called three replacement names. His was the second.

Naturally, once on-board the 737, it was obvious the flight was full and he would occupy a middle seat. Having grown comfortable flying first class for the past number of years, this was definitely an inconvenience. But, if it meant making it to Lindsay's birthday, it was a small sacrifice. Marilyn already had the present from the two of them safely stored at his parents' house, so all Buddy had with him was a small carry-on bag. Once that was safely stowed under the seat in front of him (the overhead bins were already surpassing the over-stuffed status) he crammed himself into the seat and took out the latest John Grisham novel to read.

There were numerous false starts for the flight, all being weather-related. First they had trouble pushing the plane out of the gate. Then there was a taxi delay. This was followed by a further wait at the runway.

Eventually, the engines spooled up and there was a collective sigh of relief as the big jet started to lift. For thirty seconds the plane was airborne. Then it slammed into the 14th Street Bridge killing seventy-four aboard and four on the ground.

-o-o-o-

"Honey, I'm on Florida Air flight ninety. With all the delays I don't know what time we'll get into Fort Lauderdale, so check with

68

the airline. Guess what, I got the second last stand-by seat on the plane!

"I love you and tell Lindsay I will definitely be there in time for her birthday.

"Gotta go!"

The beauty of answering machines is the person's voice can always be there for posterity. These were the last words Marilyn heard from her husband.

The rest of what happened that day is a total blur in her mind and actually no clearer than her recollections of that infamous Sunday at Woodstock.

She knows she called the airline and was told to come to the airport. She knows there were many people crying when she got there. How she got there, what was said, who comforted who is all a big unknown. Later Buddy's parents' rabbi arrived. He was probably a nice man, but she didn't know. Buddy's partners called later that night or was it another night? A memorial service was planned while they were all still in Florida. Then a week later, once his body was identified and flown to Chicago, a graveside funeral was held there. His parents flew up for it and they all said *Kaddish*, the Jewish prayer of mourning, for their lost son, husband and father.

Marilyn was devastated. She wasn't religious yet tried to mourn in the traditional manner. Based on Jewish customs, being a spouse her mourning period was over after thirty days. For any other relative it normally ran for eleven months. So, how does a nine year old mourn for her father for eleven months while her mother only one? This was a quandary for Marilyn and far too painful to contemplate.

Buddy's partner and friend Marcus Shapiro came to her home about two weeks after the funeral and told her she was quite well off financially. The firm had an insurance policy that paid out a premium on any death related to business travel and, although technically Buddy's last flight could have been considered personal, it was only because of the firm's business that he had to be in D.C. that fateful day. Everyone knew he had cancelled his prior travel arrangements that were booked directly from Chicago to Ft. Lauderdale. Shapiro also said the firm was joining the class action lawsuit on Buddy's behalf against the airline since it had been revealed they didn't properly de-ice the wings.

This was all important information, but none of it would bring her husband back. And, she missed him terribly.

Chapter 10

1986

Lindsay was a terror. There is no other way to describe her. She was indulged when her father was alive and even more so after his death. Moreover, she always needed to be the center of attention.

At school, this was fine until the past year. She had a posse who followed her everywhere. It didn't matter what anyone else wanted to do, Lindsay had the final word. That worked fine from the year after her father perished in the airplane accident. Perhaps at first it was acting out on her part, but the acceptance of her friends was probably a form of pity. Anyhow, by the time she was in her last year of public school the tide changed.

Lindsay was an outcast.

This isn't an uncommon event with pre-teen or early teenaged girls. In fact, it happens all the time. The problem is when it's your child and especially when that child has only one parent, coping is nearly impossible.

In Lindsay's case she stopped being invited to birthday parties, out to the movies, even into other past friends' homes to study. She was isolated.

Marilyn was beside herself. She didn't know what to do and even after taking her daughter to one of the most highly recommended psychiatrists in Chicago, all she was told was "don't worry; she'll grow out of it. Girls are like that and things will change."

This was cold comfort for a distraught parent. Add to this Marilyn's own frustrations. Over the past few years she had hardly dated and actually never had sex. She felt that although she was still attractive, she was beyond hope.

Her friends had tried to set her up with other single men. They encouraged her to attend the appropriate clubs at her Temple and many of the other social centers in the Chicago area, but between the duties she felt she owed her daughter and the incipient fear of dating (that only grew over time), she too had become an outcast.

One family tradition that continued was celebrating Lindsay's birthday in Florida. Even though Buddy's parents tried to say out of Marilyn's life as much as possible, she felt it would be cruel to cut them off from their only granddaughter. So, as painful as the annual trip was, she made it a point for the two of them to go the distance.

This year was no different except for a surprise that awaited Marilyn.

While Lindsay was busily tearing the paper from the gifts she'd received from her grandparents, including *Care Bears*, *Where's Waldo* books, and the brand new game *Trivial Pursuit*, there was an envelope taped to the bottom of the last box Lindsay opened entitled "To Marilyn with love."

She dutifully handed this to her mother while snidely muttering, "I thought it was MY birthday."

Her grandfather said, "Honey, it is, but it is also about time your mother had some fun too."

With this Marilyn ripped open the flap of her gift and found a ticket for a seven day Caribbean cruise leaving from Port Everglades the next day. She was dumbstruck and when she finally caught her breath said, "I can't accept this."

Her mother-in-law said, "Yes you can and you will. As Granddad said, it is about time you enjoyed yourself. Buddy has been dead long enough. You will always be our daughter-in-law and our granddaughter's mother. But, you also need some time for yourself. Go off, have some fun, find a man!"

"I couldn't do that."

"Why not? We all know you were a free spirit in your youth and I'll tell you for a fact that that doesn't go away. I'm just as horny now as when I first married Granddad."

"Grandma, watch what you're saying there's a minor present!"

"Why, Lindsay is almost a grown woman. She has hormones rushing through her body at a pace we can't imagine. If she isn't sexually active now, how long do you think it will be?"

"This isn't a discussion about sex!"

"If it isn't then I don't know what it is about. Sex is something that lasts all our lives. Some of us are lucky and have partners that not only stay with us, but are healthy forever. You are young. You deserve a life. And, Granddad and I are not going to stand in your way.

"We have discussed this off-and-on since last January and both agreed this is just what you need. We're here to look after Lindsay while you take in some sun and surf. Plus if you do meet someone it will give our granddaughter a father figure."

"I don't want another father!" Lindsay shrieked.

"Settle down young lady," her mother replied. "What makes you think I want a vacation and especially a man?" she addressed to her in-laws.

"Because, we believe that if someone as attractive, intelligent, and with the financial means that you have doesn't make a move in that direction, you will ultimately be doomed to widowhood. And whether you like it or not, our granddaughter will be deprived of a male influence, which obviously she is sorely lacking."

Granddad piped up, "I'll drive you to the port in the morning in plenty of time before your departure. You already brought clothes for the sun, but Grandma will take you shopping this afternoon to stock up on the necessary eveningwear, shoes, bags, etc. Plus you better buy a new suitcase to carry all that stuff.

"And, as her Granddad I'm going to take Lindsay miniature golfing right now so you two ladies can have some fun at the mall."

Marilyn was grinning from ear-to-ear as she wiped the tears from her cheeks. She got up and kissed both her in-laws in thanks while Lindsay sat on the floor grumpily examining her birthday gifts.

-o-o-o-

It wasn't surprising Marilyn found herself warming to the whole idea of a Caribbean cruise as she and her mother-in-law shopped for the necessary items. Around eleven the next morning, she kissed Lindsay goodbye, hugged Grandma, and climbed into her father-in-law's silver Lincoln Town Car. Within thirty minutes they were pulling up to the Holland America Line's terminal building.

"Remember what we said last night, you will always be ours, but it is time you shared your life with someone else."

74

"Granddad, what makes you think I will even meet someone on the ship? It is a big boat with over a thousand guests. There's lots of places to get lost, and like the old *Love Boat* television series, it is a contrived environment."

"You're sitting at a table of eight for the late seating. We ordered you the wine package and you're traveling as a single. If that doesn't attract eligible men, I don't know what will."

He then flagged down a porter and tipped him to take her bags inside the terminal. Once they were loaded on the cart, he leaned over and kissed the top of Marilyn's head. "Have fun and I mean it."

With that he turned away so she couldn't see the tears in his eyes.

Clearing through the embarkation process was relatively simple and before long Marilyn was walking up the gangplank into one of the "Dam" ships. Her itinerary on the Nieuw Amsterdam included their first day at sea followed by landfall in San Juan, Puerto Rico. Next was a run down to St. Maarten with the last port of call being St. Vincent and the Grenadines. Then it was another full day at sea back to Port Everglades.

She was determined to look her best and started with an hour at the spa followed by a fresh hairdo. After that Marilyn took a self-guided tour of the ship. It was only two years old, but looked like it had been launched yesterday. The brass-works gleamed and the carpets were freshly vacuumed, crystal glittered and the amount of original artwork was astounding.

Before long it was time for the sail-away party on the navigation deck around the pool. Fresh fruit punch was served nicely cooled in tall plastic glasses. It was spiked with just the right amount of rum. While on deck she glanced around to see what men were likely to be traveling stag. Most seemed to be paired off while a few were decidedly gay. However, there was one specimen who looked somewhat promising.

She stood around five feet two in her stocking feet and Buddy was a little under six feet tall. Naturally, Marilyn tended to use these measurements as her guide. But, on seeing the gent at the rail with the sad eyes, it wasn't hard for her to recalibrate. He was definitely over the six foot mark and in his bathing suit she thought he looked yummy.

Where did that come from? Maybe being on the water, without any worries, and a lot of bare skin in sight started her hormones flowing too. The question was how to meet the man. She was out of practice on the dating scene and felt that if she was too forward, he may be put-off.

Instead of acting on impulse Marilyn made a note to address this tomorrow and just enjoy the evening, gourmet dinner, and welcome aboard show in that order.

It was a semi-formal evening that first night and arriving at the table in her new cocktail dress, Marilyn felt really good about herself.

She was the last to arrive and as it turned out, there were two married couples, another single woman, and two single men already seated. One of whom was the man on deck. Maybe things were looking up!

Unfortunately, being last to the table she was seated opposite him. Everyone exchanged names and politely passed the bread as the wait staff introduced themselves. Unlike your typical road house restaurant, this being a cruise where the servers remained the same for the duration, the introductions were warm and friendly including their home country and number of years with the line.

After that they then passed around the dinner menus to the guests and took the drink orders. Since Marilyn's in-laws had pre-ordered the wine package for her when they made the booking, the sommelier showed up with her selection card for that evening. Looking at the menu she settled on a nice French chardonnay that should pair nicely with the sole meuniere she planned to have as her main.

As expected, the conversation was light and focused on where everyone came from, their respective vocations, and how many cruises they had taken both with Holland America and other lines. Naturally, their favorite ports of calls and ship amenities were also discussed. Little was exchanged in the way of personal details and after dessert Milt, the man sitting opposite Marilyn, excused himself to visit the men's room. On his return, while passing her seat he leaned over and whispered in her ear, "Care to join me for a drink after the show?"

She was thrilled but simply said, "Yes."

Nobody at the table reacted and as the plates were being cleared they collectively made their way to the theatre. The two couples wound up sitting together at one end of the aisle and acted as if they had know each other for years. This left the three single women sandwiched between them and Milt, who sat at the other end of the aisle. Since they all stayed together while entering the theatre Marilyn again was separated from the man she most wanted to meet. Unexpectedly frustrated, Marilyn would remember little of the show other than that it seemed entertaining.

However, as she left the massive auditorium, she felt a light tap on her right shoulder. Turning instinctively, she was pleased to see it was Milt.

"I know we exchanged names at the table, but let me properly introduce myself. I'm Milt Morgenstern," he said extending his right hand.

"I'm Marilyn Stone, and I'm pleased to meet you Milt Morgenstern."

They made their way to the most distant bar on the ship searching out a secluded table. Being adults on a cruise they quickly overcame the natural tendency to be coy and wound up opening up almost immediately. Marilyn told Milt about Buddy and he explained how he came off a bad divorce a couple of years ago but that his ex-wife had died of breast cancer this past November. Although they didn't have any children, Milt still felt extremely sad about the woman in spite of the fact she put him through so much pain.

Milt also said that he came from Toronto, Canada and he was in land development. Further discussion clarified this to mean land speculation and that while the real estate bubble was growing he'd worked out a formula that had proven to be quite enriching. It was simple enough that he was surprised others didn't follow it. His formula was based on selling a property when its value had climbed to an amount equal to twice the equity plus any carrying charges to that particular date, including estimated taxes on the sale. Upon settlement, he determined that half of the net profit should be set aside with the balance used for reinvestment. That way a controlled amount of capital was all that was ever in play while the other half of the proceeds were broadly invested in a portfolio of diversified holdings.

Since he believed the bubble would ultimately burst, he felt that by taking this approach, multiples of the proceeds were safely accumulating, while only the originally invested capital would ever be at risk.

Having been doing this for the past five years, Milt had taken an initial hundred thousand dollars and turned it over so many times that he was currently sitting on over six million in his non-real estate portfolio. In fact, the majority of his funds were sheltered in government-sponsored instruments earning close to twenty percent per annum. And, although he could have leveraged the six million to well over three times that amount in real estate, this way he had little exposure. Also he had liquidity so that when the market eventually collapsed instead of being be hard-pressed to salvage a fraction of his original investment, Milt would be very comfortable, no matter what happened.

He claimed, "The real kicker is that if I'm right and the market tanks, I can take some of my liquidity and probably buy back in at amounts that rival when I first got involved."

As they sipped their drinks it also came out that it was Milt's brother who had pushed him to take the cruise. He told Milt, "you're not getting any younger and dying with a fortune that you can't take with you will do you no good. You need to have some fun and can well afford to take the time."

Milt hadn't had a real vacation in over three years since before his wife first sued for divorce. In fact, that vacation was to Cancun, Mexico, where they were trying to see if they could save their marriage. They took every tour imaginable, saw *Chichen Itza*, climbed the pyramid, snorkeled in the clear water off the coast, rented a Hobie Cat sailboat for an afternoon, and watched three *Folklorio Mexicana Azteca* performances. But although they were all lovey-dovey on the trip, two days after arriving home she left him. The divorce papers followed a day after that.

Milt and Marilyn talked for a while longer, trying to get comfortable with each other without prying. Most importantly they wanted to discover areas of common interest to see if they were companionable. Milt walked Marilyn back to her cabin, and kissed her chastely on the cheek after which he said, "Would you like to meet for breakfast?"

She replied, "I like to walk in the mornings and was planning to do a few miles on the track on the promenade deck. How about you join me and we can go to breakfast after that?"

"Sounds good. Why don't I come by your cabin at seven-thirty?"

"It's a date!" she said and softly closed the door behind her.

Milt's heart skipped as he strolled down the corridor to the grand staircase that would take him up to his suite.

-o-o-o-

They spent most of their day at sea in each other's company. The speed walk turned into a lingering breakfast, which then rolled into the familiarization seminar on Puerto Rico, followed by another lecture on shopping for gems in the islands. A tour of the kitchen afterwards led to a dip in the pool. After that came a late snack, each going to their respective cabins for a nap before dressing for dinner. That night was listed as formal in the ship's daily bulletin, so Marilyn had cautioned Milt it would take time for her to properly prepare. Respecting her wishes, he waited until fifteen minutes before they were to attend the captain's reception before softly knocking on her cabin door.

"Is that beautiful lady ready for her beau?" Milt said just loud enough to be heard as she was reaching for the handle. On opening he gasped and said, "I'm floored!"

"You clean up pretty good yourself," was her reply.

She then took his arm and linked hers with his letting the door close behind them.

They looked stunning as they entered the reception hall and the ship's photographer held up his hand so he could take a picture of the impressive couple. A server arrived minutes later with a choice of punch or champagne. Milt lifted two glasses of bubbly, handed one to Marilyn, and toasted her with, "to what the future holds."

She giggled and touched his glass.

Dinner was again superb and the evening passed with them sitting together not only at the table but at the show too. From there they went to the top-deck lounge to dance. A little after one in the morning Milt accompanied Marilyn down to her cabin. At the door she said, "Would you like to come in?"

He didn't need any encouragement and after she flicked the light switch, he pushed the door closed with his foot. Resting a hand on her hip, she turned around placing her arms firmly around his neck and pulled him forward for a warm kiss. Their embrace seemed to last forever until Milt took a step back. He draped his tuxedo jacket over the chair in front of her dressing table just inside the room and undid his tie and shirtfront. Next he reached for her again and they started another passionate kiss.

While embracing he slid down the zipper at her back and the teal blue satin gown swished to the floor. With its plunging neckline her well-formed breasts were pushed up by a brassiere that didn't easily unhook. She let out a deep throated laugh and said, "Easy big boy, take your time," reaching behind.

At that point the two snaps opened and he moved forward to cup her bosoms while her right hand tugged gently on his zipper. Once he was released, she started to stroke his penis and they deeply moaned. It had been a long time for both of them and although they weren't shy, they wanted to savor this time together.

Slowly they shed the rest of their clothes and shuffled to the bed. Milt swept his arm across the two pillows scattering the chocolates left earlier by the maid when she turned down the covers. Marilyn laid back, pulled up her legs and helped guide Milt into her. He didn't need much assistance since they were both wet and well-aroused.

-o-o-o-

Although south Florida is beautiful in the winter months, there is something magical about the Caribbean islands. Perhaps it is the lingering scent of the spices grown there in the past, or maybe the hint of coconut oil used in so much of the cooking. Whatever it is, the romance permeated the air and definitely enhanced Marilyn and Milt's time on-shore.

They thoroughly enjoyed all three ports of call and engaged in shopping, touring and for the latter two even made it a point to go to the beach. Being uninhibited and on vacation, they even hit the topless beach in St. Maarten where Marilyn strutted her stuff. That was a total turn-on for Milt and he could hardly wait to get back to the ship and show how much he appreciated it.

Then, it was the last day at sea. The moment of truth had arrived. Was this a casual fling or something more long term? They both enjoyed each other's company in addition to the wild sex. Both of them had independent means and wouldn't have to rely on the other financially. But, she came from Chicago and Milt was a Toronto boy. There was a border between them and Marilyn couldn't forget her demanding daughter. Personal histories aside, the question was exactly what Milt toasted at the captain's reception, "to what the future holds."

Peter & Margaret Wong's story

Chapter 11

1996

The long range executive jet was spacious and comfortable but it was the unknown that depressed Paul and Mei Ling Chen. They had been abducted at gunpoint, hustled into a waiting limo, taken to the local airport and then forced onto this plane.

Maybe it was a Gulfstream or the new aircraft from Bombardier. Whatever it was, the plane had phenomenal range since over the past twenty-plus hours, it had only made one short refueling stop. Chen knew it was almost 5,800 nautical miles from Toronto to Beijing and figured that with the time in the air flying westward over the Pacific, they were somewhere in that area.

At that point the pilot came on the intercom, "Folks. Sorry that I haven't introduced myself or come back to visit with you, but I was under strict orders to stay up front. However, we are approaching our final destination and, unlike the fuel stop a while ago, I have been instructed to tell you that the shades are to be lowered right now and in the top drawer of the pantry you will find a sealed box. Please open the box and follow the instructions. Unfortunately, if you don't do as told there will be dire consequences.

"Also, I hope you enjoyed the flight. Pilot out."

Chen closed the window shades as instructed. He then went forward to the pantry and inside the utility drawer found a sealed flat box typically used to wrap a woman's scarf as a gift from a high-end store. He opened it and saw two black hoods. For the first time since this ordeal began he felt real fear creeping into his gut. Silently he came back to their seats and handed one of the blackout covers to Mei Ling.

"The captain was wrong. There were no instructions. But, I think you'd have to be a fool not to understand that we're to put these over our heads."

With that the two of them put on the hoods, tightened their seatbelts for arrival and held hands. Once they were on the ground and the thrust reversers had wound down to a tolerable noise level, Chen leaned over and said, "No matter what happens I love you and will do whatever I need to keep you safe."

Mei Ling leaned towards him and put her head on his shoulder. They then felt warm air rush into the cabin as the air-stairs were lowered. Two sets of feet were heard pounding up the metal steps and into the entryway. Rough hands grabbed them after releasing their seatbelts and stood them up. Their unseen greeters next forced their arms in front and attached plastic zip-tie restraints to their wrists. After that, taking them by their shoulders, forcibly led them out of the aircraft and down to the ground.

They could still hear the engines turning and soon the sound increased as jets spooled up. Next they felt the warm peripheral blast as the plane turned. Moments later the noise reached a crescendo as their transportation to this unknown destination departed.

Once their hearing had returned to normal they heard a door close and somebody, possibly somewhat aged, shuffle forward. Whoever it was, they stopped just in front of them and said curtly, "You have arrived," in English.

Recognizing the voice as belonging to the man who Chen considered his adopted uncle from Hong Kong and the leader of one of the main triads, he made the mistake of saying, "Honorable uncle how pleased..."

At that point something solid hit him firmly behind his knees and Chen buckled to the ground.

"Don't ever address me again as your uncle.

"In fact, neither of you are allowed to speak unless asked a direct question. Is that clear?"

Chen immediately replied, "Yes."

Mei Ling, being stunned at everything that was happening, delayed a moment too long. This earned her the same treatment as her husband. Groveling on the ground without the benefit of sight and her hands tied painfully in front of her, she moaned.

While on the ground, the man who Chen considered his uncle silently pulled down his zipper, extracted his withered manhood and urinated on the two of them. He then zipped up and said, "That is what I think of you. You have shamed me, lost almost a billion of my hard-earned money, and now you have to pay for your stupidity.

"Did I not make myself clear to your whore wife just now? Your lives are mine and when we get to our destination, I will explain what it will take for you to possibly survive."

In the local dialect he then said to the two minders, "Put them in the last seat in the SUV. They stink. You two will sit in the middle seats and I will stay in the front with the driver."

-o-o-o-

Having been forced to pull down the shades in the plane the Chens hadn't seen the horizon on approach. Had they, they would have marveled at the thick dark smoke rising from the jungle-like vegetation surrounding the landing strip. But, sitting in the SUV they could definitely smell it.

A mixture of wood, chemicals, gasoline, or possibly kerosene, combined with the pungent stink of human excrement scorched their nostrils. It made them want to gag, but they were both afraid of vomiting into what amounted to a sealed black cloth bag enshrouding their heads. Add to that the lingering fetidness of the old man's piss. Somehow, they held down their stomachs for about an hour until they arrived at their destination.

Both of them were forced out of the vehicle and pushed ahead into some kind of structure. Once inside their hand bindings were cut off and the hoods removed. They repeatedly blinked to clear their vision and tried to take in the rustic surroundings. Chen's nominal uncle stood about six feet in front of them behind some type of an old fashioned government issued desk and chair arrangement.

The room was dusky and also contained a lingering pall of the smoke. There was a series of dented grey metal filing cabinets along the back wall while a very high-end Mettler precision scale and antique table-top computer took up much of the desk.

"Let me make myself clear. You are in a remote part of the Guangdong province of China near the town of Guyiu. Although we are within walking distance of the South China Sea, only a fool would attempt to escape using that body of water. In fact, near here is a pier that reaches out into the shallows and soon you will have the privilege of seeing me feed my pets. That is something I like to do when I visit.

"In the meantime, let me explain things to the two of you. Simply put, you have been tried in absentia by the elders in the triad and found guilty. They wanted you immediately put to death. But, from the goodness of my heart, I pleaded your case and they granted leniency.

"Well, maybe not leniency exactly, since what I was able to negotiate is a rather harsh. Simply put, if both of you survive here ten full years from this date, you will be set free. However, there are significant restrictions on both your freedom and what you need to do to achieve it.

"Let me start by explaining what is entailed in gaining your release. First of all, I need the two of you to strip. Here are two cotton outfits you will wear while here."

"Don't we get a chance to shower or at least wash up first?" asked Chen.

Just as the brute behind him was winding up with his military grade truncheon, the old man raised his hand. This stayed what would likely be a leg crushing blow.

"That is the last time you will speak unless asked." The old man then waited as they got out of their filthy garments, which were placed by the other thug into a plain paper bag. This included all their personal belongings.

"To continue. Now that you have changed your clothes, you are also changing your names. From here on you are Peter and Margaret Chow. You are Chinese nationals and no longer Canadians. That means you, whore wife, need to learn Cantonese. I know you weren't born here, but the first demand, if you wish to leave here alive, is to speak the local dialect as if you were a native. Peter was born in this country and the language should come back naturally.

"If you survive, you will immigrate to Canada and we will set you up with modest lives. But, that is a big if.

"As for what you will be doing, let me first explain what is done here and why I am so happy the two of you have arrived.

"People living in the West take their computers and electronic devices for granted. They also cherish their disposable society. However, if you replace everything, instead of repairing it, means there are tons of old equipment accumulating as trash.

"It also means that within those electronics are precious metals to be reclaimed like silver and gold! There are also trace amounts of platinum plus a mix of other valuable metals. And, often when commodity prices go tilt, even base metals like copper take on a respectable value. With this in mind, and the fact your sense of smell is probably the same as mine, you have likely figured out that what we do here is reclaim these metals."

"How much do you collect?" asked Chen, now known as Peter Chow.

"I will allow that, and I'm glad you asked."

"We get about one hundred dump truck deliveries per month. These are then broken down, the boards, chips, connections, wiring, and everything else is removed. Plastic parts are chopped up and then we burn the mass to extract what is important. After that, metals like copper, silver, gold, and platinum are secondarily smelted to commercial grade. We have an agent that assays them and puts them on the open market."

"So where do we come in?" asked Mei Ling, now to be known as Margaret Chow.

"Your husband is going to manage the whole operation and you the staff."

Seeing the puzzled looks on their faces he continued, "Don't get me wrong. This isn't some fancy American factory. You, Peter's whore wife, will be in the melting pits with the children and your husband up here. He is charged with increasing our output by at least fifty percent per year, each year, over the next ten years."

Peter exclaimed, "Fifty percent! How in heaven's name are we going to achieve that kind of growth?"

"You will do what you have to do if you want to survive," growled the old man. "Let me make this perfectly clear. I am a capitalist. Everyone knows I am a capitalist. Our country may have been taken over by the communists, but even they know that is a failed economic model. For communism to survive, it must become capitalism."

"How can you say that?"

"Very easily. I know you never formally finished college but studied extensively. Therefore you understand the principles. That is, if year over year there is a decline in production, communism becomes a Ponzi scheme since you will always be borrowing from subsequent years until everything collapses. If it is even from one year to the next, that is unsustainable since the slightest change can cause an imbalance, throwing everything into the Ponzi scheme's downward spiral. Finally, to succeed, communism needs a surplus. Even the Communists understand the necessity of a surplus although they consider it a capitalistic invention.

"Bottom line, another thing the Communists understand, is that you Peter are responsible for me making a surplus from this operation. If you don't, you die.

"Do I make my point?"

Margaret then timidly asked "What is the pit?"

"I will take both of you there shortly. We have a truck arriving this afternoon and I think you will appreciate a hands-on demonstration of what you will be responsible for from this point forward.

"But, where are my manners. Let us first go to your accommodations and after you settle in, we will have some lunch."

-o-o-o-

Their new abode didn't surprise either of the Chows now that the full impact of what they were facing was sinking in.

A ramshackle hut with flimsy window shades in a square of similar huts was now their home. The only difference being theirs slept the two of them while the rest had bunking for one adult and up to twenty children. Each was filthy and the only good news was no vermin were visible. That didn't mean they weren't there; only that in the daylight they were unseen.

Once the two of them figured out where the canteen was, they made their way to that similarly rustic structure. On arrival they saw how big the room was and it suddenly dawned on them how many others must live in this hovel. The old man was seated by himself in a corner with his two thugs standing behind him.

"I trust you find your new home comfortable," he said mockingly. "Now, you can sample the food. I must tell you it is far from gourmet, but nourishing."

91

With this, a scantily clad youth of indeterminate age came from the cooking area carrying a tray. There were two steaming bowls on it, a couple of sets of chop sticks, a small crockery spoon, a bottle of soy sauce, a bottle of Asian chili sauce, and two paper napkins.

"Enjoy your repast," their host said.

They looked in the bowl and recognized three things; bok choy, some tofu, and a few bean sprouts. This rested on some odorless yellowish liquid slowly oozing into a mound of dirty rice. Perhaps that was where the vermin were hiding, thereby inadvertently providing a source of protein for the camp's inhabitants.

As they took their first tentative taste the old man continued, "Before I forget, there are only two meals each day. Since you just arrived, I am providing a very infrequent lunch. However, in the future, you will eat only a breakfast and evening meal. Also, you work from dawn to dusk. The breakfast is served one half hour before work starts and the second meal, one half hour after work stops. Now, once you finish your bowls, the truck should arrive so we can carry on our familiarization tour."

Upon finishing the tasteless meal (neither felt comfortable using the soy or chili sauces), the five of them trudged out of the compound along a poorly marked roadway to a clearing about the size of an American football field. There were about one hundred people clustered around a number of densely smoking pits, likely fueled by kerosene. Everyone was dwarfed by piles of discarded electronics standing higher than the average man. The chemical stench this close to the epicenter of the site was beyond belief.

While trying to take in the enormity of the scene they heard the sound of a laboring diesel engine. Turning the last corner, now coming into their sight was a full size dump truck loaded to twice its height in detritus. Slowly it made its way to an assigned spot and tipped out the contents onto a pile that didn't look like it could absorb any more.

The old man smiled and turned to the two newcomers, "This is now your domain. Peter, you will make sure that to survive you will increase our output by at least fifty percent per year for the next ten. And, that will be measured by physical weight, not market fluctuations in commodity prices. Frankly, should the price drop for any of the typical products we reclaim, your increased production will have to make up for any shortfall.

"As for you Margaret, your responsibility is to make these wretched children produce what is required to meet the demands I have set for your husband. There are more than enough of these cretins to replace any of those you lose. But, you have to be down at the pits managing them. That means you will be exposed to everything they are. Do I make myself clear?"

Both of them answered with a simple "Yes."

At that point they heard the sound of a jet on approach. The old man looked up and said, "There is my ride back to Hong Kong. But, before I take my leave, there is one more thing to show you."

The two Chens, henceforth to be known as Chow, thought they had seen everything that could possibly turn their stomachs, but they were wrong. All five returned to the so-called roadway and headed back towards the encampment. About halfway there they noticed another rough road branching off into the jungle and the group started down it. About one hundred feet from where it met the previous road, their noses first identified they were nearing the latrine. The smell was beyond belief and they were amazed that after being exposed to the smoke this was able to penetrate their nostrils.

"Once every week, Margaret you are required to take one of your smelting teams and have them burn the waste from this vile pit." At least he was willing to admit how bad it was. But, the reality was that that too would add to her exposure to untold toxic contaminants. And, unlike her young charges, he made it clear she would have to be present every week supervising this disgusting task while the children would effectively rotate once per month.

As they were walking the old man started, "Peter, I'm sure you are intelligent enough to understand why I went to all the effort to bring the two of you here. This was definitely not the wishes of my partners, but I made them understand that if you were so effective in the early days with the use of our money, you could possibly do it again. Plus, I was also able to convince them that if you failed, the pleasure they would derive from hearing of what happened to you was well worth the effort.

All Peter could muster was a grunt.

The old man continued, "Finally, I want the two of you to experience the true enjoyment I derive from this hell hole."

With that they trudged another thirty yards when he said, "This is our little morgue. And, before you jump to conclusions about disposing of the bodies by burning them, we have a more hygienic practice. Today happens to be our burial day."

He then put his fingers to his lips and let out a shrill whistle. The door to this hut opened and two four-wheeled trolley emerged pushed by two gaunt men. Heaped aboard each were the corpses of about five youths. Their stomachs were puffed up with gas while their eyes stared vacantly into the void. On cue the Chows, the two henchmen and the old manfive formed a funeral procession behind the makeshift hearses and followed in silence.

What the couple didn't realize was they were effectively on a bay and within moments the group emerged from the foliage and were marching along a sand-covered section of the same rough roadway they had followed into the depths of this depraved enterprise.

The two men continued to push their dead charges right up to a pier that extended from the end of the road. As they neared the end they tipped up the trolleys and the bodies splashed horrifically into the salt water. Within moments dark fins started to rise and one of the henchmen uttered two words, "Tiger sharks."

At that point Mei Ling, now Margaret, heaved what was left of her meager lunch into the surf.

Chapter 12

1997

The first year was a bitch and his so-called uncle's words about communism echoed in his mind.

Paul Chen, now even thinking of himself as Peter Chow, had thought he'd tasted defeat in the past, but it paled to what he now faced. He didn't set out to become a hard man. In fact, he thought he would be a doctor and it was a cruel twist of fate that saw him expelled from university. Since his parents had mortgaged their future to the triads in favor of his education, the only possible path he saw for himself was a life of crime.

However, his brilliance shone through and instead of being a petty street hood, Peter quickly rose to become a leader. He also made it a point to gain the formal education he lacked by taking night and extension courses in both business and computer sciences. By the time he was running the local tong, he had also academically qualified for both a computer engineering degree and an MBA. Neither of these appealed to Peter at this point in his life, but he put his knowledge to good use.

In fact, within a handful of years he had built a number of legitimate businesses and within a decade the revenues these produced out-stripped those from his illegal activities.

His greatest venture, was creating a vertically integrated entertainment empire that saw him running the second biggest video rental business in the world after Blockbuster. His profits though outstripped his largest competitor, since Peter was able to augment the videotapes he legally acquired for rental purposes with mass-produced pirated copies, at virtually no cost, from his Hong Kong factory.

Not satisfied with that success, he mis-timed his next venture, which was converting over the operation from videotape to DVDs. What he didn't realize was how quickly the Internet was going to become a dominant factor and within a handful of years provide free downloads that would quickly displace rentals. Although he had built a billion dollar empire, he leveraged that with another billion invested by the Hong Kong triad run by the man he nominally considered an uncle.

It was the impending loss of those funds that landed Peter and his wife in what was effectively a Chinese concentration camp.

However, if Peter was anything, he was a survivor.

Within a couple of days of settling into their new environment, he realized there were three things that needed to be done for them to survive this hell hole. First, he had to find a way to improve the conditions for his staff. Second, he had to determine how he would be able to deliver the fifty percent annual increase in output. Although the old man said it had to be based on volume not dollar value, what was also implied was that it had to be accomplished with what he had, not at increased cost. Finally, he needed to come up with a plan for how he and Margaret would be able to exist financially once they were released.

He wasted no time thinking about escape. It was clear there was no way out of this except the fact the old man believed himself to be honorable. As such, if Peter and Margaret survived, he would honor his pledge to relocate them back home. Peter was certain the lifestyle his nominal uncle would provide at the end of the ten years would be humble at best.

Mei Ling, now also was comfortable with her new name Margaret, but she had the worst of it. She was responsible for the staff, which meant their overall health, working conditions, output, and total availability for work, fell under her domain. In the meantime, she was required to be physically present with them throughout the day and inhale the same witches' brew they did. If it was enough to kill off at least ten percent of the young charges each year, she could imagine what it must be doing to her insides.

On arrival she didn't speak a word of Cantonese. Her parents had both been born in San Franciso, later immigrated to Vancouver, and finally settled in Toronto where she was born. Her father wasn't even Asian, and since her maternal grandparents remained in San Francisco, visiting Canada on rare occasions, only English was ever spoken in her home.

Learning a foreign language at this point in life was going to be a challenge. But, there was no choice. None of her charges spoke anything other than their local dialect and if she didn't learn quickly, she and Peter were doomed.

However, experts agree that for an adult to learn a foreign language quickly, the fastest way is immersion. Margaret's immersion was total and well beyond her control. As such, she insisted Peter only speak Cantonese too. Within a month she was definitely able to understand everything said to her and another month later, everyone considered her a native.

By that time she too had realized manpower was key to their survival, and how it was deployed, the pathway to success.

That meant she had to come up with a way to keep the young folks fit. There were overseers with whom to contend, who also included the cooks. Finding healthy local food stocks that could be turned into nourishing meals was key. To do that she leaned on her husband to come up with a barter scheme that could work.

Everyone within a hundred kilometer radius knew what went on at their establishment. In fact, being peasants they encouraged their young folk to try to find work there. What Margaret wanted was for those same peasants to trade food produced in their own communal fields to feed the young in her charge.

At the same time she wanted to improve the living conditions. Food, hygiene, and environment were her top three priorities. For food, she knew she would also have to work with her husband on developing an effective barter plan. However, knowing Peter as well as she did, she assumed he had already started thinking about this within days of their arrival. But, it was her responsibility to make sure he included food in whatever mix he was contemplating.

As for hygiene, that was another matter. The latrines and morgue were disgusting. They were too close to the living quarters, too close to their water supply, and so unclean it was surprising typhus or other just as nasty diseases hadn't already broken out.

Finally, there was the environment. The air in particular was most disconcerting since everyone had to breathe it, not just the unfortunates handling the burning and smelting of e-waste. It also meant improving the safety around this disgusting working area. She realized they were all essentially slaves, but as Schindler learned during World War II, improving just the living conditions of his Jewish charges meant ultimately saving their lives.

-o-o-o-

Margaret wasn't wrong about Peter's initial thinking. He too realized the importance of barter. He felt that coming up with some type of plan where he could skim off a minimal amount of their output, would both improve the lives of their staff plus somehow augment whatever life they faced after surviving this hell.

First he had to come up with a way to improve the overall daily, weekly and monthly output. That was not only mandatory, but had to be clearly visible to both the overseers and his so-called uncle.

Peter had one ace up his sleeve. He was computer literate and well-versed in the use of the Internet. Although the computer on his desk was an antique, it was still a computer and had a modem. Not the fastest com-link, but it worked. With this, he spent the first forty-eight hours online searching everything he could about what raw materials went into the making of the various machine components including mother boards, memory chips, power suppliers, screens, shielding, wiring harnesses, frames, and cases. The list was extensive.

In fact, not only were gold and silver used, there was also platinum, rhodium, palladium, and obviously copper. From this he prioritized these metals based on three scales: relative concentrations by component, ease of extraction, and market pricing for commercial grade, based on statistics tabulated over the past five years. With this, he ran a regression analysis on the output to come up with a plan for how to best use the piles of

100

waste. It also gave him an idea of what could be skimmed and how to do it.

That night when Margaret and Peter finally collapsed into bed, he said, "I have given some thought about your recommendation to improve the health of the wretches under our care and how to increase the output to meet our necessary levels.

"The two are definitely tied together since there is no way my so-called uncle will permit us to have any more food or staff than already allocated, unless we find a way to cover their incremental cost. But, to cover that we need to increase production. I know it sounds like a Catch-22, but based on the research I've been doing, there are a number of precious and what I call 'valuable' metals that can definitely be extracted. But, the relative amounts vary based on which discarded equipment is rendered down. And, it even varies based on the actual components, based on which generation of technology they come from."

She replied, "It sounds really complicated."

"Perhaps, but I've built a very basic model on that antique computer in the office and if we stick to it, I'm confident we can achieve the necessary targets. The only thing is we need to reorganize the production process."

"What will that require?"

"There is a truck due in the morning. Instead of having them dump everything on the most convenient pile they come across, I want us to find a clear enough space for that particular load. Once it is on the ground, the various electrical devices need to be set up into individual piles of the same thing. That means monitors are only stacked with other monitors, CPUs with CPUs, etc. I also want you to identify the most adept children at breaking apart the various types of equipment to get down to the components. Once those are removed and stacked into their respective piles, I'll be able to identify the order by which they should then be melted down and which metals are extracted."

"That sounds like a rudimentary assembly line."

"Actually it's a disassembly line!"

For the first time in days, they both laughed.

The next morning the truck arrived and much to the consternation of the driver who started to tip his load onto the first pile in sight, Margaret ran up to him and in pidgin-Cantonese started to yell that he was to take this load over to where the children had formed a big circle. Although her language skills were improving, they still had a long way to go. But, the driver got the drift and after issuing a few epithets of his own, slowly moved the truck forward and tilted the rear so the load could fall out.

Once everything was on the ground, since Margaret had made something of a game of it, the munchkins descended on the pile and quickly dissected it. Within an hour everything was rearranged into piles of similar goods and by the end of the day, each of these was further segmented into the components from which they were made.

The next morning, based on clear direction from Peter, the various small piles from the previous day's shipment were systematically taken to the appropriate melting area and the extraction process begun. At first all six melting stations were working on mother boards, but as the feed stock dwindled, they shifted to the next item on Peter's list, the power supplies. By the end of the day the full load had been diminished to a series of five key metals and plastic slag. This final waste was crumbled into pebbles and stacked in its own pile. Peter had an idea of how best to use it in the coming months.

On assaying the five metals, Peter found that the output was over twenty-five percent ahead of the output from the last day of processing, the one before yesterday's shipment. This was the ammunition he needed to prove they could start to achieve their target. Moreover, this he determined would be the process by which all further disassembly was going to be done.

-o-o-o-

A week later they heard the unmistakable sound of an executive jet on final approach. Peter's nominal uncle was coming for a visit.

About thirty minutes later, the man pulled up in the same black SUV as the Wongs had traveled in dripping in piss, along with his two minders. Peter and Margaret were standing in front of their so-called office building when the trio pulled up. One of the two thugs was reverently carrying a narrow velvet package a little less than three feet long.

The old man greeted them, "I hear good things about what you have accomplished already Peter, but why is the whore wife here and not with the workers?"

"She too has done much in making this possible."

"I understand, but she has a role to follow and that does not include standing idly by while I discuss business with you."

"Sir, I would hope that at this point you could accept her contributions as much as mine."

"I will let you know when and if that comes to be. In the meantime, I would like to see first-hand what you are about, and I understand you have some matters you would like to discuss with me."

"I am honored to have you here and let us look at the production line we have created. Also, I would like to know what to call you since 'sir' seems so improper."

"By the time I leave today, I will tell you how to address me in the future."

From there they went to view the operation and the old man was suitably impressed. It worked like a well-run Swiss watch with bulky discarded electronic devices arriving by one truck and by the end of the day everything it had delivered was reduced to the valuable scraps with a minimum of waste. Moreover, the quality of the individual metals were of significantly higher assay than anything that had been extracted prior to Peter's arrival. The old man was pleased.

Seeing the delight on his face, Peter took the bold step of addressing what he wanted to discuss.

He started by saying, "Sir, I have increased our output by almost thirty percent. But to make the fifty percent you demand, I need better workers. The process can only go so far and the rest is the human capital. Plus, when I say better, I also mean better able to work."

"Be blunt, what are you asking for?"

"I want to feed the workers better and I want at least twenty-five percent more workers on-hand."

"Just where do you think I will find the money to do this?"

"How about taking a small percentage of the increased production and barter with the local inhabitants?"

"Then how do I make up my lost revenue?"

"That's just it, you won't lose you will gain!"

"Here is what I am prepared to do. I will let you barter ten percent of the reclaimed copper. You cannot touch any of the other metals. I will permit you another ten percent in staff too. But, one of the overseers will do the bartering and procuring of staff. Do I make myself clear?"

"Absolutely."

"Now, I realize that if you feed your charges better, you will deprive me of my enjoyment while visiting you. But, I am confident there will always be some of these runts who will die between my visits."

Peter knew what was coming and felt the bile rise in his throat. However he swallowed hard and said, "Why don't we make our way to the morgue. You will also see how we have cleaned up that foul area."

The old man, Peter and the two thugs walked briskly to the hut containing three young bodies. They were already loaded on a cart, which was manned by two of the healthier looking children. On arrival the small cortege moved out to the pier. On reaching the end, the old man held up his hand for them all to halt. At that point he motioned to the bodyguard holding the velvet package to hand it to him.

With a lightening quick motion the old man had extracted a samurai sword, swung it in an arc and severed the head of the man who had just handed him the package.

The head fell into the sea and his body slowly collapsed into itself on the pier. With an invisible strength the old man booted the corpse over the edge and said, "That is what happens to those who cheat me. Peter don't cheat me."

In-turn, he stammered, "Sir, I won't."

"You no longer have to call me 'sir.' Please call me 'honored uncle.'"

At that Peter bowed deeply and glanced at the water. He was appalled to see the tiger sharks making a beeline to the bobbing head with the mystified eyes staring into eternity.

A few moments later there were three loud splashes as the bodies of those who had died since the old man's last visit were fed to the sharks.

Chapter 13

1999

Peter and Margaret made the most of their incarceration by ensuring all the children in their care were properly cared for. The environment alone guaranteed the death of some. But, the numbers had dropped off dramatically over the past couple of years.

Instead of three to four dead kids per week, it declined to around two each month.

In the meantime, Peter's uncle seemed pleased since he made sure to make his production numbers both years and without any increase in operating costs. As well, the local farmers were satisfied with the barter arrangement, which provided added cash and an incentive for them to grow more crops. If it wasn't for the brutal overseers, primitive conditions, terrible food, and toxic environment, they would be fine.

Through diligence they had made living in hell palatable, if not ideal.

The challenge was rapidly becoming how to ensure there was a nest egg that could come out of this, assuming they survived on one hand and avoided imminent death should they attempt to skim even a miniscule amount of the precious metals. On a daily basis, the output was measured as it cooled from the respective smelters. Gold, silver, platinum and others were weighed by one of the uncle's henchmen and the recorded results e-mailed to Hong Kong by Peter as each was tabulated. The physical product was then picked up when Peter's uncle made his near weekly visits on the executive jet.

Peter also suspected their personal surveillance went well beyond what he saw on a daily basis. This included regular, yet random sweeps of their personal space by a thug with a metal detector.

To test his theory about how deep their minders went, Peter once secreted a poorly smelted gold sample that deliberately contained lead and other elements. He put it in an envelope and clearly marked on the cover "for further discussions with my uncle."

Two days later, the old man appeared both unannounced and days ahead of any expected visit. Again he carried the velvet wrap with the samurai swords inside.

Since they were not expecting him, and the fact he had obviously landed at another strip since they didn't hear his jet approach meant both Peter and Margaret were at their respective workplaces. The first Peter was aware of his arrival was when a shadow loomed over his desk.

"Where is your whore wife?" the old man barked.

"Honorable uncle, she is naturally at work minding her charges."

"Don't 'honorable uncle' me you wretched ingrate. Send someone to fetch her!"

Peter did as demanded and they waited in silence as the old man visibly grew angrier by the second. A few minutes later Margaret entered out of breath.

"Now that you are both here, I understand that the two of you have concocted a scheme to steal from me. You both know how I deal with thieves and that is now your fate."

"Sir, what are you talking about?"

"Show him," he shouted apparently to the walls.

At that point one of the minders appeared. He went to the desk drawer and withdrew the envelope with the sample inside and presented it to the old man.

"What is this?" he demanded.

Peter immediately determined what had happened and smiled broadly.

"Honorable uncle, please look at what I have written on the cover of the envelope. A few days ago we had a problem with the smelting and thought we'd stumbled upon a new alloy that would make more sense to keep in its raw form rather than further melting it down. That is why I put some aside and made a note that I should discuss this with you on your next visit. Obviously this stooge doesn't read or he would have understood what I had written. "

With this the old man flicked out the sword and with a swish the head of the overseer neatly fell from his neck.

"I loathe incompetence as much as I do theft," he said.

For the first time since he was a child, Peter thought he saw some compassion in the old man's eyes.

"I am sorry for doubting you. You have both proven you are loyal and I feel foolish."

This revelation was amazing and they both held their tongues.

After a few moments the old man softly said, "I want to make this up to you. Peter, what would you like?"

Tempted to say their freedom, he instead said, "I know this may sound crazy living here, but one thing I really miss are my cowboy boots. I had a wonderful pair of Tony Lama hand made ostrich skin boots and they were incredibly comfortable."

"Consider it done, what size are you and I will bring them with me on my next visit. However, that sounds somewhat trite. Is there anything else you would like?"

"Would you trust me with your swords?" he said softly with baited breath.

Surprisingly, the old many said "Yes, these are yours."

And with that he handed over the heirlooms, which he'd acquired from his predecessor. That man had personally removed them from the hands of a Japanese officer who offered the swords in exchange for his life at the end of the Second World War. Since the prior triad leader was as brutal as the old man, he tested the sharpness of the blade by removing the occupier's head.

After he left, Margaret accosted her husband with, "What kind of simpleton are you? Cowboy boots and samurai swords when you could have requested virtually anything!"

"Love, I know what I am doing."

"Do you? For the first time in my life I think I married a fool."

-o-o-o-

Ironically, Peter had in fact been skimming from his uncle. The problem was he was secreting it in such a way he was positive nobody could find it. But, the real problem was until that day it didn't matter since he had no way to get his precious hoard out of China.

Obviously, he couldn't sell or barter it since that would immediately alert his uncle that he was in fact cheating. So, he

110

waited until an opportunity arose where he could further his plans to give the two of them some reward from this hell hole.

Since their second week in China he was able to collect trace amounts of all the metals. However, the one he concentrated on was platinum. Peter knew the going rate for platinum was over $14 per gram (or $400 per troy ounce) while gold was about seventy percent of that and silver a fraction of the gold standard. So, if he was going to risk it all, it might as well be for the metal most likely to be worth the most.

How he accumulated his stash was quite simple. Part of Margaret's improvement strategy for the children was to make sure they were as comfortable as possible while working. One thing Peter suggested was putting matting under their feet to cushion them. Since most of the kids didn't have shoes, let alone proper footwear, this made total sense.

The mats were woven from the discarded plastic slag that was first re-melted and then extruded into fibers. Peter, with his engineering background figured that the wire harness at the end of the cathode ray tubes would work well as an extrusion mold and every month had the children produce enough material to form a fresh set of mats.

The mats in use were collected on a weekly basis and stored in a hut behind their shack. Peter made it a point to personally shake these out in the middle of the night and collect the scraps that fell from between the fibers. These he bound in tissues and buried at various points throughout the compound known only to him. He also did a rudimentary separating of the findings so that what remained was closer to eighty percent platinum and around twenty percent gold.

111

A week after his uncle gave him the swords, the man returned with the boots. These too were ostrich skin like Peter's old pair and accented with red flashes of smooth leather. They sported a full two inch traditional cowboy heel. Peter was ecstatic with the gift and paraded around the camp with them on.

That night, well after his wife was asleep, Peter stole out of the bedroom and into the office area. There he set to work with the small samurai sword called a *tanto* on the inside heels of his new boots. First, he carefully cut out the insoles. Next, he worked the sword around the periphery of the back of the heel leaving the nails in place. Then he scooped out the internal layers of leather making up the impressive structure, something the company was very proud of. Finally, he fitted the insole back and tamped it all around making sure there was a tight seal. Now, not only did he have a place to store and hide his nest egg of powdered platinum, but anyone checking the boots with a metal detector would think it was the nails that set off the machine.

The next night he started to collect the various deposits he'd scattered around the compound. Before he did this he weighed each boot on the Mettler scale so that he had a baseline of how much he would ultimately be able to hide this way. Based on his calculations of the estimated dimensions for each cavity at two inches by three inches by one inch Peter determined he could hide up to about six cubic inches or 100 cubic centimeters per boot. If he packed the platinum as tightly as possible, and with a density of nearly 21.5 grams per cc, he could theoretically store up to a kilo per shoe. At the going rate of fourteen dollars a gram, each one would be worth twenty-eight thousand dollars. Not a bad start, although not nearly enough unless he found a way to prove he had a shoe fetish or the price skyrockets.

BOOK TWO – THE MIDDLE YEARS

Joseph's story

Chapter 14

2006

The opportunity the young Chen couple faced was both formidable and extremely rewarding. Here they were just having passed through customs at Ben Gurion International Airport, 19 kilometers southeast of Tel Aviv, looking through the crowd of meeters-and-greeters trying to find somebody with a hand-held sign with their name on it. They were told there would be a driver to take them to their new home in Haifa, but their flight was almost an hour late, so they were hoping he was still around.

This was Israel, warm, welcoming, and the soul of three religions. Although neither of them were remotely religious, it was impossible not to be caught up with the tides of emotion flowing through the crowd.

They were collaborating with a team in Montreal and another at the Hadassah Medical School in Jerusalem on their primary research; the root cause of Alzheimer's disease. But like the hundreds of scientists around the world, the two of them differed in their respective opinions. Over the next few years they felt their perspectives would meld so they could defend a unified thesis. This would place them at the forefront of the research and add a PhD to both of their current board certified geriatric specialist designations through the American Board of Internal Medicine. And they knew that unlike most theses, theirs may incorporate a dissenting opinion in the outcome. However, that was very much still down the road with this being their first day "in-country."

Joseph spotted the man with the sign first. They were about the same height but their ride had a shaven head and a small black goatee. On seeing the couple looking at him he waved and made his way through the crowd.

"Hi," he said. "My name is Dov and I'm here to drive you to your new home. Shalom!"

They both replied with the same greeting knowing it meant hello, goodbye and peace.

Joseph said, "Dov you have absolutely no accent."

"That's what growing up in Baltimore will do for you. I made '*aliyah*' with my family when I was fourteen and love it here."

"Where do you live?"

"In Haifa at the university. I'm hoping to be one of your grad students since I've already completed my bachelor's degree in microbiology and applied to have the two of you as my advisors for my masters."

"I'm sure we're going to have a number of applications to consider when we arrive," said Juliette to make sure they weren't going to be backed into a corner.

"That's for sure. It isn't often we get a husband-wife team with the credentials you two have."

It took almost an hour and a half to get from the airport parking lot to the university. Joseph had checked Google Maps before they left for Israel to see what to expect and the driving time was very close to the one hour and seventeen minutes Google estimated.

The campus was quite compact and much smaller than the Chen's were used to. However, it was bright, modern and provided an opportunity to really excel on the global stage.

Their first stop was to meet the Dean of Medicine, Dr. Russell in his office. He had made it clear to Dov that before he took them to their new quarters, he wanted to meet the couple.

He greeted them warmly with, "Shalom, and my most personal welcome to our humble university."

Joseph replied, "Dr. Russell, it is our pleasure to be here."

"As my husband said, Dr. Russell, we are so honored to be both at this wonderful center of medical discovery and in Israel itself."

"You are going to fall in love with this country no matter what your religious leanings are. It gets into your soul. But, what I'm really saying is that the essence of Israel and it's warm, energetic people helps drive discovery. That is why we are all here!"

"Doctor, on behalf of both of us, that is exactly what captured our imaginations and why we decided to not only travel thousands of miles, but to commit to as many years as it takes to achieve our research goals.

"I know this all sounds like a lot of hot air but we believe the opportunity afforded us is something that could only be tackled in an open environment like Haifa University."

"That is why when the two of you first wrote, I made a personal commitment to determine if this institution was the right one for the both of you. What really captivated me was in your proposal I detected the two of you may actually not be in

117

total simpatico on the expected outcome, and that the challenge goes beyond developing a simple test regime."

"That is entirely true," said Juliette. "My husband is of one opinion and I'm of another. Much of this is in the details and not the overall efficacy. But, we think the dissonance will keep us on track and result in a much better outcome."

"You have definitely set a series of challenges for the two of you and I look forward to your success. Please know that my door is always open and if there is any way I can help, don't hesitate to let me know."

Dov, who had remained silent throughout all of this while standing in the background, then quietly opened the door so they could take their leave. The couple shook the dean's hand again and they then made their way back to the car.

"I'm exhausted," sighed Juliette.

Joseph groaned, "Me too."

"Your accommodations aren't far from here and I know the shipping crate you sent ahead has arrived."

"Nuts," said Joseph. "We were hoping it would be a day or two so we could acclimate before having to set up our home."

"From what I understand, you two aren't required to be in the lab for another week. Why don't you let me be your guide and we'll tour the country for a couple of days before you get started."

Juliette perked up and said, "That's a wonderful idea, Dov! Let's take tomorrow to sort things out and plan on the following day as our initial tour. What do you think?"

"I think I'll pick you up Tuesday morning and we'll head down to Tel Aviv. My plan is to take the coast road and hit the key sites on the way. Then we'll give it a couple of days so we can be in Jerusalem on Friday. You'll be able to see the Arab crowds that go to the mosques during the day and the Jews at the Western Wall that night. It will give you a perspective on this beautiful yet complex country.

"In the meantime, why don't you get some rest and I'll call you tomorrow. If you're up to it, I can show you around Haifa later in the day."

Joseph replied, "Sounds like a plan."

-o-o-o-

The time difference caught up with them much faster than they expected. Within a couple of hours they were fast asleep. And, they slept until eight the following morning, which gave them a burst of energy to attack the shipping crate and start setting up their new home.

Dov called around noon to ask how they felt and was pleased to hear how much they had accomplished. He then inquired about their late afternoon and dinner plans. The couple said they felt that if he would pick them up around four, they could grab an early nap to be fresh enough for some sightseeing.

Promptly at the agreed time, Dov rang their doorbell.

"Shalom. This is looking like a real home!" was how he greeted them. "Are you ready for some exploring?"

Juliette said, "Can you give us an idea of what you have in mind?"

"Let me surprise you."

"OK."

With that they set off down from the campus and headed into town.

119

Dov took them to the waterfront where they admired the two huge cruise ships, both starting to make arrangements for departure. They also saw a couple of Israeli navy vessels moored slightly to the east of the cruise docks.

From there he swung through some of the refinery area looping around to point out some of the sights while moving through the older parts of the city. It was nice to see how the city elders had not only preserved these buildings, but encouraged making many into quaint shops, bars and restaurants. But, what really impressed them was seeing a building called "Beit-Hagefen Arab Jewish Center" giving hope that their sojourn would be peaceful.

They continued heading south passing into a residential area that rivaled Beverly Hills. Similarly, the street with magnificent homes wrapped in exotic foliage wound ever-upward.

At the top of the rise, he stopped and they all got out to admire the view, taking in a breathtaking panorama of the modern industrial city spread out below them. He then marched them to the entry to the visitors' gate to the Baha'i Gardens, where they first peered down at the golden dome.

The lush plantings were breathtaking and they slowly descended the wide stone staircase, gasping at the overwhelming view and mingled fragrances of over a million blooming plants.

"I had heard of this place and actually Googled it a couple of weeks ago," said Juliette. "But, I am totally blown away seeing it in person."

"Ditto for me," said Joseph.

By the time they were ready to leave, their stomachs were giving signals their "normal" dinner time was approaching. "Dov,

120

we don't know about you, but Juliette and I are starting to get hungry."

"Me too," he said. "In fact, I have a great place I'd like to take you. It's about twenty minutes away. Are you up for it?"

"Sure," they said in unison.

With that the three of them piled into the car and started to work their way through the mountains.

"Dov, what are all these trees?" asked Joseph. "It looks like a forest."

"It is," he replied. "It's the Jewish National Fund's Carmel Forest. There are millions of trees here planted since the birth of Israel, mostly paid for by your countrymen."

"This is far more dense than I ever thought possible for tree growth in such an arid country," Joseph said.

"Israel may be tiny, but it is a country of contrasts. We go from some of the harshest desert, to the lowest point on the globe at the Dead Sea, to the highest agriculture yields worldwide in the north. So, why should you be surprised we can grow forests like these?"

"This country is amazing."

"Well, wait until you see where we're going for dinner!"

About fifteen minutes later they entered a Druze village. Dov was able to find a parking spot immediately in front of the restaurant where he had made reservations for this evening.

The owner greeted him effusively and welcomed the Chens to his establishment. He then took them to a table with a wonderful view of the town through the window. After asking for their drink orders, Dov asked, "Have you ever had Israeli lemonade?"

Thinking what could be special about lemonade made in Israel, Juliette said, "No, as you know we just got here and haven't had a thing."

"Then you're in for a treat!" Dov said, and ordered the same for all of them. With that the host left them with menus.

Dov next said, "Just order a main course. You won't need any sides or salads."

Within minutes, immediately before the drinks arrived two waiters showed up with trays full of mezzes. Many were eggplant based, but there were also different salads, dips, and wonderful falafel, all accompanied by warm pita just from the oven. Immediately after, three frosty tall glasses of lemonade seasoned with fresh mint arrived.

"*L'Chaim*" said Dov as he raised his glass and after a clink with sip, they dug in to the spread in front of them. By the time the dishes of grilled chicken and lamb showed up all three were nearly sated on the appetizers.

Dov started the conversation with some basic statistics. "You all know that Israel is the Jewish state and our claimed homeland for over three thousand years. What you may not realize is the population is split seventy-five percent Jews, twenty percent Arabs and five considered 'others.'

What you've seen today are two factions of the 'other' group. The Baha'i are their own religion while the Druze another. Although the Druze are also an Arabic sub-set, they traditionally pledge allegiance to the country in which they reside. That's why they are accepted into the Israeli army and there are many accounts of Druze fighting Druze throughout the numerous wars this country has seen."

"That's just like the American Civil War," said Juliette.

"So true," replied Dov.

Their conversation carried on for more than two hours touching on numerous interesting facts about the country, its people, the wave-over-wave of conqueror and how they impacted the various histories. Dov also made sure to extract some information about the Chens' own expectations of their time in Israel.

Chapter 15

2007

The couple shared an office. It wasn't big, but it was functional. However, the lab put at their disposal that was a miraculous site. Over forty feet long and almost as wide, it had every convenience at their fingertips. As well, they had access to over ten graduate students all vying for a spot on their team. Naturally, the budget only went so far and only allowed them to hire two grads each. So, with a team of six they were committed to determining at least one documentable cause of Alzheimer's disease.

Juliette had been studying the work of Maria LeDuc, a senior fellow at the Bloomfield Centre for Research in Aging at the Jewish General Hospital's Lady Davis Institute in Montreal. LeDuc had spent the past fourteen years researching in a direction where she'd faced scepticism and outright derision within the scientific community. She was challenging the accepted explanation for the past 25 years of the cause of Alzheimer's: the formation of "plaques" on the brain that destroy neurons.

Instead, LeDuc had been convinced the enzyme Caspase-6 is a root cause and gathered evidence that its activation precedes the plaques. Then, in later stages, these entangle elements in the brain ultimately leading to Alzheimer's. The Chens' fellowship was based on collaborating with LeDuc to either prove or disprove the effect of Caspase-6.

They estimated their study would take at least two and probably three years to complete. Moreover, they wanted to

124

establish a series of articles on the subject so the community would be fully informed of the outcomes as they were determined.

One thing about which they were certain was there was an abundant supply of test subjects with families that were hopeful this type of research would be able to identify the presence of Alzheimer's long before death and autopsy. Sadly, to-date that was the only accepted protocol.

The biggest single hurdle they faced was the lack of a simple test for caspase-6. With this in mind, Joseph determined that if they were able to prove the causality with Alzheimer, then having a test to identify both the presence, and more importantly the concentration of caspase-6, would become the most reliable indicator of the disease. And, a true measure of their success.

To accomplish this they decided to split their resources between developing a test and proving the enzyme as the disease agent. Although one would think coming up with an effective test would be the easier of the two, the effort for both was about the same.

However, the sooner they had a simple test, the faster they could process patients. Moreover the more patients they could measure the greater the reliability of their research.

A complicating factor was that caspase-6 was thought to be an indicator for Huntington's Disease and traditionally not attributed to Alzheimer patients. As such, lab assay testing for HD was well known and the fact it wasn't being used to confirm HD, since Huntington's was a genetic defect, meant turn-around time was less critical. But since an Alzheimer diagnosis was still much more an art than a science, the sooner it was diagnosed the faster various remedies to slow its progress could be applied.

Over the first six months the team used the standard assay techniques to extract and measure caspase-6. Then serendipity intervened.

One day there was a power outage while the grad students were analyzing a series of samples. Dov, who had just come back from a stint with the Israeli army reserve, was a boy scout at heart. He had a series of green glow sticks in his backpack that was always tucked under his workstation.

When the lights went out everyone stayed where they were. There was a maze of delicate glass directly in front of them representing a few months' worth of hard work. The last thing anyone wanted to do was possibly damage this array and set back all they'd been working on so diligently.

Dov realized the seriousness of the situation and said, "Hey everyone, I have some glow sticks in my bag. Let me grab a few and we'll at least be able to move out of here until the power comes back online."

He leaned over and snagged some, then he snapped them to start the photo-chemical reaction, and shook each one carefully to bring them to full illumination. Once they were all at their peak he got up and started to move to the other stations, handing them to the researchers so everyone could use them to safely exit the lab.

As he passed the most comprehensive section of the array a number of spots within the glass maze started to also shine. Just then Joseph looked over and saw the pinpricks of green light in the glass tubing.

"Holy shit, I think we just found our mechanism to identify the presence of caspase-6 in living samples!" he shouted.

126

Everyone gathered around the display and started to wave their glow sticks over it marveling at how clearly they could see the miniscule structures. When the power came back on, they all now knew where their focus would be.

Over the next few months they used this technique to analyze every sample that came into the lab. With these results they were able to determine the level of efficacy and were amazed at the accuracy of their findings when further analysis was done to compare against the slower older methods. In the meantime, on behalf of the full team, Joseph used his own funds to start the commercialization process including patent filings, working out intellectual property issues with the university, and sourcing venture capitalists willing to move this from the lab to mainstream.

-o-o-o-

While studying for their medical specialties in Baltimore the couple made it a point to explore the wonderful historical sites within a two-hour driving range of their home. There they could step back over 150 years of history to study the Civil War, or almost 250 years by visiting the preserved memorials of the War of Independence in Philadelphia.

In the same amount of travel time in Israel they could go back millennia, especially when visiting Jerusalem.

Joseph became totally enthralled with the iconic city. He read every book he could find on its history and how it affected three religions.

They had made it a point to not own a car in Israel. The distances they traveled were often short except for their weekend excursions. For those they used the excellent public transit

127

system. Again, they could make it from Haifa to Jerusalem in around two hours and the trip was about fifteen minutes shorter if they were going to Tel Aviv.

But, once they had exhausted the typical tourist sites including Masada, Nazareth, Bethlehem, Caesarea, Jaffa, and Eilat, Jerusalem became their destination of choice.

After their first visit to the Old City they were hooked. It didn't matter which of the four sections they visited, Christian, Arab, Armenian or Jewish, they were captivated by the history, people, and blend of architectures.

Often the couple planned two weeks ahead with a view towards whether they would make it a same day or overnight jaunt. The primary determinant was avoiding the Jewish Sabbath in the sacred city. Jerusalem was effectively closed up tight from sundown every Friday until an hour after sunset on Saturday. Planning was rarely a problem since the couple would book mid-week time off from the university and, not being Jewish, they had no problem spending the Sabbath in the lab.

Moreover, Haifa is a much more cosmopolitan city than Jerusalem with fewer religious restrictions. As such, they had complete access on Saturdays or any of the Jewish festivals, along with all the resources they may need.

Joseph declared, "Honey, as long as we live here I want to study the history of this fascinating place almost to the same level as our scientific studies. Naturally, I want to visit as many ruins as we can. But my real goal is to embrace Jerusalem!"

"Anything you say dear," was her laconic reply. She had already experienced his archeological ardor in Baltimore when he insisted they visit every Civil War site after examining in detail the battle histories. Then, he augmented this with trips to both Philadelphia and Washington, DC to reflect on how democracy arose out of the American Revolution. So when Joseph made this announcement at the end of their first month in-country, it came as no surprise to Juliette.

He was an avid reader and a remarkable student. In addition to the stacks of books he brought home from the university's library on the history of Jerusalem, he used every online source he could find. Then, once these were exhausted, he went to the Hebrew sources.

Joseph's attitude was that they were already learning the language just by living in Haifa, so it wasn't much of a stretch for him to try to find historical source materials in the native dialect. Where he drew the line was classic Greek, although he had a smattering of Latin from his high school days. That too came in handy.

A typical excursion to Jerusalem usually started with a nine o'clock departure from the Egged bus station, which would get them into the city before Noon. They would then either walk or take a taxi to the most likely spot where tourists would gather in proximity to Joseph's latest site of interest. There they would wait until an English-speaking tour bus arrived and surreptitiously sneak into the group. Once that batch returned to their bus, they would then find their way to the next site Joseph had mapped out.

They used this approach for a few months until Joseph decided the information the tour guides were supplying was inaccurate. After hearing for the umpteenth time that the tomb the visitors were facing was King David's when it was obviously constructed nearly two thousand years after the king's death by early believers in Islam, Joseph couldn't hold back.

"That is a load of crap you're telling these people who have paid good money for this tour!" he shouted.

"Vat do you mean?" said the agitated guide.

"I mean anyone with a basic education knows that King David was long dead when this tomb was built and his bones were never buried in it. In fact, nobody knows where his bones are and it was Mohammad's followers who first built here. That structure didn't last and was rebuilt a number of times over the next thousand years. Then when the Mamluks couldn't stand the bickering between the mere thousand Jews and slightly fewer Christians left in the city in the early 1400's, they claimed it for themselves."

"Are you some foreign Chinese goy, suddenly a maven on Jewish history?" he shouted back.

"Joseph, you are embarrassing me. Please, let's go," said Juliette pleadingly.

"No honey, this man is wrong. In fact, many of these guides are wrong. The history is right in front of them in any language they choose but instead they still feed this crap to the tourists."

"Joseph that may be so, but, this isn't our tour and it isn't our responsibility to correct them."

By this time the guide had marched up to his accuser and said, "Look, I don't know vat you tink you are but I had to pass a very detailed examination after four years of study to become a tour guide and I only repeat vat I have been taught. If you tink vat

I'm saying is wrong take it up vith the autorities at de Israel Tourist Office."

"That is exactly what I plan to do!"

"Hey, vere is your name tag? Are you even on my bus? I don't remember seeing you getting onboard!"

"Honey, let's go," implored Juliette.

"OK," Joseph said resignedly and took her arm brusquely pushing past the confused tour guide.

Once they were around the corner and heard the bus engine starting up Juliette said, "I know you are a stickler for accuracy and I know you have studied these sites from every perspective imaginable, but you embarrassed me beyond belief just now. Please in future let us hire our own guides, and if you disagree with them, you can discuss it one-on-one. That way the two of you may learn something."

"All right, I promise."

Before the next excursion Joseph dutifully went online and tracked down a large number of independent guides. He first contacted them by e-mail and asked a detailed list of questions. His goal was accuracy. After a week of back-and-forth digital discussions he settled on three he felt worth interviewing. With everything in place, this trip to the Holy City started with a series of face-to-face interviews in the lobby bar at the Prima Royale Hotel. This compact tourist hotel, where they often stayed, was well-situated, being virtually across the street from the far more luxurious Dan Panorama and less than a ten minute walk to the Jaffa Gate, a significant entry to the Old City. Their route also took them through the Mamilla Mall, one of Juliette's favorite shopping centers worldwide.

131

The first meeting went well and Joseph felt confident he could trust the information this man offered. And, the second was about the same. However, it was the third potential guide who was so infuriating, starting with his overbearing demeanor.

"Shalom, I'm Danial," said the last interviewee extending his hand first to Joseph and then to Juliette. The two of them shook the proffered hand and they all sat down at the table.

"Is there anything we can get you, Danial?" asked Joseph.

"A cup of coffee would be fine," was the reply.

A waiter was hovering as the introductions were underway and left to get a fresh cup for their latest visitor. They didn't have time to even start a conversation before the man was back pouring the strong rich elixir into their cups. One thing the Chen's really loved about Israel was the spectacular coffee. Even the most common coffee shop served blends that put North American vendors to shame.

With that done, he left and their discussion started in earnest. Joseph said, "I have met with two other potential guides and as I said in my e-mails we are usually in town around twice each month. Since we arrived in the country I have tagged along with many tourist groups listening to the garbage they're being told by obviously misinformed or worse, incompetent docents. When I confronted one of these so-called experts a few weeks ago my wife said I embarrassed her. So, I had to promise her that I would hire our own guide for when we are in town."

"That sounds prudent."

"Yes, I think it is. And today I would like to make a decision on who I will hire on an on-going basis."

"*Beseder*," said Danial.

132

Joseph pretended he didn't know the man meant "OK," and pushed on saying, "Whatever, my concern with you isn't your education or your references, it is the fact I have seen you before on a tour we tagged along with about six months ago. And, even though it appeared the group really liked you, you told them that the cave under the Wall was built in the Second Temple period when in fact it was hundreds of years later."

"What makes you such an expert?" he snapped.

"Because, I'm an academic and make it a point to read a number of source books plus check out a broad range of online sources to learn as much as I could about this place."

"*Atah tofesh,*" the man said.

"*Lo, atah tofesh,*" Joseph shot back.

Danial replied, "You speak Hebrew?"

"We both speak it and read it and yes I have examined all the major sources not only in English but in Hebrew."

"I underestimated you," he said.

"Yes, and if you promise never to tell us the local folklore as opposed to the latest archeological determinations, you're hired."

Danial said, "Yes, that is agreeable."

Todah rabah.

Bevakesha.

With that Joseph and Juliette now had their guide. Unlike the other two interviewees, they had actually seen this man in action. Moreover, they had tagged along for much of his tour and except for the tunnel reference was accurate.

Over time Danial proved to have a wealth of knowledge well beyond anything Joseph was able to derive from the tomes

133

he had devoured, irrespective of their source language or how well-respected the author.

Chapter 16

2010

Israel was an amazing adventure. In the three years Joseph and Juliette lived there they saw so much and accomplished even more. Their international experiences exceeded all their expectations in every dimension to the point they were concerned about settling in when they returned to North America.

As one would expect with their combined degrees and practical experience gained over the past years, they had their choice of facilities from around the world. However, they decided to narrow their choices to where they respectively grew up. This included either San Francisco or Toronto, Canada. However, the opportunities afforded by the Lakebeach Hospital in Toronto were greater than anything they could find in the Bay Area of California.

The fact they were both now working at the foremost gerontology facility in Canada was in itself intimidating. Sharing the lead role for advanced care in dementia was something they could grasp academically. But they needed to see how it would work in practice.

When they applied for the position it occurred to them they would have a better chance if they broke with convention and submitted their application as a team. Although unorthodox, the practice wasn't unknown and with their combined publishing efforts it made the review process that much easier for the hospital. Moreover, their offer to work for a single salary since Joseph was able to fall back on his trust fund clinched the deal.

From the hospital's perspective they were getting the two best and brightest in the world at the price they may have had to pay for someone far less esteemed to run one of the hardest sub-specialties in their domain. In fact, patients where dementia was questionable, because of the advanced progress of often chronic diseases adversely affecting their general health, fell under their purview.

To the young couple this was a dream opportunity where they could both continue their studies of medical subjects other facilities would fight to have, while providing a level of care well above the global norm for this demographic.

And, since they had decided to settle either in San Francisco to be near Juliette's family, or Toronto where Joseph grew up, being in Toronto sealed the deal. Here was where they would raise their family. Plus since Juliette was American-born, their children would automatically be dual citizens.

Their domain was physically situated on the sixth floor and occupied the full western wing. This part of the hospital was designed in the 1980's and reflected modern touches compared to the rest of the facility that dated back to just after the WWII. It was also kept fresh with unmarred paint and spotless surroundings. As well, there was an incredible collection of art hanging in the corridors, rooms, and common areas. Obviously, the donors were wealthy and at some point probably needed the tax receipts.

However with the exception of perhaps Los Angeles or New York City, one wouldn't expect original art from Chagall, Miro, Degas, Warhol and a myriad of other well-known artists to hang in most hospitals save for the C-level suites and possibly the board room. At Lakebeach, it was throughout, with some of the most impressive located in the two "quiet rooms" on their floor.

These suites were set-aside as a comfortable place where grieving relatives could gather after the passing of a loved one. Each offered two chambers separated by French doors so that the front area could be a retreat, while the latter, the more inmost space, was where tears were common and arrangements for remembrances made. So, soothing images adorning the walls provided solace to the families.

Since the couple were splitting duties, they would often work opposite shifts. That was something the two of them endured in Los Angeles. But in this case, they also shared the same workspace so that both at home and office, they would encounter their respective bad habits on a protracted basis.

Joseph realized he would have to clean up his act in the pristine hospital office environment, especially with a hand-signed Henri Toulouse Lautrec poster staring directly at him. It would appear unprofessional to overload his desk with the typical heap of dog-eared journals, notes, monographs, and record files that normally occupied every available space in his past work surroundings. Plus, there was no way Juliette would put up with a mess like that when she also needed to use the same desk while on-call.

She adored the hospital's art collection and in off-hours would tour the facility compiling a personal catalog of its holdings. For her this was both educational and enlightening. But what Juliette didn't discover until they'd been in the hospital for a full three months, was that the artwork on display was only a fraction of the total collection. She only realized this when the Lautrec in their office was unexpectedly changed to a different one and Juliette asked someone what happened to the previous poster.

"They's changed ever' so offen," mumbled one of the custodial staff. "They's hun'reds more downs in da tombs."

Hearing this only excited her more since now Juliette could increase her knowledge of the hospital's holdings by viewing all the replacement art recently mounted. She thought it would be interesting to see how long it would take before one she had already seen hanging would resurface. Also, would it be hung in the same location as it had previously occupied?

Milt & Marilyn's story

Chapter 17

1990

"Go fuck yourself!"

"Is that any way to talk to your father?" said Marilyn in despair.

"You are NOT my father! You are a lame imposter who is fucking my mother!"

"I am your step-father. I legally adopted you. And, as your elder, I deserve some respect."

"Respect is earned not given. As far as I'm concerned you can shove respect right up your ass."

"You are not yet legal age and I am personally responsible for you. Therefore you still need to do what you are told."

"As I said before, go fuck yourself!

"I am seventeen and will soon be eighteen. Maybe I'm still your charge only because I didn't emancipate myself when I had the chance. So I will do what I want when I want and you can scream at me all you like. In a few months, when I can, I am going to walk out."

"And what will you do for funds?"

"The first hundred thousand of my trust fund comes available when I turn eighteen."

"That won't last long the way you spend money."

"Yeah, but at that point you won't have a say in what I do!"

This typical exchange had taken place on a regular basis since Milt had married Marilyn. Lindsay hated him with a passion and no matter what he did, it was never enough.

Marilyn had thrown in the towel a long time ago, but Milt thought he could at least find an accommodation with the girl if not a true relationship. She was bitter, angry, and felt he was an interloper even though her mother had remarried over twelve years ago. There was never any chemistry between Milt and Lindsay and the acrimony only grew over time.

The only good news in sight was that the girl was planning to attend the University of Maryland in a year, once she graduated high school. And the parents had agreed as soon as she was away at college, they would finally decide exactly where the two of them were going to permanently settle.

Since they had married, Milt still retained a home in Toronto but commuted to Chicago for two weeks at a time. He officially became an American resident and eventually a dual citizen. But, with the different medical systems the two of them realized there may be an advantage to moving to Canada so that Marilyn could also become a dual citizen.

The only obstacle was Lindsay and they agreed that as long as she was living at home they would not disrupt her education by moving to another country. Everyone knew that would shortly change and immediately on her departure for college, they had plans to spend some time in Toronto exploring housing options.

On the other hand, Marilyn had reservations about Lindsay attending the University of Maryland since it had a reputation of being a party school and it wasn't hard to overlay her own college-era experiences on her daughter. As far as she knew, the rebelliousness Lindsay exhibited was mostly a result of her remarrying, which the girl focused by fighting with Milt. She probably wasn't a virgin, but also not apparently promiscuous like Marilyn was at her age.

The question was how much would that change once a brat like Lindsay was on her own and away from any positive family influence.

-o-o-o-

Near the end of August the three of them packed up the used Dodge minivan they had bought for Lindsay, wished her well, and sent her on her way heading due east. It was a simple run from Chicago to College Park, MD along the interstate highway system.

The next morning the two parents boarded the short commuter flight to Toronto.

Milt had previously parked his car in the airport garage. Having sat idle for the typical two week period it was covered in dust. He turned on the ignition and hit the windshield washer button at the end of the turn signal stalk. Then he moaned when nothing came out. Naturally, the wipers started to automatically sweep the filthy window effectively grinding the accumulated detritus into the glass. He immediately switched them off, but the damage was done.

The good news is that being in a northern climate he had a substantial snow brush in the trunk and grabbed it to try to clear the window enough to see. That way he could at least drive to the nearest gas station to buy a bottle of washer fluid. After a noble effort, the glass was clean enough for him to maneuver as long as they didn't drive directly into the sun.

Leaving the airport, he turned right onto Dixon Road and looked for the first place that was likely to have the necessary cleaning agent. However, by the time they hit the first stop light, there was a carwash immediately to their left. Talk about serendipity!

Once the vehicle was clean, they bought a bottle of washer fluid to avoid the same problem in the future then made their way to downtown. In about thirty minutes they arrived at Milt's condo near the corner of College and Bay Streets.

This was an up-and-coming part of town somewhat like downtown Chicago, very similar to where North Michigan meets East Chicago Avenue. Both locations are lined with condominiums whose original sales pitches included promises of wonderful views of the respective Great Lake. The trouble is typically only twenty-five to thirty percent of the units actually face the water. As for the rest, they face the wrong direction, are too low down in the tower, or have an obstructed view.

Although in some ways the Bloor Street corridor in Toronto was perhaps further developed, and in many respects considered to be "higher end," especially with the Yorkville shopping area nearby. Bottom line, the two cities were extremely similar and Marilyn felt comfortable in both.

Milt's condo was really small and more a pied-a-terre than somebody's permanent residence. Therefore, they needed to find something more substantial if they were going to make Toronto their primary residence.

With Milt's past ties in the local real estate market, it didn't take him long for him to line up a number of properties they could view over the coming days. However, before leaving Chicago the couple agreed that for their first day as official empty nesters they would act as tourists and take in the sites.

They started with the CN Tower, explored Chinatown while enjoying some dim sum upstairs at the Pacific Restaurant, then visited the Art Gallery of Ontario. This was located just down Dundas Street and is famous for having one of the largest collections of Henry Moore sculptures in the world. Moore's work is one of Marilyn's passions. After that, they headed back to Milt's condo for a nap, some nookie, and a shower before dinner.

Although reservations weren't necessary, they purposely made one for an outside table at one of the Greek restaurants on the Danforth. It was a beautiful summer night and they thought being cooped up inside the shoebox that substituted as a condo suite was a waste. On arrival Milt ordered a big pitcher of red sangria. Although the drink is Spanish in origin, when it comes to a warm weather refresher, it was hard to beat on any patio.

The both had the roast lamb following an appetizer of fried calamari. Their dinner also included a Greek salad, roasted potatoes, and rice. By the time they were finished, they were beyond full. This necessitated a stroll down the Avenue to try to work off some of their meal. Both were glad they didn't order some baklava for dessert. Neither had any room left.

They took the efficient Bloor subway line there and back, making them feel like true urbanites, which was considerably different from how they lived in the Chicago suburbs. By the time the two arrived home, Marilyn had made a decision.

"Milt, today has been a wonderful day and the more I think about it, the more I'm convinced I do not want to live in the suburbs anymore. Why don't we concentrate our search around here?"

"That sounds like a good idea. Do you have any physical boundaries you would like to set?"

"Why don't you grab a map so we can mark out some that make sense?"

Milt dug in the pile of material he'd received from one of his real estate colleagues and brought out a well-used map of Toronto. He then opened it on the kitchen table.

Marilyn gazed at the chart and asked him to mark exactly where they were at that moment. Once Milt put a red dot on the intersection she said, "What about from the Harbourfront to just north of Bloor Street and from just west of University to just east of Yonge Street? Is that good for you?"

"That sounds perfect. I'll call the agent again in the morning and tell her to narrow down the search."

Chapter 18

2000

It only took a couple of months for Milt and Marilyn to settle on a wonderful two-bedroom condominium at Market Square. This avant-garde complex, located at the corner of Front and Church Street, sits across the street from the historic St. Lawrence Market. When first built the area was in need of gentrification. Now it is one of the trendiest areas of the city, situated on the periphery of the financial center, making it convenient for Milt for when he actually went into his office. But more importantly, it's in close proximity to some of the best upscale shopping Marilyn could ever desire.

Their unit was spacious. It was also located on the top floor so high enough in what's considered a low-rise building for them to see Lake Ontario. In fact, summer evenings there was nothing more relaxing that sitting on their balcony and watching the world go by.

Marilyn had become a dual citizen meaning she now had full medical coverage in Canada. Milt's business continued to expand even though he had significantly cut back his hours to often less than one day per week. They were living a wonderful life.

The only issue was Marilyn's daughter Lindsay.

She had met the man of her dreams in college, married him, and thankfully moved to the Palm Beach area in Florida. Marilyn's son-in-law is a periodontist making enough money to keep her daughter happy and as far away from Milt as possible. However, each winter the two of them still make the trek down to celebrate Lindsay's birthday. Marilyn claimed it was a tradition and refused to stop even if her daughter was almost thirty years old and still a bitch. Anyhow, Milt figured it was a small price to pay considering how happy he and Marilyn were the rest of the year.

The two of them really loved their condo and its convenience.

One night around nine-thirty there was a loud knock on their front door. Since they hadn't been contacted by the concierge in the lobby before the dreadful racket, they figured it must be somebody from inside their building.

Even though each suite had a peep-hole in the front door, Milt had his guard down thinking the caller was a neighbor. On opening he saw the superintendent from the adjoining structure in their complex, and obviously under some duress, when without preamble he declared, "You have a leak. It's destroying the unit below you and I need to check out your suite right now!"

Milt knew their own super was off for a month having some minor surgery that unfortunately required a prolonged recovery. With this in mind he suspected this man was filling-in. However, it took him a full thirty-seconds to remember his name.

"Nelson, come on in. I can assure you everything is bone dry," he replied after the pause.

"Honey who is it?" asked Marilyn from their second bedroom that they had set up as a comfy den.

"It's the super from next door. He's covering for Robert and said we have a leak."

"Not from our suite!"

For the next fifteen minutes the three of them opened every cabinet, checked the two bathrooms, and the front hall powder room, ran an empty dishwasher, then turned on every faucet in the place. All seemed dry.

After that their unexpected guest left and probably went downstairs to see if there was any change in the leak situation. Since he didn't return that night, they assumed all was well.

Wrong!

Two weeks later, Robert the super for their building was back from his month away. The trouble was now he was at their door.

"Guys, I'm really sorry to bother you but that leak downstairs has persisted and they're going crazy. Let me test a few things my stand-in may have missed."

With that he checked caulking, grout, and every other type of sealing in their suite. He also examined the glass door to the shower stall in the master bathroom. This was determined to be warped and he sadly declared it proved they were at fault. Milt didn't argue and said he would cover the cost of any and all repairs.

The next morning Marilyn contacted a contractor they had used in the past and made arrangements for him to re-caulk their shower plus order a new glass door. Over the next week the work was done and all seemed well.

Wrong again!

Two weeks passed and the drip was back. This time the building manager got into the act. She was a new hire and had been with there for only a few months.

However, her reputation had preceded her as someone who went entirely by the bylaws and building rules until she decided she didn't like you. Up to that point Milt and Marilyn were neutral about her and figured she felt the same about them. However, that was all to change.

This time, around ten in the morning she arrived with the plumbing contractors that the building typically used for the common element repairs. Declaring an emergency she demanded entry to their unit and had the three plumbers who accompanied her start poking holes in the wall. By the time they finished there were a couple of eight by ten inch gaps in the en-suite bathroom and another of the same size under the vanity in the guest bathroom. Although the cause of the leak remained undetermined the manager insisted it was caused by Milt and Marilyn.

Again they agreed to repair any damage caused by them and within a couple of days had brought back the same crew they used previously.

This time the leak definitely seemed to be fixed. However, the building manager wasn't convinced. Instead she ordered her own team to return a week later augmented with an official looking legal document.

This she claimed said they were able to punch more holes around both bathrooms until the root cause was determined. Since water only flows downhill and there was a constant drip in the lower unit, by definition this had to originate in Milt and Marilyn's suite.

At this point Marilyn put her foot down and said they could do what they wanted in the en-suite bath, but could not touch the guest bathroom or powder room.

The men were there for the rest of the day accounting for approximately seven billable hours for each of the three. In that time they took off almost all the tiles in the shower stall and from around the sunken bathtub. They then punched holes into the ceiling and walls and surrounding the bath. Then they inserted fiber optic cables attached to mini-television monitors and examined every possible source of the leak. The eureka moment came when they discovered a pinhole with a miniscule drip emerging from it about mid-way up the cold water feed. Obviously, it must only spray when the tap was turned on.

This discovery resulted in the removal of nearly two additional linear feet of tile to determine how high up the wall water had penetrated. As well they lifted the shower floor to see if the rubber water barrier had been compromised. Naturally, once they did all that, it was clear the bladder was filled with water while the steel wall studs were rusted from the floor to the top of the now exposed area.

Marilyn was beside herself. However, once Milt got home from work, he said his insurance company would take over plus he would put his best real estate lawyer on the case. He believed that would cap their exposure and get this mess on a professional footing. Moreover, he knew from past experience that if the damage had been caused by exposed pipes, the problem would be his. But, now that the plumbers had confirmed this problem resulted from pipes hidden behind the wall, it was the building's responsibility.

Just as the crew was preparing to leave, the building manager came up again and forced her way into the suite to examine the damage. Milt said it was OK, while Marilyn shouted "Get out!"

Although it was unlikely the excessive physical damage to the bathroom was at the request of the manager, Marilyn was not going to let her into their suite. To her mind, the only consolation was that she'd refused to let them destroy the guest bathroom. Otherwise they wouldn't have had any bathing facilities until this mess was repaired. However, this was now well past the point of being a simple repair and instead was going to be a major renovation. Who knew how long they would be inconvenienced.

The process now comprised submitting a claim, getting quotes, getting permits and then commissioning the work. Neither of them thought it would take three weeks just to get through this phase alone.

This started with a series of pictures augmented by expert examinations that had to be sent to the adjusters. Interviewing possible contractors followed next. Unfortunately, the larger ones were booked months into the future and the really small ones didn't want to take the risk associated with working in a condominium. Getting three quotes was a much bigger deal than they ever thought it would be. But, their insurance broker said their coverage demanded them.

Ultimately, they were able to put together the necessary documentation and as soon as they got the green-light for the permits, they nailed down a company with a fifty-year history supported by stellar recommendations.

Together with the contractor they went to pick tiles, fixtures and finishing materials. The latest fashion was more ornate than the original style used when that bathroom was originally constructed. And unbeknownst to Milt and Marilyn, newer techniques were far more labor intensive.

The following Monday a team of four burley men showed up right on time. They had completely demolished the old en suite by that afternoon, right down to the bare concrete. At that point the head of the contracting company arrived and said, "This is a snap. We should be finished by the end of this week, or the beginning of next."

At ten the following morning the phone rang and Marilyn answered. To her dismay the contractor informed her that since they were now ahead of schedule, nobody would be there that day. The following morning the excuse was the team was picking up materials from the distributor. Finally one person came around noon and made questionable progress on installing the new steel studs.

On Monday they finally delivered the rest of the materials including bags of cement, piles of tiles, boxes of grout and a tile cutting saw. All of this was stacked in three spots; the den, the dining room, and across one wall of their bedroom.

However, for the next couple of weeks when it came to actual workers, it was effectively the same pattern…one showed up for three out of five days. The renovation was now well behind schedule and although there was a "drop dead date," everyone knew there was no way that would be met.

Progress, if it could be called that, was being made but at a snail's pace. Plus it seemed every excuse in the book was fair game by a company supposedly with stellar references.

One issue that cropped up close to when the project was originally scheduled to be completed, really annoyed the couple. Being Jewish they were coming home from Temple on Yom Kippur only to find that two workers had actually shown up. But as Marilyn and Milt opened the door around 1:00PM, they were already packing up.

151

According to one of them, a neighbor had banged on the door a short while ago to say that since many in the building were also Jewish it wasn't appropriate to work on the holiest day of their year.

Knowing this to be bogus, and there was nothing in the by-laws prohibiting this, they pleaded with the workers to stay. But, by this point there was nothing that could be done to keep them on-site.

A real concern the couple had was that friends from the States were planning to stay with them the following weekend. That is why the work had originally been timed for completion two full weeks ahead of the visitors (and why the drop-dead date was in the contract). But, anticipating at least some unforeseen delay, they had allowed some slack.

They also knew that additional time had to be provided for the installation of the glass shower doors plus a proper full suite clean-up to extract as much of the plaster dust and fine grit thrown off from the tile saw.

As the visit loomed closer, the number of workers seemed to increase and they stayed longer. One Friday evening Milt and Marilyn arrived home after a dinner out to find the men were just packing up. Their foreman said, "If the security people hadn't stopped us, we were planning to stay the whole night to get this finished."

A likely excuse, but it was apparent they had made solid progress. But even though they weren't making noise, the security guard was within his rights to make them stop. So, there was little Milt or Marilyn could say.

Since the upcoming weekend marked the arrival of their guests, a full-court press was underway to wrap things up. The glass doors had been ordered, final tile cuts made so the saw could be removed, grouting and caulking were both nearing completion, plus all the plumbing hook-ups were tested and proven leak-free. At noon the day before the company was to arrive, everything but the shower door installation was finished on the punch-list. This allowed the cleaning crew to arrive that afternoon and clear out by six-thirty that evening. All was done with the exception that the shower door not being installed meant the guest bathroom would have to be shared by everyone.

Milt and Marilyn thought the workers would never leave and even though there was one remaining inconvenience, figured they could live with it for a little bit longer.

The visit went well and a week after the date the doors were first promised, Milt called up the head of the contracting company and said, "You told me the doors were coming from Scarborough. Naturally I thought Scarborough, Canada not England. I guess they're still on the boat."

"That's a good one. I'll have to share it with the guys," said the contractor. "No, they are coming from just around the corner but we didn't want to interfere with your guests."

Groan.

A couple of days later when Marilyn was out getting her hair styled and Milt was at his office he called home to check voice mail for messages. There was only one:

"Mr. and Mrs. Morgenstern, I'm Fred, the owner of the shower glass installation company and I'm calling to tell you how sorry I am that your glass has not been delivered. Normally you

would have had at least two full week's use of the new shower and in the past we have always had 100% perfect service from our suppliers. I can't say why we've had so many rejects over the past few months, but it is a reality. Frankly I won't accept anything less than perfect and that is why you have been waiting so long. I know it is cold comfort that you aren't alone, but I promise you that tomorrow I will be going to the primary supplier myself and confirm the glass they have produced for you is in fact ready for installation.

"Please trust me that the delays are necessary. If you got sub-par glass you would be after me to replace it in no time and I really want to avoid that.

"If you want to call me back here's my number, otherwise I'll call you tomorrow."

That night at dinner Milt asked, "Honey, are you staying home tomorrow to wait for this Fred's call?" "Are you crazy? I've already spent more than five mornings at home over the past two weeks waiting for them to arrive. Now we find out they haven't even accepted delivery of the glass. It's obvious everyone is lying through their teeth and if they really need to get hold of me, they have my cell number."

That weekend there was a family function in Rochester, NY and they were looking forward to getting out of town to be away from the reminders of their disastrous renovation. Not surprisingly, nobody had called all week to say that the glass was ready.

On Sunday morning at the hotel in Rochester, while Marilyn was taking a shower without concern about leaks, renovations, or just about anything else Milt called to check the voicemail back home. There was only one...Fred.

"Mr. and Mrs. Morgenstern, it's Fred again and I want to say that I normally don't work on Saturday. But, with the pressing nature of your glass installation I thought it best to come in to the office and call you. I was going to call yesterday, but got tied up and forgot.

"Anyhow, your glass is in. It is perfect and if I had caught you at home, I could have set up the installation for Monday. Anyhow, it's obvious you are out. So I'll call tomorrow morning and try to set something up for Tuesday."

"Shit!" screamed Milt, ready to throw his cell phone across the room.

"Honey, what's wrong?"

"I just called home and you aren't going to believe this. Fred from the glass company called yesterday to say that the glass was ready and flawless."

"That's wonderful!"

"No, it's not. He also said he meant to call on Friday but got tied up and forgot. Now, instead of installing tomorrow, the earliest will be Tuesday or later in the week. I have to call him right now and tell him that he MUST get his crew to our place on Tuesday morning or he won't get paid."

"Fred, it's Milt Morgenstern calling and I am not happy. If you had called on Friday as you said you'd planned we could have worked out scheduling for Monday. But, now with us out of town for the weekend, we have to rely on you somehow to confirm you will definitely be installing on Tuesday.

155

"Again, it looks like we're at the bottom of the pile. That's what we've been experiencing since this mess began. All I can say is I hope you get there Tuesday."

If Milt had called from a landline instead of his cell phone he would have probably slammed it down so hard the receiver would have cracked. Except for the phone call and local weather, which was constant rain the whole weekend, everything else was wonderful.

Monday evening Fred called their home again and this time was able to talk to Milt directly. He made a formal commitment the glass would be delivered the next afternoon.

Around 2:30PM on Tuesday security called to say the installers had arrived. On reaching the suite they said, "Since the door is mounted on another piece of glass, we're going to have to let everything set before we can actually install it. That means we'll be back on Friday."

What the hell did that mean, thought Marilyn. However, it soon became apparent that the side pieces of glass enclosing the open area reaching from the low-rise tile wall to the ceiling were attached using silicone. This material had to cure and solidify before the door hinges could be affixed and these newly set pieces of glass able to support the weight of the door.

On leaving the installers said that somebody would call on Thursday to set a time for hanging the glass door on Friday. Good grief!

The tide must have changed since around noon on Thursday the concierge called up to say, "Those door guys are here to finish your job."

This was good news in spite of the fact this reno was the talk of the condominium wags.

Marilyn was out with friends for lunch and Milt called her as soon as he hung up with the front desk.

"Honey, you aren't going to believe this but the door guys are here!"

"Milt, will wonders never cease? Now the question will be when can we use the shower?"

Then in a near whisper she said, "I mean use it together."

"You took the words out of my mouth," he responded with a definite lilt in his voice.

Forty-five minutes later the two installers left and the bathroom was now intact. What should have been a couple of weeks took over three months to complete. But, the next morning the two of them could scrub each other's back as well as the rest of their anatomy while luxuriating in a soothing spray.

Chapter 19

2009

The Florida trip was a disaster this year.

No sooner had they arrived for their annual birthday visit than Lindsay started in on Milt.

"Milt, the kids are getting older and starting to ask questions so I've put mom in the guest room and you'll have to sleep on the couch in the den."

"Are you crazy?" asked Marilyn. "We're a well-adjusted married couple and there is no way you are going to have us sleep apart!"

"This is my house and I'll do what I want. And, you WILL do as I say. Otherwise you can leave!"

"Ladies, settle down. I'll sleep on the couch," Milt replied trying to calm the waters.

"Milt, you can't always give in to her. She has dominated your life since we started dating and it isn't fair."

"Fair or not, it is her home and we need to abide by her rules."

The trouble was this was only the start and within two days the situation had deteriorated to the point the couple decided leaving early was their best option. However, they refused to let Lindsay drive them to the airport.

So, instead of enjoying some winter sun and time with their grandchildren, they returned to the snowy north.

Milt was visibly upset and buried himself in his work. Where normally he would spend an average of a day or two in the office he now was there nearly every day, and often much longer than the typical nine-to-five. Plus, Marilyn was hearing from his staff that he wasn't quite himself.

With this in mind, she decided they needed to make up for the aborted southern trip. Going online she found some last minute cruise deals that sounded wonderful. Considering they hadn't taken a cruise since they first met, Marilyn thought it was time to make up for that omission.

Within moments she'd booked a one-week Western Caribbean cruise on a brand new ship leaving out of Fort Lauderdale that Saturday morning. The itinerary looked lovely with stops in Key West, Cozumel, Roatan, and Montego Bay. And, the airfare was included in the final price with carriage on one of the best-rated charter airlines in the world.

She called Milt's administrative assistant and told her what she was doing, then asked his aide to quietly clear his schedule for the upcoming week. On his arrival home that evening the printouts of the tickets were sitting on top of his dinner plate.

"Honey, I can't believe you did this," he exclaimed.

"You need the break and I need my husband back. Are you upset?"

"Hell no! I agree and I need this almost as much as you do. I'm ecstatic!"

-o-o-o-

The flight down was a typical charter flight with cramped seats, champagne, and a McMuffin for breakfast. But, who cared. They were off for some well-earned R&R with an open bar, lots of food, and sunny warmth. Throw in some afternoon delight and the package deal was sealed.

Never having been to Key West, in spite of the dozens of trips to Florida they'd taken, both found the town to be charming. Their only complaint was their on-shore time was too short. To compensate they took the trolley tour and avoided shopping other than a new hat to augment Milt's colorful collection.

As it turned out, they weren't the only ones to think the excursion time insufficient since late returnees delayed the ship's departure for Cozumel by almost an hour. Who said if you're not aboard on time, the ship leaves without you?

It seemed everyone was already aboard were leaning over the starboard rail watching the final three laggards hurdle down the dock. As they scampered up the gangplank, a cheer went up clearly yelling for free beers from the latecomers. Since it was all in jest, the drinks never arrived. However, since everyone was on vacation and in a party mood, the crowd moved freely around the top decks once the ropes were thrown. As the ship now got underway, the revellers soon lost themselves in the Caribbean sunset.

Cozumel was a port known to the couple from their past trips to the Mexican Riviera. They had visited a number of locations on both sides of the country and knew where the best local shopping finds were hidden. On disembarking, they broke away from the crowd and hoofed it into the downtown core. After a few blocks they headed off the main street and cut into the alleyways with the best of what the town had to offer.

Here they ducked into the various local goods shops looking for both trinkets and gifts, especially for the grandchildren. Although they knew they wouldn't see them for some time, especially in light of Lindsay's latest stunt, they'd have felt wrong not buying something for them.

Marilyn fell in love some beautiful silver pieces and convinced Milt to buy a pair of new cufflinks. As well they picked up a few things for the condo, just because they said "Cozumel" on them. Neither of them were packrats, but they couldn't resist the temptation of the perceived deal.

After a day of shopping including stopping for cold *cerveza* on a sundrenched patio where they listened to a Mariachi band, they returned to the ship. That night was the captain's dinner and unlike their prior cruise, this one was downright casual in comparison. Milt had brought a blazer but no tie with him as his most formal attire while Marilyn only packed a short skirt as hers. However, they had a few hours before the main event and decided sex, snooze, and shower would be the best order of operation.

The next day they arrived in Roatan just before sunrise. Looking from the ship, the land appeared raw and uncivilized. They quickly realized they were in a third world country and the light drizzle only seemed to dampen their spirits. However, after a hearty breakfast they joined the queue to disembark onto the bobbing tenders that would take them to their shore excursions.

Milt had suggested the "Walk through the Rainforest" as something that would be ideal for this port call. Marilyn was somewhat skeptical at first, but figured it would be interesting to see the Mayan ruins along with the flora and fauna of this tropical island. Also, by the time they made landfall, the rain had stopped and the sun was peaking through the clouds. The humidity likewise started to climb seemingly adding some excitement to their adventure.

Over sixty people piled into two local buses that looked like they were from the nineteen fifties. Peeled paint, nearly bald tires, cracked vinyl seats, and engines that labored to supply a minimal amount of air conditioning was the group's transportation to heights well above sea level.

With puffs of blue smoke, the two vehicles chugged out of the port area and meandered through the town. What greeted the tourists was a mix of run-down shanties and storefronts that looked like they came from a Humphrey Bogart movie, and probably just as old as one of those classics. However, it was the roadway itself that gave everyone pause. Huge craters filled with red-brown water ran down the middle of each strip of crumbled asphalt. But, this was only a prelude to what awaited them as they climbed the heights.

Their guide kept a running commentary about the island, the country's history, his education both in Honduras and the graduate studies he completed at UCLA in Los Angeles. The question was whether this was to impart some knowledge on these unsuspecting tourists or to distract us from the ever-deteriorating roadway.

After about fifteen minutes of incessant grinding it was apparent the group had climbed a noticeable way. Out of the left side of the bus the guide pointed out the island's sole airport down below and the control tower unexpectedly located right beside their bus. He said that arrangement was unique in the Caribbean but worked well, since having the tower at this elevation provided a nearly three hundred and sixty degree view. He was right, but as they turned away to head up the next incline the question was whether the bus would actually make it.

Theirs was the second vehicle in the convoy and the passengers watched in rapt attention as the preceding bus made one attempt after another to climb the incline. Each time they got a little further up the hill, but in doing so cut deep ruts in the muddy ground and sprayed the bus waiting behind with a thick coat of red slime. Finally, the first crested the hill and pulled into a parking area. Now it was their turn.

This driver took a long run to gain some momentum and veered to the right to avoid the tracks from the earlier bus. He got more than half way up the hill before trying it again. Surprisingly, this time the wheels held and as he pulled into the parking lot everyone cheered.

"Fifteen minute stop to examine the local crafts on display. Please try to buy something since this is the only marketing these artists are allowed to do by law," said the guide.

Milt and Marilyn went from stall to stall carefully avoiding the puddles and deep mud pools. They looked desperately for something to buy, but everything appeared that it would fall apart once they were back on the bus. However, rather than leaving without anything they made a point of purchasing some postcards.

Once back on the bus, one of their fellow tourists asked how much farther to the rainforest tour and how much higher would that be?

"You'll all be pleased to know it is only fifteen minutes away from here and downhill!" was the happy reply.

Sure enough, the bus turned around and effectively drifted down the hill they'd climbed with such difficulty. At the bottom the driver turned right and as he picked up speed sent another spray of mud that obscured all the windows. While the sun was breaking through the last of the clouds, it quickly dried the mud into a hard coating. It was obvious that any further sightseeing from the vehicle would be through the front windows only. In fact, the only thing that seemed to work flawlessly were the windshield wipers.

True to his word, fifteen minutes after leaving the hilltop they turned into what was definitely a tropical canopy. Thick green leaves obscured the sky from trees wrapped in vines. This was definitely jungle-like and adding to the mystery was a small zoo directly in front of the unloading zone for the various tour buses. The good news is that all the buses were similarly encrusted.

We all piled out and gathered in a loose semi-circle around a new guide who was also a government employee and dedicated to this particular site. He started with an overview of what we would see, the type of terrain on which we would be hiking, and some history on the Mayans who had inhabited this area hundreds of years in the past.

Everyone listened attentively until there was a collective gasp.

One minute Milt was standing next to Marilyn and the next he was sliding down the slight slope on his behind.

"Somebody please help me!" he cried.

Marilyn, afraid she too would suffer the same fate made a tentative step forward but the gentleman standing next to her put out his hand and said, "I'll get him."

Within moments three other men from the cruise ship rushed forward and gently helped Milt rise from the sloppy earth.

He was covered in the reddish mud not only on his backside, but on his hands, up his arms and splattered across his back. Once on his feet, Marilyn joined him and helped him into the men's rest room, which was in a hut immediately to their left and down a few steps.

"I'm so embarrassed," he stammered.

"Honey, don't be. The ground was slippery and it could have happened to anyone."

"No, I felt my feet going out from under me even before I started to fall."

"That's because it has been raining since before we got here and this is the rainforest."

"I hope you're right since my butt is really starting to hurt."

After a few minutes of wiping him down with damp paper towels the couple joined the tour. Milt purposely didn't push himself, and tried to make the most of it. He really enjoyed the scattered Mayan ruins even if they were replicas since the originals were in a museum on the mainland. But, when they got to the butterfly preserve, he was amazed. The iridescent fluttering bodies literally took his breath away. For the next ten minutes he vacillated from looking in awe to snapping pictures as fast as his digital camera would allow.

Eventually, the tour ended and everyone re-boarded the ancient buses. From here they proceeded into Coxen Hole, the nominal capital of the island to do some shopping before heading back to the ship. This time they picked up some real souvenirs including a few Marilyn wanted to give to her close friends back in Toronto and Chicago.

Once back aboard the ship she made a point of examining Milt carefully and in spite of her quiet assurances immediately after his accident, something didn't feel right about the whole thing.

The next day was a day at sea, which offered Milt the opportunity to recover from his fall and Marilyn a chance to visit the spa. He made a point of taking it easy and found his greatest exercise of the day was bending his elbow on a regular basis to make sure the cold beer made it into his mouth.

That night he was well enough to dance and they made the most of the shipboard entertainment. Plus since landfall wasn't expected until mid-morning, they didn't turn in until well past midnight.

Montego Bay loomed large on the horizon as they went down for breakfast. They'd decided they would prefer a sit-down waiter served meal rather than their normal buffet on the Promenade Deck. This gave them the chance to find a choice table with a picturesque view of Jamaica as they steamed into port. It was fascinating to watch the indistinct greens, blues, magentas, and tans morph into clearly defined trees, structures and beaches. As they enjoyed their coffee they watched the docking process while the massive ship nudged the pier with nary a tap. It was all so smooth that it took a moment to realize all motion had completely stopped.

They had at least an hour before their tour was scheduled to congregate in the movie theater in preparation for disembarkation. Since this was their last port of call, it seemed that everyone on board was determined to take at least one excursion. Milt and Marilyn had booked the leisurely sounding

166

rafting trip on the Martha Brae River. To their minds it was a perfect ending for the trip.

This time the buses were much newer and well-equipped. The travel time was slightly over an hour from the port and with the hundreds of tourists ahead of them, they spent much of the pre-river time in the gift shop. There wasn't anything of interest to buy except for a couple of rum punches at the attached bar to mellow them even further.

Eventually they were escorted to the riverside where they were helped into one of the many thirty foot long bamboo craft. Their guide was relatively talkative and provided a running commentary on the sites as they passed them. Before long their romantic river cruise was almost over. At this point, Robert, their vessel's captain stopped his poling and reached for a ditty bag laying on the deck and tied by its draw-string to a cleat near his feet.

"We rely on both tips and the tourists buying our hand carved gourds," he said. "Won't you please take a look at my handiwork and let me know what you think?"

"This is beautiful," gasped Marilyn.

"How much?" said Milt.

"What are you prepared to pay?"

"How about ten dollars?" Milt replied.

"No Mon, this took me nearly a day to carve. I can't sell it for less than twenty."

"Deal!" Milt said.

A few minutes later they slowly made their way to the final dock where the rafts were collected by truck to be driven to the starting point. The couple thanked Robert then Marilyn stepped lithely out of the raft. Next, Milt tried to get up.

To his shock, his limbs wouldn't respond to his commands. He just sat there.

"Milt, what's wrong?" Marilyn said in alarm.

"I can't, I can't, I can't" he stammered.

With a sense of shock both she and Robert lunged towards Milt causing the raft to suddenly move from the dock. However, Marilyn was soon able to also step aboard and take a firm hold of Milt's right arm. Robert, already there, was on Milt's left while they gently lifted him to his feet as the boat drifted back into the mooring.

Within seconds Milt seemed to recover and was able to step from the raft. Although shaky, he made his way to the waiting tour bus and climbed aboard on his own steam. Marilyn hovered over him as his complexion slowly came back to normal from the pasty white of a few minutes beforehand. By the time the bus was full and pulled away, everything seemed OK.

Their next stop was a local craft market. Although Marilyn had her eye on a few things, she refused to leave Milt's side. So instead of first buying some knick-knacks for their home, Marilyn started to look for some sort of assistance for Milt.

There were probably fifty artisans in the compound, each with their own tent-like structure. By the time Marilyn got to the tenth or eleventh she saw exactly what she thought would be perfect.

Standing in the far corner was a four or five foot high black and white walking stick with the image of Bob Marley carved at the top. Within seconds she was haggling with the carver who took her outside the tent to examine the mahogany tree from which he hacked the original piece of wood. Obviously, he was trying to impress her with his skill and foresight, which is why she settled on fifteen dollars for the craft. After that Marilyn had Milt sit in the shade while she examined the various dyed cotton offerings ultimately settling on a royal blue bathing suit cover-up.

The rest of the cruise passed without incident and the couple relaxed relegating Milt's mishap to the backs of their minds. Then before they knew it, it was time to disembark.

Their ship docked in the middle of the night and when they awoke the next morning it was a mad dash to the main dining room for a final breakfast. Next step was to head to the theatre while carrying any carry-on luggage with them. On arrival passengers were put into groups reflecting whether they were staying in Florida or flying off to the cold north. Since Milt and Marilyn were heading home to Toronto, they were in one of the earliest groups to depart the ship.

-o-o-o-

They boarded the shuttle bus for the five minute ride from the port to Fort Lauderdale Airport. Once there, everyone grabbed their luggage from the under-bus storage area and got into the appropriate line for their carrier. Naturally, the charter airlines had the longest lines and once they'd checked in, they proceeded through security. Somehow they got to the gate early enough to grab seats in the waiting area. It was obvious the airport was in need of renovations and including sufficient seating facilities.

Fifteen minutes later passengers from the south-bound leg of their aircraft marched through the terminal. As Milt and

169

Marilyn looked a week ago with wan skin and expectant eyes, these folks too made it clear they were now starting their vacation.

Expecting to board within the next forty minutes, everyone waiting for Milt and Marilyn's flight were surprised that those from surrounding gates with later posted departure times had already started to board.

At first nothing was asked by the passengers nor announced by the airline. Then it became clear those waiting for this particular flight were getting restless. Ultimately, a man sitting beside Milt got up from his seat and approached the desk. He spoke loud enough so they could hear him ask, "Is there something wrong with our flight?"

The gate attendant mumbled something and he came back to his seat visibly disturbed. However, whatever was mentioned at that point he kept to himself.

Since it was approaching the noon hour, people who had eaten breakfast over five hours ago aboard the ship were starting to become hungry. Within about five minutes after the man who had approached the airline attendant sat down, about twenty individuals now stormed the desk. After being told, "Everything is under control," it was becoming clear something was definitely wrong with the aircraft

Rather than sit around getting progressively more hungry, the passengers wanted to know if they could leave the boarding area to buy some lunch from the airport concessions. After about fifteen more minutes an announcement was made:

"Ladies and gentlemen on Sun Charter Flight 090, we wish to inform you your aircraft encountered a minor problem on landing and we are attending to it. In the meantime as a token of

170

our appreciation we would like to offer you lunch vouchers. However, these must be used at the establishments in this departure wing. That means they cannot be used anywhere past the security area. Please line up in an orderly fashion so we can provide you your coupon."

"Well, that clarifies things," said Milt as he rose from his seat to get vouchers for the two of them.

"Honey, as far as I'm concerned we're still on vacation," replied Marilyn.

Once these were in-hand, they headed to the airport's version of one of the best recognized chain restaurants. Checking out what was being offered, it was obvious had the national management team been aware of the poor quality of the offerings compared with the exhorbitant prices being charged they would have been embarrassed.

The couple selected sandwiches, drinks, and potato chips for their lunch. Although there was no restriction on using the freebies for alcohol, neither of them felt the need for a drink. If they had realized at that point the extent of the upcoming delay, they may have imbibed.

After lunch, the passengers re-congregated in the boarding area and tried to wait as patiently as possible. Around three that afternoon the captain appeared at the podium and took the microphone, "Ladies and gentlemen, it is with extreme disappointment that I have to tell you our airplane is not able to fly. The problem is that one of our two batteries died on arrival. FAA rules require two fully operational batteries at take-off and since we do not qualify, we can't leave.

"There is some good news though. That is, Miami International has a supply depot for 737 aircraft like ours and we've ordered a fully charged battery from their stock. I have been assured it is on its way up here."

Milt mumbled, "I hear a 'but' coming."

Sure enough, "That is the good news as I said," stated the pilot. "However, there is some bad news. If the battery doesn't arrive within the hour and the installation completed in that same timeframe, our crew becomes what is considered 'illegal' and cannot fly. Naturally, I will keep you informed as things develop."

At that point the pilot headed back down the jetway to the crippled plane. About fifty minutes later a number of Broward County police officers started to quietly position themselves around the waiting passengers. One was at the counter when the captain, along with the rest of the crew, emerged all toting their overnight bags. The captain picked up the microphone again as the police officer surreptitiously sidled up to him.

"Ladies and gentlemen, I'm sorry to say that the battery is still being transported from MIA. We are now at the point that even if it showed up this instant we would be overtime once it was installed. As such, we are leaving.

"However, I have been assured by corporate that a fresh crew is being flown down here as we speak. They are on a flight to Jamaica and will be diverted to Fort Lauderdale to take you home. Their estimated time of arrival is five this afternoon."

With that the law officers quietly moved to surround the crew and escort them out of the airport.

172

"What the hell were they thinking," shouted one of the passengers, "did they really believe we were going to riot? Typical American over-reaction of bringing in law enforcement and escalating a bad situation into a terrible one" he continued.

Many grumbles were heard in acknowledgement while the passengers settled in to wait some more.

By this time Milt was starting to exhibit many of the personality traits that preceded their vacation. It was clear he was upset, but there was an apparent tremor in his right arm augmented by eye fasciculations. Marilyn was becoming concerned.

Five o'clock came and went with no further announcements. However by six o'clock, the passengers especially those with small children, were hitting the end of their rope. One young father approached the counter asking about dinner arrangements. This prompted another appearance of law enforcement along with somebody supposedly senior management from the airline who looked like she wanted to be anywhere but there.

"Passengers of flight 090, I'm the local management representative and I want to personally express my sincere apologies for this unforeseeable delay. We are doing everything in our power to get you out of here tonight," she said.

Milt burst out with, "What about the bullshit phantom crew that is on the way down here? Anyone with half a brain knows you can't board a flight to Jamaica in Canada and divert it to Fort Lauderdale. There is no way Homeland Security would let them into the country if they hadn't pre-cleared US Customs in Canada."

Marilyn was aghast at her husband's outburst, especially since it generated a flurry of heated comments causing the officers to put their hands over their guns. At this point the man appearing to be the ranking lawman grabbed the mike and said, "Listen up. The airline is doing everything it can. In the meantime you are in the U.S.of A. and will abide by our laws. I have been told there are meal vouchers for dinner and if you are prepared to clear back through security you'all can leave the premises. But, you must be back by ten o'clock tonight."

Somewhat mollified, many of the passengers again queued up for meal tickets while some could be seen on their phones making dinner reservations.

"Milt honey, what would you like to do?" asked Marilyn.

"Well, I definitely don't want to have dinner with your bitch of a daughter," he shot back.

Marilyn got out her cell phone and called one of her cousins who had a place in the area. She hoped they were in town and on connecting she gave whoever answered an abbreviated account of what had happened. The good news is they were free for dinner.

Fifteen minutes later they were waiting for Marilyn's cousin outside in the warm evening air. Once in the car it was agreed they should still stay close-by and decided to hit the restaurant strip in Hollywood, Florida. That was only about twenty minutes away using the back roads.

They found a cozy Spanish restaurant and had a convivial dinner. Steve, her cousin's husband has always been a bit of a tech snob and wanted to show off his latest i-Phone.

At eight-thirty he demanded, "What's your crappy airline's name again and the flight number?"

Milt responded and after a moment of finger contortions on the smartphone screen Steve grumped.

"What does that mean?" asked Milt.

"It says here your flight has been canceled and passengers are to call the airline for further information. Here, you can use my phone."

Milt clicked on the hyperlinked number and was connected with a recording that said, "To all passengers on our delayed flight 090 from Fort Lauderdale to Toronto, please proceed to the desk in the departure area to receive further information on which hotel you have been assigned for tonight."

"Holy crap!" exclaimed Milt. "I can't believe this. Steve, can we settle up and have you drive us right back to the airport?"

He made it in record time and they were in front of the vacant desk within twelve minutes. A line had started to form, but it was obvious less than half the passengers from the ordeal were present. After waiting fifteen minutes recounting what everyone had done for dinner, two ground hostesses appeared.

One grabbed a microphone and said, "Ladies and gentlemen we are pleased to tell you that we have made arrangements with local hotels to accommodate you for tonight."

A heated exchange immediately started with the most clearly heard shout of "Why couldn't you tell us this in the boarding area rather than having us line up yet again?"

Milt tapped the shoulder of the man in front and said, "Do you mean to tell me you didn't know why you were lining up?"

"Yeah, they just told those of us who stayed in the departure wing, as we returned from their crappy meal offerings, to come here."

"You're kidding. We were at dinner in Hollywood with cousins and it was after one of them checked the airline's website on his i-Phone we discovered that it said to call their 1-800 number. I did over half an hour ago and the recorded message said we were being put up in hotels for the night."

"No shit! The stupid airline put out a notice to the general public that long ago but didn't tell us, the passengers, until just now?"

"Sure looks that way," said Milt.

Slowly the line snaked forward with each family group receiving yet another voucher along with instructions to wait outside the door immediately facing the counter. There shuttle buses to their specific hotels would arrive. Milt and Marilyn were booked into the Embassy Suites just north of the airport and their vehicle showed up in mere moments.

"What a shame they couldn't have done this in the mid-afternoon," said Marilyn. "They already would have known the flight crew was over their limit at that time plus getting another crew was impossible. Instead they put everyone through delay after delay. Just think of the ill will it caused.

"If they had only done what they have now done a while ago, they would have built trust in the company. I can tell you I don't care what compensation they may offer, I will never book them again."

Since it was now eleven o'clock and the two of them were weary beyond belief they simply undressed and got into bed.

176

Airport pick-up was at six in the morning with the new departure time set for eight.

At five-thirty they met the rest of their fellow travelers, who were booked at the Embassy Suites Hotel, gathered around the coffee urns in the central breakfast nook on the main floor. Everyone seemed more rested than the previous night, but it didn't look like any had slept that well. Perhaps had they all had another hour of rest, their demeanors would have been better.

At 6:00 AM sharp the two bus drivers rounded up their charges and everyone piled on the shuttles. Within minutes they were back at the airport where the line-up to the check-in counter was already well formed. However, as they had come to expect nobody was on the desk. Naturally, it didn't take long for the grumbling to begin.

At first Milt seemed somewhat quiet compared to the other men in the queue. But, after about ten minutes while the line continued to grow with the arrival of buses from the other hotels the airline had used and nobody appeared at the desk, Milt's voice started to arise above the din.

He echoed the same complaints as the others, but his became clearly audible.

"Milt, please lower your voice," shushed Marilyn. "You're starting to embarrass me."

"I will NOT lower my voice. I have been quiet too long. This treatment is intolerable!" he nearly screamed.

Others joined in with even louder complaints and before long two ground personnel accompanied by four Broward County police officers arrived. One of the cops stood on the scale between the counters to elevate himself and shouted, "This is the United

States of America. In case any of you don't know we have very strict laws on who can board an aircraft and just as importantly who can be thrown off one. If everyone doesn't assume a proper level of decorum, nobody will be issued a boarding pass. Do I make myself clear?"

A few mumbled "yes sirs" could be heard while the line went silent.

Considering the new departure time was less than an hour from this point and they had just started to process the hundreds of passengers, tension remained high. Although everyone had been cleared by TSA security the previous day, they all had to go through it again before trudging the full length of the corridor to arrive at their gate. The only good news was that as soon as they got to the gate, there was no further wait to board the aircraft. Surprisingly, by five minutes after the hour the plane was full and the doors were closed.

However, once everyone was seated, it was clear nobody was really happy.

As the passengers boarded the plane each was handed a one-page letter on airline letterhead. The majority of the text was what one would expect including an explanation backed up by an apology. Yet it was the bottom line of the last paragraph that further angered the travelers. It read:

In consideration of circumstances beyond our control the company has agreed to provide a $250 credit to be used within one year. It may be combined with any promotion underway at the time of booking. However the voucher applies to each family unit that was booked on this flight.

It was the latter part that most angered the people. That meant the $250 credit would be split based on how many people constituted a "family unit ". For a couple a $125 savings for each person wasn't too bad. But, sitting immediately behind Marilyn and Milt was a family of eight. For them, this apology was meaningless and as it turned out most family units on board were composed of at least four people.

Milt shouted as soon as the plane started its push-back from the gate, "What kind of additional crap is this!" Before long his cry was picked up by a number of others, to the point that once the tow-motor was detached from the plane, the aircraft sat in place until the captain came on the intercom.

"Ladies and gentlemen, I understand from the cabin crew that there is still some disgruntlement with regard to our terrible delay. Right now I want to speak to you as a fellow traveler and not a representative of the airline. We too had our schedules disrupted. We too were fed false information. And we too want to get home as quickly as possible.

"I know the compensation offer sucks. But, what I recommend is that everyone write the company as soon as you can. In fact, my name is Captain Bruce McLennan, and reference me in your letter.

"To my mind, everyone should have been offered $250 per person and please tell them I told you to say that. Now, if everyone takes a deep breath and calms down I will get this bird taxied out and into the air just as quickly as I can. Thank you."

The rest of the flight was uneventful.

Not long after returning home it was clear that Milt started to have persistent problems. First his legs began to numb, then his speech occasionally was slurred.

"Honey, could you please pass, passssss, pass, the butter?"

"Of course Milt."

"I donnn know why sometimes I cannn...t make myself clear," he said in a frustrated tone.

Although they had high speed internet access and were avid surfers, plus they received annual medical checkups, neither they nor their doctors put it all together. They missed the signs of early onset amyotrophic lateral sclerosis, better known as Lou Gehrig's disease, or ALS for short.

There was a fifteen year difference in age between Milt and Marilyn, but this disease isn't age specific. However, once Marilyn really started to suspect he might be suffering from something serious, she sat him down at the computer where they checked out Wikipedia. For ALS it said:

ALS...is a debilitating disease with varied etiology characterized by rapidly progressive weakness, muscle atrophy and fasciculations, muscle spasticity, difficulty speaking (dysarthria), difficulty swallowing (dysphagia), and decline in breathing ability. ALS is the most common of the five motor neuron diseases.

It wasn't like either had avoided the subject and at Milt's next scheduled doctor's appointment the following month, they confronted the man with their suspicions.

He said, "Look Milt, this isn't something to be taken lightly. I will set you up for some tests and we'll see."

"Doctor, I respect your opinion, but right now, with what we've researched, I think I have ALS."

"I don't want you to jump to conclusions. That's the problem with all this Internet stuff these days. People come into my office and have self-diagnosed dysentery when all they have done is eaten too many bananas."

"Doctor, this is much more serious than that, and if we're right, Marilyn and I don't have much more time together. Definitely not quality time."

"I have to agree with you. But, that is only IF you are right. There are other conditions out there that are far less scary and with much better long term prognoses. Let's take it one step at a time."

"OK, but I'm not going to get all giddy over the chance it could be something else. Frankly, I'm more interested in your advice on how best to use the time we have. We have always enjoyed an active and fun sex life. Is that going to crash?"

"Look Milt, I don't even want to start this discussion until we have something concrete to talk about. See my front office and they will schedule you for what has to be done. When the results are in, then we will talk."

Milt met Marilyn in the waiting room. She had offered to come in for the discussion, but he thought it better that she wait for him outside.

"What did the doctor say?" was out of her mouth before he'd made it to the front desk.

"He wants me to take some tests to rule out various things. I'm setting them up now."

By the time they left the office Milt had the paper requisitions for blood work, urine, a stress test plus a priority appointment with a neurologist, only with a four-week wait.

181

Obviously, the only reason he was able to snag something so soon is because his doctor said it was urgent. Milt started to realize what he thought urgent meant had another meaning in the medical profession.

However, rather than hold things up since he wasn't having a cholesterol test as part of the blood analysis (which normally requires twelve hours of fasting), they headed downstairs to the on-site lab to get things underway.

Milt hated the site of his own blood. In college, he had no problem sticking himself with needles in his biology class, but anything else made him squeamish. In fact, at his summer job between junior and senior years he worked in a chemical warehouse. One day, a fifty-five gallon drum of some dense liquid slipped off the two-wheeled truck and while trying to get out of the way an edge scraped Milt's forearm. There was no pain, but a significant amount of blood immediately welled up. One look at the wound and he fainted.

With this in mind, whenever he had to have blood drawn, Milt made it a point to have something to read with him so he could concentrate on anything but what was happening. This time he was so distracted by his own fears he marched into the room with the one-armed chair and just melted into it. Marilyn didn't have to come fetch him afterwards, even though he was fully awake yet far from alert.

The weeks until the neurologist visit passed with a slowness neither of them ever thought possible. Although they were active doing everything they normally did including seeing friends, eating at nice restaurants, visiting various art galleries or museums, and attending cultural events, there was a pall on their activities.

Milt didn't seem any different physically although the things he considered symptoms hadn't changed. But, there was an enormous elephant in the room that needed to be confronted.

Once the day arrived, Marilyn drove the two of them to a clinic in one of the downtown hospitals. In Toronto many of the main teaching facilities had been merged into a world-renowned institution called the "University Health Network," or UHN. Originally independent facilities, the Toronto General Hospital, Toronto Western Hospital and Princess Margaret, they were now an integrated unit. Additionally, the Hospital for Sick Children and Mount Sinai hospitals are in close proximity. Friends visiting from Boston once commented how similar the two cities were with respect to their downtown hospital infrastructure.

Marilyn pulled into the uber-expensive parking garage behind one of the large buildings. From there they made their way through the labyrinth of corridors up to the designated spot at the appropriate time. Thinking they were the only ones with an appointment at that particular time, it was a rude shock when they realized every one of the dozen or so people in the over-crowded waiting room had been scheduled for exactly the moment. If this was the standard routine, it was apparent waiting was something they would have to get used to.

Eventually Milt was called and this time Marilyn insisted she see the doctor with him.

As per usual even though his family doctor had forwarded his full chart, the person escorting them into the examining room also took a full medical history. This young person who appeared to be a student then did a cursory physical check-up and, after telling Milt to put his clothes back on, ushered them into the specialist's private office.

On entering, the doctor was finishing up with one chart and invited them to take a seat. He then stood up and offered his hand to both of them.

"The results of your preliminary work-up by Doctor Nanacsik should be here shortly although I have looked at what has already been entered into the computer. I've also reviewed your family doctor's notes. As I believe he told you, the diagnosis for ALS is pretty much ruling out everything else. That means it takes time.

"I know that is the last thing you want to hear, but it's the truth."

Getting over his surprise that the youth who had just taken his vitals was at least a resident and not a student, Milt gasped out, "If I have ALS, just say it and tell me how fast it will progress."

"Look, I don't want to sound evasive but it definitely depends on the individual."

"So, that's a non-answer."

"Milt!" said Marilyn, "Give the doctor a chance. He just met you and I'm sure he wants to help as best as he can."

"Honey, if I have ALS, and I believe I have, I don't have that much time. Therefore, I want to maximize what we can do before I become a raving lunatic."

"Milt, you know that isn't how the condition progresses."

"No doctor, it takes everything but your senses. You remain fully aware of what is going on around you, but over time your ability to function diminishes until you die of respiratory failure. How am I doing?"

"Just fine. But, you don't have to lose quality of life in one fell swoop. There are treatments available that slow its progress."

"Yeah, like *Riluzole*."

"Yes, you have done your homework. But as I said, we are getting ahead of ourselves. Let's set up the necessary on-going testing regime and I'll see you again in two weeks. At that time, we should be able to rule out a number of things."

-o-o-o-

The testing progressed and the results came back as expected time and again while Milt's symptoms stayed pretty consistent. Finally, his neurologist said, "I'm sorry but it's looking as though you were correct from the start. You definitely have ALS."

"To say I'm relieved is a lie. But it is good to finally have something definitive," said Marilyn. "What do we do now?"

"I'm going to prescribe *riluzole*, which should keep you pretty much physically where you are right now. We'll also continue with monthly visits and monitor your condition. In the meantime, keep your life as regular as possible. If you find there are increasing symptoms or new symptoms suddenly appearing, please get hold of my office. Also, if pain becomes a problem we should be able to manage that too."

"What about sex?" the couple said almost in unison.

"I take it you're active, so don't stop. If one position becomes painful, try another. There is no reason to curtail sex. This isn't affecting your heart and staying active is a positive contributor to your overall well-being."

185

Milt replied, "Well, at least that's a relief."

For that comment Marilyn gave him a shot in the ribs.

"Any other questions," asked the doctor.

"The hard one," said Milt, "how long do I have?"

"Again, that's difficult to say. The average is thirty-nine months from diagnosis, but it's incredibly variable. Listen to me now, I want you to go and live!

"Now, get out of here."

Peter & Margaret Wong's story

Chapter 20

2005

Even in Hell, one adapts or dies, and the great strength of the human spirit is adaptation. For Peter it was devising ways to increase production on an annual basis with the hope his so-called uncle would honor his promise to release them. His ulterior motive was to pad his nest in some manner so that should they gain their release, they wouldn't be entirely dependent upon the treacherous old man.

Margaret found ways to become close to both her charges and the limited number of townsfolk she interacted with on a daily basis. Since the overall quality of food had improved, so had the longevity of their young workers. The workforce's overall attitude was more positive, which ensured Peter made his annual numbers.

Even the uncle got over the fact there were rarely corpses to feed the sharks during most of his visits. It appeared the ever-improving hoard of precious metals provided more fulfillment than witnessing an aquatic food frenzy.

However, it was clear that those who had grown up in this toxic environment were better equipped to cope with it, especially as it marginally improved. For Margaret, having lived all her life in North America, being there was a physical hardship that she knew was taking a toll on her lungs and possibly other parts of her body.

Peter was well aware of her suffering having to bear witness to her labored and distressed sleep cycles every night. He knew there was nothing he could do here, but once they were free of this sentence, life would improve.

He also was aware that placing the physical hardship on Margaret was his uncle's design, since he demanded they both had to survive the full ten years to be set free. Based on Peter's calculations, they were down to only an handful of days before they'd know their fate.

Over the years Peter became ever-better at hoarding what he saw as their legacy from this incarceration. Ironically after timidly requesting the first pair of cowboy boots, every year for the past six, he'd received a new pair on his birthday. His uncle didn't realize he how much he was personally contributing to Peter's theft.

Within days every heel was meticulously modified so that it could be filled with the accumulated platinum dust. As long as he could smuggle all seven pair out of China and back into Canada, Peter estimated there would be over six hundred thousand dollars worth of the precious metal socked away, especially since the price per gram had almost doubled over the time they'd been imprisoned.

Compared to the amount of cash Peter had handled in the past, this was negligible. However, he had to deal with current needs and realities. He figured that if his uncle honored the terms, he would be returned to Canada with a modest living. The six hundred thousand dollars worth of platinum dust would be a good bulwark against the unforeseeable, but he knew it was far from a fortune.

Because of the risk, he kept Margaret in the dark. She had no idea what was stored in the heels of his boots, only that they all seemed very heavy and wondered why her husband was so enthralled with them. Perhaps if he had left some of them unaltered she would catch on. But, Peter made a point of modifying the heels immediately upon receipt, and his wife never handled them until after they had been loaded with platinum.

-o-o-o-

The two of them had watched the date in May creep ever-forward with mutual trepidation. Then, on the appointed day there was the unmistakable sound of an executive jet on approach. Thirty minutes later the latest version of the same SUV showed up with only a driver and Peter's uncle aboard.

As per usual they were both waiting for the man standing almost at attention in front of the hut that acted as their office. They were silent, mostly because they were shaking. This was it.

"Why so glum," was how he greeted them. "This is a very big day," he said with a broad smile.

Peter wasn't sure if it he was seeing a Cheshire cat or the big bad wolf, but cautiously replied, "Honorable uncle we are happy as always to see you, and appreciate the significance of this date."

"If you honestly appreciate it, then for the first time in ten years I grant you permission to embrace me."

Peter didn't waste a moment and lunged forward with his arms outstretched.

"You too Margaret."

With this she joined her husband in wrapping her arms around the old man.

"Now that that is over with, I want to conclude your involvement with this operation properly.

189

"Margaret, I want you to go down to the work area and bring me the two people who have been with you the longest AND show the most promise in potentially running this place."

She didn't hesitate and nearly flew down the path. While away Peter's uncle carried on with, "I have some clothes for you aboard the plane. Last week I was in London and realized you were going to fulfill your obligation to me and the triad. With that, I needed to move ahead on my promise. As well, there are internal travel documents aboard, plus we will get your passports attended to as soon as we arrive in Hong Kong, starting with photographs.

"As for the immigration paperwork, I tapped into the excellent network you established so many years ago and everything is underway. They expect to have your visa issued next week and our people in Toronto are already looking at possible housing. Unfortunately, you will have to take a driving test when you settle in. Naturally, you will also take some lessons since as far as the Canadians are concerned you are Chinese immigrants who never learned to drive.

"I see your wife returning with two able bodied young men."

This was the first time in Peter's recollection he hadn't called Margaret a "whore."

Peter was starting to relax. Just then the old man said, "Nephew, do you still have those beautiful samurai swords I gave you?"

"Of course honorable uncle, would you like me to return them to you? Obviously, we can't carry them on an airplane."

"No, but please fetch them for me."

190

Peter made his way hastily into the cabin and returned with the swords wrapped in their velvet cloth. His only fear was that he may have accidentally nicked the smaller one while modifying one of the fourteen heels. However, when his uncle extracted it from its sheath, the pristine edge glimmered in the sunlight. He returned the *tanto* to its protective cover and then removed the long *katana*.

"You have kept these in good condition," said the old man.

"Thank you, honored uncle," replied Peter.

"Nephew, I want you to take this from me," he said while balancing the sword on his two hands and presenting the blunt back edge formally to Peter.

"No, honored uncle they are yours."

"I insist," he said without any room for argument.

"Now, feel the balance, the grace of the weapon, its sheer power." said the old man.

"Yes uncle I feel it."

"Good, now pick which man's head you will remove with it."

"What?"

"Nephew, have your ears filled with wax in the past moments?"

"No uncle, but you want me to execute one of these men?"

"Absolutely. One will inherit what you and your wife have built on my behalf. Knowing how equitable a man that I am, he will remember this lesson and make sure he overachieves."

"But uncle I do not want to kill one of these men. They have been loyal to you and either would be worthy of taking over."

"Nephew, maybe I didn't make myself clear. If you don't kill one of them, I will kill your wife. Based on our agreement, both of you have to survive to leave this place. If I kill your wife then you will be doomed to remain here for the rest of your life. And, to be crystal clear you will no longer be running this place but working in one of the pits."

"Yes uncle, I understand."

With this Peter glanced at both men. They were standing together with fear etched in every muscle of their bodies. Neither was past their mid-twenties, but they were strong, dedicated, and honest. How can he kill one of these two?

Sensing his hesitation the uncle said, "Peter you have killed before. If my memory is correct nine men have died at your hand. Most were shot, but not all of them. Why should this murder be any different? In fact, it will round out your total to an even ten."

With this the blade flashed in the morning light almost as fast as a bullet. A soft hiss was heard followed by the sound of an over-inflated basketball hitting a poorly maintained court. Then the body collapsed forward with blood shooting out of the severed neck. Margaret retched on the spot while the sole survivor made a beeline to the trees.

"Don't worry about him. Once his courage returns, so will he. I will be driving us to the aircraft and my man will stay to whip him into shape.

"Isn't it about time you and your wife cleaned yourselves up?

"And, before I forget, let this be a lesson to you that this fate befalls anyone who crosses me. If I find you stole a single gram of anything from this enterprise, you too will both feel the sharpness of this steel.

Peter handed the sword to his uncle and bowed in the traditional sense. The old man wiped the blood on the back of the corpse and replaced the weapon in its scabbard. He then wrapped the two in the velvet cloth and handled the bundle to Peter. "As I said, they are your gift from me. Treat them with respect."

-o-o-o-

On arrival at the plane they found a Harrods bag crammed with new casual clothes for both of them. Peter's uncle encouraged them to head into the lavatory and change. He took a stab at their respective sizes, but since nothing was truly high style, he was confident what he picked would fit well enough.

When they had both changed he said, "Peter, I see you're still partial to cowboy boots. Those look like the first pair I bought you."

"They are, honorable uncle. The rest are safely packed."

"What I propose is the two of you will spend the next week in Hong Kong. There you will stay in a moderate tourist hotel and shop for some appropriate clothing. I will take care of your passports and once in-hand will book your flight to Canada.

"You will also have a chance to choose your new home from a number that will be presented to you. Also, you will be impersonating the real Peter and Margaret Wong who live here but have extensive family in the Toronto area. You can be assured they have been well-compensated to grant you their identification. That way the passports will be bona fide except we will substitute your pictures."

"It sounds like you've figured out everything," said Margaret who for the first time felt she could address this terrible man directly.

"Yes, my dear I have. Your husband set all this up many years ago when the wealthy population of Hong Kong felt threatened by the 1997 deadline for repatriation by China. He put together a phenomenal network that I'm proud to say is still in operation. The only sad thing is he no longer derives an income from this enterprise, nor will he in the future.

"That brings me to another thing. You two are supposed to be retired family members of others who have already immigrated to Canada. As such, your financial needs are not great. It is imperative you do not suddenly get big eyes once you're back in the West.

"I know how enterprising you are Peter and how tempting it will be for you to come up with some way to augment the stipend I will be paying you. One word: don't!"

"Yes, honorable uncle."

"You need not add the honorable."

"Yes uncle."

After this exchange they all rested until their approach to Shek Kong airfield, which is open to private use on the weekends. However, the site of so many Peoples Liberation Army Air Force planes lined up along the tarmac only served to remind the Wong's how far they still had to travel to freedom.

Another SUV was waiting for them on arrival, and the driver carefully loaded their baggage into the rear. He grunted when he lifted the bag holding Peter's boots. With this the uncle said, "I think we will use Fedex to ship your goods directly to the address for the home you select, so you don't have to worry about customs at either end of your travel."

They then made their way to a modest high rise tourist hotel that didn't compare with where they had stayed in the past. But considering they had just left incarceration one level above hell, it was paradise. Peter's uncle checked them in and after dropping their meager possessions in the room escorted them downstairs to the waiting SUV.

Their first stop was a photo store where their passport pictures were taken.

After that he gave instructions to his driver to take the three of them shopping.

One thing about Hong Kong is in spite of the re-annexation, shopping options had remained exactly the same as they were beforehand. You name it, you can buy it. The only limitation they faced was that anything they bought had to conform to a senior couple who planned to spend their retirement in Canada so they could be with their family. However, by the time they returned to the hotel, their bags filled the closet from top to bottom. Plus, there were the handmade items that would be ready later in the week.

They then went for an early dinner after which the old man left the two of them alone.

In spite of the wine, fatigue, shopping exhaustion, and full bellies for the first time in a decade, they made passionate love a number of times before the first rays of light broke through their east-facing window.

-o-o-o-

The week passed quickly. Much of it was spent in preparation for their "immigration" to Canada. They started by viewing real estate listings of homes in areas where they would blend in as newly arrived retirees. The uncle had instructed his contacts to concentrate on properties that were vacant and where a lease could be signed and occupancy taken within an extremely short timeframe.

Having been out of the country for ten years, Peter and Margaret were amazed at how changed the Greater Toronto Area was. They spent hours examining MapQuest and Google Maps, especially their respective satellite views to get a feel for what awaited them. And, based on this they settled on a three-bedroom bungalow on the north side of Steeles Avenue near the Pacific Mall. This again placed them in York Region, but far enough away from their old home in Richmond Hill so the likelihood of bumping into anyone they knew was extremely slim.

As promised, Peter's uncle sent one of his henchmen to pick up the belongings they wanted shipped. This included six pair of Peter's boots since he planned on wearing one pair for the flight. He figured that if they were confiscated by security, he would still have the six others waiting for him when he arrived.

Finally, the day of their departure arrived. They were booked on a 5:00PM Air Canada flight, which would arrive in Toronto around eight the following night. Total flying time would be approximately fifteen hours non-stop.

Peter's uncle drove them to the airport and hugged both fiercely as if he wasn't their captor for the past ten years. He was a complex man, but for some reason had a warm spot for his so-called nephew. As he ushered them from check-in to security he stopped and said, "You have been far better than I could have ever hoped. I know you aren't blood, but you are as close to blood to me as anyone could be. For that I am truly sorry I had to put you through what I did. Hopefully in time you will forgive me.

"I know you think me cruel and have seen me do some terrible things. But you too Peter, have done many of the same. That is why I know you will respect my demand that you do not cross me. You know the outcome.

"But, before you board the flight I have something for both of you," the uncle said, taking two small jewelry boxes from his coat pocket.

"For you Margaret, I have chosen a string of flawless diamonds and for you Peter, here is a diamond men's solitaire ring set in platinum. These two items are valued at over five hundred thousand dollars. They are yours and if you ever need to exchange them for cash, contact me first.

"I know I have put limits on you, but I also know that financial situations change. That is why I'm trusting you with these gifts, and the fact you will contact me if you need help."

"Uncle, we don't know what to say but thank you," stammered Peter.

Since their flight was being called, they said hasty goodbyes and cleared through security.

Peter was so overwrought with his uncle's unexpected generosity he absentmindedly placed his boots in the bin and loaded it on the conveyor that ran through the x-ray machine. It was only when he realized the belt had stopped and there were three people examining the screen that he became suddenly concerned.

As it turned out, they reached some type of agreement and let his possessions flow down the line. Once he could reach the bin without leaning into the enclosed covering Peter immediately took his boots to a nearby chair and slipped them on. Margaret was waiting for him and couldn't understand why his face was suddenly so flushed. She still didn't know he had a small fortune in platinum crammed into the heels of each of his well-worn Tony Lamas.

They boarded the 777 aircraft with the appropriate grouping based on their boarding passes. On entering they saw the economy section was laid out 3-4-3 with them in the center section, mid-way back. Not bad, but nowhere near the luxury of first or business class that they'd regularly flown commercially in the past. However, to maintain their new personas as retired Chinese immigrants their only option was modern day steerage.

The couple settled in and looked around. Neither spoke for a moment then, like giggling teenagers blurted in unison, "I wonder, who are the old man's spies?"

Peter responded, "It could be anyone; the couple sitting next to us or those across the aisle. We should be circumspect in what we say and make sure we keep our voices down."

Stating what was in the back of both their minds Margaret said, "Will we find our son?"

"A day doesn't go by that I don't think about him. Is he well? What is he doing? Is he married? Did he finish college? Does he even live near where we will be?" Peter replied.

This outpouring of emotion caught Peter unaware and he had to stifle a sob. Once he caught his breath he then said, "I

198

miss him terribly. I hope somehow we can reconnect with him. Only time will tell."

At that point the departure announcements started so they made themselves as comfortable as possible for fifteen-plus hours in their aluminum and carbon fiber tube.

Once airborne, they picked up their conversation but focused on reviewing the past week. They started by recapping the events of their day of release, the shopping, meetings with immigration officials, picking where they would live, the sumptuous meals compared to what they had eaten for the past ten years, and the final parting gifts from Peter's uncle.

As the flight droned on, they watched a couple of movies selected from their individual entertainment centers and mostly dozed between meals. About an hour before arrival they were given the customs form, and Peter filled it out for the family unit. He felt a lump in his throat seeing the red maple leaf. Never being much of a patriot he was surprised how much just having an official document in his hand was so comforting.

Since the only baggage they had was carry-on, and they landed at the brand new Terminal One, the couple whisked their way down the moving sidewalks into the customs hall. On entry they made their way to the shortest line and on reaching the guard on duty presented their documents. Peter knew they were genuine even if their pictures were bogus. However, the guard did a further examination of their passports and sent them to secondary inspection.

Not expecting this, they were somewhat disturbed. However, once they were in front of the officer everything seemed to go relatively smoothly.

"Where were you born?"

Margaret said, "China near Beijing."

"And you sir?"

"The same."

"What family do you have in Canada?"

"Just about all of them," said Peter.

"Such as?"

"Our son, our brothers and sisters."

"Is that all?"

"Yes officer."

That seemed to satisfy the man and perhaps speaking with a distinct Chinese accent also benefitted their cause. At that point he opened both passports and stamped them.

"Welcome to Canada!"

On exiting the customs hall they saw a man in a dark suit with a sign that read "P. Wong" in both English and Chinese characters.

"We are the Wongs," said Peter on approaching the man.

"Your uncle sends warm regards and welcomes you to your new home." With that he reached forward and took possession of their carry-on baggage. "Follow me."

Being late spring, the weather was still warm and the sunset was almost a half hour away. So, they had a chance to view first-hand the changes that had occurred at the airport and then along the way to their new abode.

The unnamed driver left the airport and took the 409 to the 427 and then turned onto the 407ETR toll road. As he stayed on that course, the two of them marveled at all the development that had sprung up on both sides of the highway. When they left, or in truth were abducted, the 407ETR had just been opened. Much of the development they were now seeing was at that time still far in the future. Now, the road was a mature passageway with millions of square feet of office space, manufacturing and commercial centers bordering it. Another example of building something and they will come.

At the Kennedy Road exit they headed south and just before a main street that Peter figured must be Steeles Avenue, especially since an Asian mall that rivaled anything they saw in Hong Kong was on the left, the driver turned into a side street. He followed it around to a quiet cul-de-sac and then stopped in front of a very pretty bungalow.

"Welcome home," he said as he exited the vehicle and grabbed their bags from the elevated tailgate.

The two of them got out and followed the man into the house. On opening the door they were pleased to see the place was fully furnished and sitting off to the right the pile of boxes they'd shipped via Fedex.

Chapter 22

2009

At the time Peter and Margaret were heading back to Canada, Joseph and Juliette were immersing themselves in their studies in Israel. Neither couple was aware of the other, nor where they were respectively located on the globe. It would be years before they would all reside in the same city, and at that point, their physical separation was still about the same distance, only shifted eastward.

For the first few years the Wongs found it difficult to assimilate. Having been out of the country for so long, and with the overriding necessity to live a covert life whereby they never reveal the fact they aren't actually new immigrants, placed a terrible emotional toll on them.

Some of it was the roller-coaster of making up for being associated with the wrong people in college, to unimaginable wealth, to forced incarceration in a place that rivalled Devil's Island, and now to assuming a middle class existence. They were thankful to be alive, but were unsure of the life they were living. Even though Peter's crime-filled past was always just below the surface, the harsh realities they faced in the Chinese metal recovery operation were still too fresh to ignore.

They did their best to blend in to their community and surroundings by shopping at the local stores, getting a modest Toyota Corolla sedan, and keeping a very low profile with visible spending well within the expectations of a retired couple. Ironically, neither of them felt they were actively looking over their shoulders. Their issue was a vague feeling of constant displacement.

One thing that probably helped both of them is they physically aged much more than one would have expected as a result of their China experience. They both looked at least ten years older than they really were. Moreover, they acted more like the age they appeared to be so that anyone meeting them would think they were well into their seventies, as opposed to barely in their sixties.

Being in Canada meant they were able to take advantage of the socialized medicine. Days after their arrival they took a cab to the closest registration facility to make sure their health cards would be available as soon as they hit the minimum ninety-day residency requirement. In the back of both of their minds was a belief that after all they had been through, they likely needed some form of medical attention. With over a decade of never having seen a doctor and being exposed to toxins well beyond anything possible in North America since the Second World War, this was a nagging fear.

They had some difficulty finding a family doctor because of how the medical establishment conformed to government imposed quotas, but before long they had one who spoke fluent Mandarin and Cantonese. To keep up appearances, they tended to continue to speak only in the dialect they used in China, even at home, and when asked their birth dates fudged their replies so the difference between how they looked and the age they claimed was much more in line.

"Mr. Wong, how do you feel today?" asked Dr. Woo.

"About the same as I did at my last visit."

"Are you taking your blood pressure medicine as prescribed?"

"Yes doctor and I'm also making sure we get a walk in our neighbourhood almost everyday. In fact, when the weather is bad, we walk at the Pacific Mall. That way Margaret and I keep up our strength."

"That is a good regime. How long do you walk or is it by distance?"

"Our goal is an hour and we try to keep up a good pace. We do not saunter."

"Very good. Any other problems you want to discuss?"

"Not about me, but I am concerned about Margaret."

"What about her?"

"She has developed a wheeze and a cough that won't go away. Sometimes she also has trouble swallowing."

"Yes, I noticed the first two things you mentioned when I saw her at her last visit. Is she also here today?"

"She is outside, but told me I should see you first."

"Why don't you send her in and if I need to talk to the two of you together, I will ask you to come back."

Peter went out to the waiting room and told Margaret it was her turn. About twenty minutes later the doctor poked his head out of the door and asked Peter to join them.

"I'm not going to beat around the bush, but I am concerned about your wife," he said to Peter.

"I have examined her and took some throat swabs. As well, I looked as deeply as I could and there are some things that are disturbing in her throat. Margaret said she has never smoked, but I am sure that back in China she was exposed to some pretty nasty airborne particulates. So, with this in mind I want her to

204

see an ear, nose and throat specialist to rule out anything really bad."

Peter said, "Doctor, what are you saying?"

"Margaret may have a form of throat cancer. Naturally, we won't know for sure until the test results are back.

"I've already asked my staff to make a booking and to put a rush on it. Since the two of you are retired I will assume that once they have a date you will be able to fit it into your schedules?"

"Of course," they answered in unison.

-o-o-o-

Blood tests, breathing tests, bone scans, and doctor appointments followed in such rapid succession they felt like social engagements. In fact, looking at the calendar stuck to their refrigerator door one would think it was a very busy social schedule, except for the follow-up requisition forms appended to it. There was much to be done to first diagnose a condition and then determine its spread or prognosis. By the latter part of the year it was apparent Margaret was ill and with a worsening condition. After all they had been through, Peter felt this newest challenge the most acutely.

And, for the first time in his life he was truly afraid.

Fear never entered his psyche when he was forced out of college. It didn't arise during his years running a crime syndicate. He was immune to it building the second largest entertainment rental empire in the world. Even when he stared down his uncle's thugs in Toronto when they were kidnapped and then again so many times in China, never did fear chill his bones. Now dread was his constant companion seemingly already displacing Margaret, even while she still lived.

Peter tried to suck it up, but there were times, especially in the shower, when he let his tears freely flow.

One pledge he made himself was that whatever Margaret needed or wanted she would have. Even if he had to tear open one or more of his boots to extract the platinum, he would do it. What good would that hidden wealth serve if his wife was no longer alive to share it with him?

As her medications increased along with her treatments, it became obvious these may prolong her life, but at some point they would no longer improve it. They had discussed respective end-of-life preferences and filed all the appropriate documents. But again, theoretical exercises bore little resemblance to the reality when it was staring you in the face. Decisions had to be made and it was rapidly falling on Peter's shoulders to handle them.

Some initial ones were eased by the presence of a social worker provided through a supplemental health insurance coverage they purchased as soon as their government health cards were issued.

The woman was very comforting and said, "Margaret I want to talk to you about something you may not want to discuss. Please understand this is difficult for both of us and it isn't going to happen tomorrow or six months from now. In fact, it may be over a year away. But, what I want you to tell me is that since you realize there will come a time where your husband will no longer be able to provide you the assistance you need, you will have to consider some other solutions. With this in mind, let's go through a list of places and see which ones you would like to consider."

With this they were able to come up with three facilities starting with Lakebeach Hospital at the top of the list. Considering it had the best reputation for senior care, especially palliative if it came down to it, everyone was pleased with the choice.

In the meantime Peter remained her primary caregiver and dutifully served his responsibilities. He made the meals, encouraged her to go out as much as possible and tried to lift her spirits every chance he got. He knew it was a losing battle, but there was no way he would throw in the towel. The cost was too high and too personal.

Sadly, after eight months he hit a stumbling block. The sheer volume of pills, even though they were in blister-pack containers split into breakfast, midday, evening, for each day in the week by the pharmacy, had become too easy to mix up. As well, he was physically weakening. The strain of Margaret's care was taking a further toll on his body. The day of their parting was rapidly approaching and he dreaded it with all his heart.

One morning he awoke to find Margaret on the ground next to her side of the bed. He asked her what had happened and she said she fell trying to go to the bathroom a few hours ago and was too weak to get herself up from the ground.

"Why didn't you wake me?" he said with tears in his eyes.

"Because you were sleeping so soundly I didn't want to disturb you. I see what is happening and know how precious sleep is to you. I know how exhausted you are from looking after me."

"What do you mean? It is my honor to take care of you. Maybe we waited too long to be married after living together for so many years. But, when I finally proposed and you accepted, I took on the obligation to love you for better or worse."

"I know my love, but look at me. I'm a broken old woman too weak to get myself back in the bed and you have become a tired old man. I think it is time we make that call and at least you will gain back some strength."

They made an appointment with their family doctor for the next day. While there, it became painfully apparent something had to be done, otherwise it was likely the caregiver would die before the patient. This was not an uncommon situation since in cases like this, the person responsible for the care of the sick spouse literally burns themself out.

To alleviate the situation, their doctor said they should give careful consideration as to where Margaret would be most comfortable. He mentioned a number of near-by facilities, many of which catered to the aging Asian population. However, without revealing their past ties to the area, and referencing the form filled out with the social worker, Peter asked about Lakebeach.

That hospital had been well-known for its breakthroughs in treating the elderly for decades and in the evening when Margaret was in her deepest sleep, Peter had often quietly crawled off to follow the progress of her condition on the web. This naturally led to links which connected to treatment, diet, care, and various institutions. On one occasion he noted Lakebeach's name along with a number of their leading specialists.

"Mr. Wong as much as I would love to get Margaret into Lakebeach, as you probably are unaware, there is a significant waiting list for up to two years for a bed. Maybe it's shorter if you're prepared to pay for a private room. However, these are prohibitively expensive especially for someone like you, a pensioner living on a fixed income."

"Doctor, with all due respect I don't think you are in a position to know my financial situation," Peter said suddenly without a trace of a Chinese accent. "I can well afford to cover the cost of a private room. Your task is to find one and as quickly as you can."

"Who are you?" the doctor asked.

"I am Peter Wong. However, I have strong family ties to resources that can well cover the cost of my dear wife's care."

"Mr. Wong, I will take you at your word. But, for a moment there I was unsure of just who you are."

-o-o-o-

Peter realized that in the heat of the moment he had nearly let everything slip. He made one silent vow to be more careful in the future and another to do whatever it took to make sure Margaret was comfortable, while receiving the best care possible. Even if he had to carve into all of his boot heels and sell his precious accumulation of platinum dust. If that's what it took, he would do.

In fact, one of the other things he had been doing during his midnight computer surfing was following the ever-increasing price of the metal, which based on his current holdings was now worth well over a million dollars.

Therefore, money would not be a problem. He was confident that as long as he kept his commitment to his uncle to

209

remain within his secret identity, he would come up with a way to sell the precious dust so that the old man never found out.

Two days later the dreaded call came.

"Mr, Wong, this is Tilly in the admitting department of Lakebeach Hospital calling with some good news. A private room had opened up and if you can bring Margaret to admitting by ten o'clock tomorrow morning we can get her settled."

"Good news," thought Peter. Perhaps to the hospital, but not for him. Obviously, notice was extremely short for these things.

BOOK THREE - THE PRESENT

Chapter 23

2010

Milt's condition continued to deteriorate. It was almost exactly a year since the diagnosis was confirmed. Now it was apparent the effects of ALS were gaining momentum. Both he and Marilyn saw what was happening to his body.

At Milt's urging, Marilyn started to enquire about facilities that would be able to help him in his fading months. She had always heard of Lakebeach, but considered it more of an old folks' home. However, over the years it had morphed into a full-blown hospital specializing in diseases and conditions that tend to affect many other than just geriatrics.

Although ALS can hit much younger people, Lakebeach was better equipped than most senior or nursing homes for providing care to patients who were already more advanced in age.

They set up an in-home evaluation by a social worker who had been provided through the community care organization. It was at this point Marilyn realized one of the key benefits of socialized medicine. This care was both covered by their publicly funded insurance and once in the system, it could assist at every stage along the way. Had they chosen to live in Chicago, even though President Obama had passed his monstrous health care bill, the fact it wouldn't kick-in until 2014 meant they would have had to rely on private insurance until that time and manage the process entirely on their own.

The great uncertainty for Marilyn's family back in the States was that nobody really knew how their medical coverage would look in 2014, nor if the "Obamacare" bill would survive the 2012 election where the Republicans were vowing to repeal it. All they needed was to maintain their current majority in the House and achieve a simple majority in the Senate. However, if their Presidential candidate won the election, it would sound the death knell of a poorly written bill.

Anyhow, all that was irrelevant since the two of them now lived in Canada and that was where Milt was receiving care. Marilyn fully intended to cast a mail-in ballot as was her due as a dual citizen, but the outcome would have no bearing on the couple when it came to Milt's condition.

Their particular unknown was if there would be a bed for Milt at Lakebeach when he needed it. In the interim he'd remain home until she could no longer provide the necessary support.

Up to this point, he'd been relatively mobile and they were getting on with their lives as best as possible. However, large muscle control was evaporating and Milt was having trouble walking in addition to feeding himself.

His doctor had warned him that based on the ALS Functional Rating Scale (FRS), which descended from 48 to zero Milt should expect to lose one point per month irrespective of where in his body the disease started and what his initial score was. Sadly, being nearly eighteen months since he started to notice symptoms it was apparent he had deteriorated to about half of what it had been.

Sitting in front of his doctor with Marilyn beside him, Milt waited expectantly for the current verdict. It wasn't long in coming.

"Milt, it's time to face reality. The disease is progressing and I'm afraid may actually be accelerating. With this in mind, it's time to make plans for the future. I'm not saying tomorrow or even in a few months, but the time will come when Marilyn will no longer be able to be your primary caregiver."

"Doctor, I know," Milt said with difficulty. "What do you propose?"

"I have some forms here listing facilities that are expert at handling ALS patients."

"Marilyn and I have discussed this and as far as I'm concerned the only place I would like to go is Lakebeach."

"That is a very good hospital, especially for the aged. But, I'm not sure it is ideal for ALS cases."

Marilyn answered, "Doctor, we've done some research and they definitely have ALS patients, especially those in the latter stages. Milt says he would be comfortable in that environment and frankly I want him to be as comfortable as possible." Having said this she extracted a tissue from her purse and dabbed at her eyes.

"Oh damn, I promised myself I wouldn't cry."

"Honey, it's OK. I love you and I know you love me. This is tearing up both of us."

"Folks, you have the choice to list one or multiple facilities. Why don't we make this as simple as possible and only list Lakebeach. That way you're in their system and should a bed become available, you should be able to get it.

"Forget what I said about the other institutions. It's your decision and Milt, since you are still competent, you have the say. Plus, Marilyn you have the legal guardianship for Milt's medical decisions for when he isn't able to make them. And, you've also made it clear Lakebeach is your only choice."

"That is correct," she said before Milt could reply, seeing that he was already fatigued.

"The only caution I offer," said the Doctor, "is that once they call, you only have forty-eight hours to accept the bed. Sorry, I keep saying 'bed', but since you have additional private insurance, you will be registered for a private room as well as semi-private.

"Anyhow, when they call, you have to be ready to accept or Milt will drop to the bottom of the list and have to wait until the next go-around."

Marilyn acknowledged with, "We understand."

-o-o-o-

Four months later Milt was having trouble swallowing his food. He was exhibiting other advanced symptoms including breathing difficulties and very little motor function left in his arms. Just as they were questioning their decision about limiting his choice to a single facility the phone rang.

"Mrs. Morgenstern, this is Tilly at admitting at Lakebeach Hospital. I wanted to let you know that a private room on our sixth floor will be available this week. We need to know if your husband Milton is prepared to commit to the room."

"Yes," she said with a hoarse voice and tears in her eyes . "When do we have to come in?"

"Today is Monday, why don't you arrive Wednesday morning at ten?"

"OK, we'll be there for Wednesday at ten. Do we need to bring any of his in-home assistance devices, or his walker, or wheelchair?"

"No, only use what you need to safely transport him here."

"Thank you so much."

On Wednesday, Marilyn carefully maneuvered Milt into the converted minivan they bought when he was first diagnosed with ALS. It wasn't the easiest vehicle to drive but it was both the most practical way to travel. Plus, it was distinctive, especially when parked in the handicapped spaces at the mall or other locales.

Milt had progressed to an electric wheelchair some months ago and had mastered the hydraulic loading mechanism. However, today's emotions overwhelmed him and Marilyn had to both load and unload the unwieldy device. The only good thing was that once in the seat, he didn't have to get out of it until he was formally in his room and wanted to be put in the bed.

However, before that they had to go through the intake process, set up an account in the business office, and then tour the facility, so that Milt could familiarize himself with where he could go internally on his own. He wasn't bedridden and as long as somebody could get him into his chair (and make sure the batteries were charged overnight), he was free to roam at will.

By early afternoon they had completed all the necessary steps and Milt chugged into his room on the sixth floor. It faced due south and he had a clear view of the CN Tower. When built in the mid-1970's the tower was the largest freestanding structure in the world. However, although it had been eclipsed a number of times since then, it was still impressive.

The room was airy and had a number of impressive pieces of art hanging on the walls. In fact, Milt had noticed what appeared to be a significant collection as he toured the place. He made it a point to try and reconnoiter in the future to see just how extensive it was.

A hot lunch was waiting for him and he said, "Marilyn, why don't you let one of the staff feed me. I'm going to have to get used to it and you should go down to the cafeteria. You need a break."

Not sure if she was dismissed or Milt was just being his normal considerate self, Marilyn thought she could use some 'me time' and said, "Sure honey. I'll be back in about an hour."

The adjustment for both of them was hard and it took about a week for it to sink in that this was the way it would be until the end.

-o-o-o-

Marilyn made it a point to get to Lakebeach as early every morning as she could. She liked being in Milt's company even the days he was non-communicative. Some of it was psychological, just knowing their time together was limited, and the other the physical tie that had grown over the decades of their happy marriage.

Therefore, it was no surprise one morning when Marilyn was in the midst of reading a book while sitting in the recliner in Milt's room. She glanced over to see how he was doing, and saw a tent forming from the light sheet covering his lower extremities.

"You gotta be kidding," she said with a smile in her voice.

He replied in his now grating voice, "No, I'm not."

With that she went to the door, closed it and then sat in the stacking chair that was next to the bed. Extending her arm, Marilyn reached under the sheet and started stroking Milt. For the first time in weeks she saw a real smile on his face. However,

217

in his advanced condition she was unsure of just how this would end.

After a slightly longer period than she expected he ejaculated and sighed in gratitude. She rolled back the sheet so it wouldn't adhere in the mess and said, "You have obviously been saving that up!"

"Yeah, I have."

"Maybe next time we can find a way for me to enjoy it too?"

"Be my guest!"

With that Marilyn made her way to the adjoining bathroom. After washing her hand she grabbed a handful of tissues to clean up Milt. What surprised her was his erection had hardly subsided.

"Down big guy, I don't think you're quite up to another round."

"You never know."

"Talk like that and you're getting me wet."

"That's the idea."

"Is it now? Maybe next time. It's almost time for them to deliver your lunch and I don't want to shock the staff."

"OK, that's a promise. Next time you too have to get some pleasure," he said more clearly than he had spoke since arriving at the hospital.

With that Marilyn replaced the covering and the tent pole slowly receded.

That night back at home Marilyn decided to go online and check out exactly what sexual activity would be appropriate for the two of them. It turned out anything that wouldn't cause pain or undue stress on Milt's joints was considered acceptable.

The only downside of this web surfing was she happened to stray onto some porn sites and before she realized what she was doing she had masturbated to a wonderful orgasm. Maybe it wasn't as deep and fulfilling as when she has had sex with a man, but satisfying just the same.

-o-o-o-

Marilyn had no family to speak of in Toronto other than a handful of Milt's relatives who had befriended her. All of hers were in the States mostly split between Chicago and Florida. She kept in touch with her daughter on a regular basis throughout the year as well as their annual visit to Florida for her birthday. Naturally, there was no trip this year and future ones would be without Milt. From Milt's perspective, he only went to satisfy Marilyn. There was mutual animosity between him and his step-daughter, which had not abated since Milt's becoming ill. He was just as glad she never came to visit and he wasn't sorry he'd never step foot into the state of Florida again in this life.

However, his relatives did visit and they also did their best to support Marilyn. They knew the situation was terminal and hoped that the relationship built over the years would remain in Milt's absence.

One day Milt and Marilyn had both dozed off. He was in the bed and she in what had become her favorite recliner. She had some knitting in her lap when a male voice softly said, "Hello, Aunt Marilyn."

It was Jon Davidson, Milt's favorite nephew.

"Jon, how lovely to see you!"

219

"And you. How's Uncle Milt doing?"

"Not bad under the circumstances."

"Let me answer for myself," Milt grumbled. "I'm not bad for a dying man."

"Glad to see you've not lost your sense of humor."

"Never had one so how could I lose it?" he quipped.

"What brings you to town?" asked Marilyn since Jon was living in Northern Virginia, just outside Washington, D.C.

"We're moving back."

"What, you've been there about ten years and now you're moving back?" she said.

"It's actually closer to eleven years and we came to the realization the economy was going to take a long time to recover. For consultants like me, there is virtually no work. In fact, most of the meetings I'm going to are networking gatherings ranging from one-on-ones to larger groups. The point is there isn't anything doing and nothing on which to share or collaborate.

"We started talking about this a couple of months ago when we woke up one morning and my wife asked me what we were doing down here with everything dried up and our children and two wonderful grandkids back in Toronto. With that I didn't need any more encouragement, and I'm up here meeting with past contacts to see if there is anything specific I can do that would put my accumulated experience to work.

"As of this morning I had coffee with a man who is running one of your innovation centers. I've been involved with one in Virginia. In fact, you may recall the funny looking black glass building near Dulles Airport that looks like something built by the Mad Hatter. That's the Center for Innovation and

Technology or CIT for short and I really learned a lot about mentoring from working with them. So, when my old friend up here heard that, he said I should come onboard with their organization as a mentor.

"There I can help small companies not only grow but as the economy improves, introduce them to some of my American contacts as appropriate."

She immediately said, "It would be great to have the two of you back here under any circumstances. At least you'll have health coverage. I can just imagine what it's costing you down there."

"Was costing us, is what you should say. When the monthly fee for the private coverage we had been paying for the past year recently almost doubled as a result of our so-called Obamacare, what a load of crap that is, we cancelled it."

"How can you live without insurance?" grunted Milt.

"The same way millions of other Americans are. We're taking a chance nothing major will happen and if it does we check into a county hospital. They cannot turn you away although they may not be able to offer the full course of care. For anything else we can go to a walk-in clinic and pay the hundred dollars per visit.

"As for prescriptions, we can get those filled here for a fraction of what they cost down there. We're up enough that that isn't a problem like it is for others who have to take a bus to Canada just for their drugs."

"Sounds pretty bad," said Marilyn.

"Oh, it's worse than you can imagine. Let me tell you something I was told by somebody in the know about this stupid health plan the Congress recently passed. As you all know,

221

virtually nobody has read it and those who have don't really understand it. Anyone who says they do is lying since most people have only focused on the parts that pertain directly to them.

"For example, there is one senior networking group I belong to that meets one Friday every month. A couple of months ago, on the Friday immediately after the bill was passed that fateful Tuesday night, I was talking to the vice president of marketing for one of the largest hospital groups in the state. She told me that the management team had been on-call since the passage of the bill."

"What do you mean?" Marilyn asked.

"What she told me made me sick.

"It turns out that within hours of the passage all hospitals were mobbed by people with pre-existing diseases demanding immediate care."

Milt asked, "Isn't that what Obama promised?"

"No Uncle, what the bill covers are pre-existing diseases after January 1, 2014. Since this is only 2010, that means the funds necessary to cover the cost of providing this type of care will not have been pooled for nearly another four years."

"In many cases the people will already be dead," said Marilyn.

"That is precisely what these people were crying at the hospital doors. They said that if they had to wait for almost four years without treatment they would surely die. You can imagine how this weighed on the staff charged with providing care and being unable to deliver."

"It must have been heart wrenching," Milt said with difficulty.

"Believe me it was. Just looking at this woman's face I could see how troubled she was. Here the President had in his typical political fashion promised something that he knew wouldn't be delivered to the vast majority of the people currently in need. That's just a sample of the rot that's infected the country and why we are planning to leave."

"Here we thought you were a true American patriot," Marilyn commented.

"Aunt Marilyn, believe me I am. I became totally enamored with the country, the hard working people, the dedicated government servants in Washington, a military willing to stand up for what is right, and I could go on.

"The problem is the leadership, or the lack of it. I don't want to get on my soapbox and rant about all that I see going on. It isn't fair the President bailed out the bankers who were at the root cause of this. He was wrong to nationalize the car industry, General Electric, and so many other things. They too have only added to the burden. He has driven up the debt by over a trillion dollars and saddled the country with a healthcare bill that will likely cost more to run than the funds it will manage. Moreover, he did that without tort reform as a sop to his legal buddies in the ABA, saddling Americans with down-range costs that will skyrocket even higher than imagined.

"But, unlike my wonderful friends, I have a legitimate exit and we are going to take it. So Uncle, hang in there. We're going to want to see more of you once we're back."

"Jon, thanks for coming," he said.

223

Marilyn walked Jon out and gave him a tight squeeze. "It's good to see you and I wish you only good things from this point forward."

With that she gave him a kiss on the cheek and headed back into her husband's room.

-o-o-o-

"Hello?"

"Hi Lindsay."

"Oh, hello mother."

"How are my babies?"

"They aren't babies anymore mother."

"OK, how are my beautiful grandchildren?

"They're fine."

"You sound distracted and why the cold reception?" Marilyn said noting the distinct sound of typing on a computer keyboard in the background.

"Because I know why you're calling and the answer is no."

"If you know why I'm calling why are you being so negative?"

"Because I will not come up there to see Milton."

"Your step father is on his deathbed and has been asking for you."

"That's too bad, I'm still not coming."

"After all that he's done for you?"

"Yes, but what exactly has he done for me?"

"Let's see, he made sure you never had to spend a penny of your trust fund, he was the one who insisted that you went to the best schools and got an excellent education, he gave you all

224

the guidance he could, and he was a male role model in the house."

"But, he wasn't dad."

"No, he wasn't. And, believe me if I could have brought your father back from the dead I would have. However, that doesn't excuse you for being so cruel to the man."

"Why not? He isn't my father and he imposed himself on my life."

"No, he did not! He was the best thing that could have happened to us after your father died in that plane crash."

"He was your sex toy."

"Now you've crossed the line!"

"Mother, you can't guilt me into this."

"Perhaps not, but this may be the last chance you get to see a man who truly loved you even if you didn't love him, alive."

"That's what I'm trying to tell you. I don't care if it is my last chance."

"How could someone I gave birth to, somebody I raised, turn out to be such a bitch?"

"They say the apple doesn't fall far from the tree."

"In this case it fell a mile away."

"Whatever, OK I'm booked on American 1552 arriving at around two o'clock on Monday the 25th. It's still a few weeks away and my plan is to stay for four days if that's alright with you."

"Why couldn't you just say that at the beginning of the conversation?"

"And miss all this fun?"

Chapter 24

2010

At nine o'clock Peter dropped off Margaret at the main entrance and then parked their Toyota Corolla in the rear parking lot of the famous Lakebeach Hospital. She waited patiently for him in one of the comfortable chairs while he trudged in with her small suitcase. She packed very little and the bag would have definitely qualified as carry-on for any airline.

A friendly attendant came to greet them and suggested Margaret use a wheelchair while she shepherded them through the laborious admittance process, starting in the business office.

At this point, the only money that would change hands was the additional cost of the room for a one-month period along with a parking pass for the car. This was easily handled on Peter's credit card. The only potential financial burden would be later months since the charges would definitely accumulate.

Once the business formalities were out of the way, they took the nearby bank of elevators up to the sixth floor.

Along the way Margaret commented on the wonderful paintings adorning the walls including those in the elevator. It seemed the hospital possessed a collection that would rival any art museum she had visited throughout her extensive travels. However, she made it a point not to mention her past although it was easy to admire all that she saw.

On arrival at her floor they made their way to a bright airy room near the nurses' station across from an open sitting area with a couple of cozy groupings. One of these included a big flat screen television tuned to a morning news show.

Nobody was currently sitting there, although a number of medical staff seemed quite busy behind the long counter of the station. Some were typing away at computer terminals while others were gathered in small groups possibly discussing various cases, or even sport scores from the previous day's games. At that time of year professional hockey, basketball, and even baseball were all still active.

Peter quickly unpacked her bag and sorted out what Margaret had brought. A few minutes later a beautiful young Asian doctor came into the room and said, "Mrs. Wong welcome to Lakebeach Hospital. I am Dr. Juliette Chen and please feel free to call me Juliette."

She continued, "I'm one of two doctors who manage this unit and it is our goal to make you as comfortable as possible and to give you the best quality of life we can. You are not confined to bed, and are free to roam the facility. All we ask are two things. If you are unsteady when you decide to go anywhere, please use a wheelchair. Second, if wish to leave this unit to perhaps go outside for some fresh air, please ask the nurses for an electronic wristband. That will prevent the security system from sounding the alarm.

"Believe me, the first time you hear the alarm it will shock you. And, if they deem it necessary and shut down the hospital to undertake a search, you will never forget it."

While Juliette was giving the welcome speech, the two of them stared at her in total fascination. Was it the last name, or perhaps her stark beauty that gave them an undeserved hope their lost son could possibly marry someone like her. Obviously, she captivated both of them and they shared the same thoughts.

"Well, if you don't have any questions, please settle in and feel free to contact me, my husband Joseph, or any of the nursing staff if there is anything you need."

With this Juliette left them open-mouthed.

Peter immediately got up and closed the door saying, "My dearest could it be?"

"Husband," Margaret gasped with a throat constricted by emotion more than her progressing cancer, "is it too much to believe?"

"We didn't ask her anything about when he came on shift."

"No, we did not. However, I expect to be here for some time so it won't be long before we see if it is truly our Joseph."

"If it is my dearest, there is no way we can let him know that we know who he is."

"Don't worry my husband. I may be dying, but there is no reason you should suffer the same fate because we stupidly become indiscrete. It is imperative we remain Mr. and Mrs. Wong.

"Anyhow, we don't look anything like we did when he last saw us. And, my medical records are based on the false date set ten years earlier than my real birth date. It is because your uncle insisted we list those in our visa applications. So, even if he suspects we seem somewhat familiar, my records will disprove any suspicions."

"You are right. But, it would be magnificent to see him again. If it is our Joseph, and Juliette is our daughter-in-law, just think what he has made of his life!"

The next morning their dreams were answered. A good looking male Asian doctor came into the room just after Peter arrived for the day.

"Hi, I'm Doctor Joseph Chen. But, as you've probably already seen how informal we are here so please, call me Joseph."

The two of them were speechless. Finally, Peter was able to say, "Joseph, I'm Peter Wong and this is my wife Margaret."

"Do I know you? You look familiar and I'm sure I've heard that voice somewhere before."

"No, I don't think so," said Margaret.

"Somehow it seems like we've met. There's something about both of you that seems to make it feel like we know each other. Guess we have some common blood!

"Well, let me get down to business. As you already know, Margaret you have advanced throat cancer. The two of you have agreed that it is your wish, Margaret, to spend your last days here at Lakebeach in our palliative care unit. Here we do not take any aggressive measures to extend your life, which you understand means should you cease breathing or your heart stop, we will not make any effort to apply lifesaving techniques."

"Yes Doctor, I understand," said Margaret.

"Good, and you Peter have co-signed the do-not-resuscitate form, correct?"

"Yes Doctor."

"OK, since your wife is not bed-ridden at this point, she is free to roam the grounds as long as the nursing staff is aware of when she is leaving the unit. Margaret, you can also leave the building for short visits to family or other sites until you aren't physically able to get around. My only caution is you take the appropriate mobility aids like a walker or your wheelchair."

"That's fine, but it's doubtful we'll leave the premises," said Peter. "We really don't have any close family here and I wouldn't want to take any chance of possibly hurting my wife."

"That seems odd since it says in your wife's history that you arrived in Canada a number of years ago as retirees from mainland China. From what I understand you need sponsors to get into the country and those are usually blood relatives."

Peter came up with some lame answer that was thankfully cut short by a page over the intercom for Joseph.

-o-o-o-

The Wongs settled into a routine. It was a hard adjustment for both of them, especially sleeping apart, but they persevered.

After testing traffic patterns for a few days, Peter ultimately would leave each morning at precisely eight o'clock. He discovered it didn't really matter what time he left between seven and nine, since the cross-town back-up was the same every day at those times.

He'd arrive at the hospital fifty to fifty-five minutes later and since for the first month Margaret was able to feed herself her empty breakfast tray would sit on the moveable stand awaiting pick-up by the kitchen staff. However, the extra coffee she ordered would be awaiting Peter's arrival, safely placed on the night table beside the bed. She would always wait for him so they could enjoy their morning coffee together.

After that they would review the daily activity going on in the hospital. There was always a mix of volunteer events plus

230

paid entertainment, booked long in advance, and that happened on at least three days each week. These ranged from musical troupes to drama to lectures. Most of the lectures were entertaining in nature rather than academic.

They often went for a walk, if Margaret was up to it. Or, Peter would push her in her wheelchair. This was followed by either a nap before lunch or sometimes watching a little television.

After Margaret's lunch, Peter would usually go to the cafeteria for a bite. Otherwise, he would head out of the hospital to one of the nearby restaurants. These were predominately sandwich places. Margaret would have a longer nap in the afternoon, freeing Peter to spend some time alone. Not having many places to visit he'd often bring a book or read a newspaper in the open sixth floor reception area facing the nurses' station.

It was also a chance to people-watch.

Within a couple of weeks he could discern certain patterns to what was happening on the floor. These went beyond the staff delivering meals, nurses pushing pills, doctors making rounds, assorted volunteer activities plus visits from the on-scene social workers. He noticed definite routines with respect to family members as to when they came to visit their loved ones.

He could also tell when somebody died through the follow-on activity. Often it would start with a flood of family members suddenly appearing at an unexpected time. A few of the medical staff would often intercept them en route to the deceased person's room followed by a social worker or two hustling down the hall after the entourage. Then a relative would usually detach him or herself from the rest and head to the quiet room to start making phone calls. Shortly after the medical and social workers disappeared, the rest of the family gravitated to the quiet room.

Depending on the time of day, the deceased was either removed by the hospital staff to be transported to the basement morgue to await the mortuary staff. Or they would remain in the room until the arrival of the funeral home people with their gurney. In either case, once the room was clear the cleaning crew immediately arrived to prepare it for the next occupant.

That person usually arrived the next day or the following one.

The other thing Peter noticed was the visitors, even the spouses of the patients, weren't very friendly. Nobody seemed to go out of their way to introduce themselves. Most seemed too wrapped up in their own anguish and were reluctant to share or commiserate.

However, all that was about to change.

About mid-way through the third week of Margaret's arrival, one afternoon Peter was quietly sitting on one of the couches outside her room trying not to nod-off. His head kept bobbing up and down while his eyelids drooped. Then, he felt a presence next to him and looked cautiously to his left.

The woman sitting next to him was quite pleasant looking and he gauged about the same age as he was. That is, he figured she was close to his real age, not the one on his fake birth certificate. He had noticed her a number of times since he started his vigil, and the man he figured was her husband occupied the room next door to Margaret.

Seeing he was actually awake she said, "Hi, I'm Marilyn Morgenstern."

"I'm Peter Wong," he said while extending his hand.

She took it and followed with, "Guess we're in the same boat with the same destination."

"Guess so. Is that your husband?"

"Sadly, yes. We've had a good life and Milt is my soul mate. He's my second husband but we've been married so long it's like he was my only one."

"Margaret and I have been together forever and I don't know what I'm going to do when I lose her."

"We both face the same fears and I have to tell you I'm trying to make the most of what we can while we still have each other, even in this place."

Chapter 25

2010

Friendship can develop either over time or when extenuating circumstances exist, almost immediately. Just look at how quickly bonds form in the military. Moreover, those are often life-long.

In the pressure cooker environment of a hospital lounge or surgical waiting area this is rare, although short term discussions may take place as a loved one recovers. But, in the environs of a palliative care unit, there is always the chance the friendship that blossoms becomes a lasting one.

In the case of Peter and Marilyn, they became close very quickly. Within days they had told each other things they hadn't shared with anyone else in decades. Ironically, Peter stuck to the fiction that had been created for him up to the time he and Margaret were incarcerated in the backwaters of China.

Marilyn recounted her wayward youth and even told stories about her experiences at Woodstock. She didn't hold back and actually laughed recalling how devastated her parents were discovering the photo of her totally nude, while tightly embracing a man she couldn't recall even meeting, being prominently displayed in a copy of *Life Magazine* that was sitting open on their living room coffee table.

In time their conversations became truly intimate. Neither one was aware of how they slipped into such a casual manner of opening up to each other. Only Peter had to pull back every so often when he realized he had lost the carefully cultured Chinese accent he normally used. When in deep conversation about things he hadn't discussed with anyone in years, it was often hard to

234

make sure that not only a modicum of truth survived while the manner with which he was delivering the story stayed true to the persona he was portraying. That is, he was supposedly a Chinese immigrant who arrived in this country as a retiree. Not somebody who grew up in Canada, was a major crime figure, had run a billion dollar enterprise, and then was kidnapped by the triads who wanted him dead, only to survive and make penance for losing a fortune of their money.

And, nobody could know that Doctor Joseph was his son or Doctor Juliette his daughter-in-law.

Before long there wasn't a topic that was out-of-bounds and they started to talk about their relationships with their spouses.

Marilyn was more open both because she had nothing to hide, but Peter was a willing participant. He was as revealing as he felt he could be, but was a good listener more than talker. And, Marilyn desired an ear.

At one point she became so explicit about past encounters Peter actually said, "Are you propositioning me?"

She stopped in her tracks and slowly said, "Peter, I can't say that I am not attracted to you, but I want you as my friend not my lover."

"I just wanted to clear the air."

"Perhaps, but in the vein of total disclosure as horny as I am, and Milt can only satisfy me to a very limited extent, I am not looking for an affair. But, should that change it would be with somebody I probably don't know, and someone I don't consider a friend."

"Point well taken," he replied.

The irony is Marilyn's comment actually opened up a path that hadn't been explored in the past between the two of them. When she implied that Milt was still able to satisfy her, Peter was intrigued.

"What did you mean about your husband being able to partially satisfy you?"

"Well, why don't we head down to the cafeteria to discuss this, where there's a little more privacy."

-o-o-o-

They both got a cup of Tim Horton's coffee and retired to the most discrete corner they could find.

Marilyn started the conversation with, "Peter, as you know we all have needs. Those don't end and when Milt was finally diagnosed we asked the doctor about continuing sexual relations. He said the only limitation was to find ways that would not put undue strain on Milt's body."

"What exactly does that mean?"

"It means that I have to be sensitive to his joints, his breathing, and excess pressure on any one point on his body."

"Oh, I think I get it. So, I understand how you could do that in the privacy of your own home but it's impossible here."

"Nothing is impossible."

"What do you mean?"

"I mean that we may not hang a sock on the door or a hat like Dustin Hoffman did in the movie *Meet the Fockers*, but we do have sex in Milt's room."

"You've got to be kidding. How?"

"Well, it started out pretty simply. That is, he'd get an erection and I'd relieve him. Then I thought, what about me? So I

236

masturbated with my other hand. Am I making you uncomfortable?"

"A little, but I'll get over it."

"If you want I'll stop."

"No, this is intriguing."

"OK, well over time I came to realize that if I followed the same rules his doctor outlined at the beginning there is no reason we can't enjoy full intercourse. So, I learned how to lower the bed to its lowest level and after a bit of foreplay would climb up on Milt.

"Naturally, I'd have to do most of the work. But, it is obvious we're both enjoying ourselves."

"Wow, I have to hand it to you."

"We started with my hand, we've progressed from there!"

"Glad you're able to keep a sense of humor."

"Humor and sex is all we have left I'm afraid. What about you and Margaret?"

"Us, I have to tell you the truth. The last time we had sex in any form was the night before she checked-in to this place."

"That's sad. It is obvious you are frustrated and I'm sure she is too. Just because she is an ailing woman in one sense doesn't mean her sex drive has diminished."

"You're probably right."

"I know I'm right. Why don't you ask her?"

"Frankly, we haven't talked about sex in years. Most of the time it just happened."

"Well, all that changed when she became a patient."

"You can say that again. That's why I haven't bothered her."

"Don't you think it is time you asked her what she wants? Maybe full intercourse is out of the question. That isn't the only way you can pleasure a person. But if you don't ask, you don't know."

"I thought you were going to say, 'don't get!'"

"That too. The point is in spite of her condition she is awake much of the day, aware of what is going on, and has probably been celibate because she doesn't want to disappoint you."

"Disappoint me?"

"Sorry, but it doesn't matter where she was raised that is a common failing of all women. We believe it is pleasuring our man that is important, even at the risk of ignoring our own needs. Again, I say ask her. What have you got to lose?

"If she says no, then respect her wishes. If she says yes, then enjoy yourselves."

-o-o-o-

In the later years, the Wongs were never comfortable talking about sex. Perhaps it was familiarity with what they respectively liked. Or, maybe it was a natural aversion to discussing something they felt was unnecessary. Bottom line, Peter found himself tongue-tied when he went back to Margaret's room.

He left Marilyn in the cafeteria and was in a conundrum while taking the elevator to the sixth floor. On one hand he was physically frustrated but unwilling to admit it to himself while on the other he really didn't know what his wife wanted. Like a teenager with a condom drying out in his wallet, he was afraid of rejection while just as fearful of consent.

238

Peter quietly closed the door behind him and approached Margaret who was propped up on the bed reading a magazine. Then, with a near stutter he started a conversation he never envisioned having with his wife of so many years, "Honey, I want to apologize if I have been neglectful of you."

Being one of her better days she was able to say, "What are you talking about?"

"We haven't had any sexual contact since before you came in here and I'm sure you're just as frustrated as I am."

"Peter, I admit I am frustrated. But, I've tried to put it out of my mind. This isn't quite the time or place for that type of thing."

"On the contrary, there is no prohibition that I know about and if you want, I can just massage your tender parts."

"That sounds nice, but what about you? I can hardly pleasure you in my condition."

"Let's concentrate on you first."

"OK, but where did all of this come from?"

"I was talking to Marilyn from next door."

"Who is Marilyn?"

"She's Milt's wife. He has ALS and since he's lost control of his arms and hands, he really can't pleasure Marilyn. But they've found a way that works for both of them."

"This sounds like a weird conversation between two strangers. Are you boinking her?"

"No dear, I am not!"

"I'm just kidding. So exactly what have they been doing? Just thinking about it is getting me turned on."

"They started with manual manipulation. Maybe that's a little too sterile or something. Anyhow, Marilyn said it started by her stoking Milt. Then it escalated to her masturbating at the same time. Now, they lower the bed to its lowest setting and she climbs on top of him."

"Sounds nice. Maybe we should try the same thing. But, let's start slowly. I don't think I'm ready for you to jump my bones just yet."

Over the next couple of weeks their lovemaking intensified and within a few days of their initial discussion Margaret felt comfortable enough for Peter to try full intercourse. Their only fear was their lovemaking was noisy enough to attract the medical staff at the nursing station just outside of her room.

It may not have been the most ideal of venues, but it's amazing that no matter how deprived people have been they have found a way to have sex in all manner of places beyond reason.

For a number of weeks everything went well. However, there came a point where Peter started to suspect Margaret was either dozing off or blacking out while they were making love. She seemed to both recover and enjoy the experience by the time he climaxed. But, he was left with a nagging suspicion she wasn't enjoying it as much as she had when Marilyn had first revealed her secret to Peter.

Over time, these apparent episodes became more frequent and longer in duration until Peter wound up saying, "Honey, do you think we should stop?"

"No my love, just because I'm not as participatory as in the past doesn't mean you should be deprived."

240

With this assurance, they continued to have sex. Then, one day the world collapsed.

Peter was on top and unexpectedly the door opened. Although they had timed their liaisons so they wouldn't normally take place when one of the staff was likely to intrude, there was always the chance some random visit could occur, in spite of their door being closed. Unlike a hotel room, there was no "Do Not Disturb" sign they could hang on the outside. So, although it hadn't happened in the past, this day the head nurse walked in.

At first they didn't hear her or realize she was there until the woman screamed, "What the hell do you think you are doing!"

Peter quickly rolled off and zipped up while Margaret laid placidly before trying to reach for the bed sheet.

"We were having a conjugal relationship," said Peter somewhat defiantly.

"No you weren't. You were raping this woman and there are laws against that!"

"That woman is my wife."

"That doesn't matter. She obviously was having sex with you without consent."

"She is my wife. We have always consented and she consented today."

"Did you ask her?"

"As a matter of fact yes! I said 'honey, do you feel up to fooling around?' and she said 'yes.'"

"But what about when she was unconscious? At that point she had rescinded her consent and as long as you continued your rutting you were raping her.

"I'm going to have to get Dr. Chen in here to handle this mess."

"Please don't do that," said Margaret openly crying at this point.

"I'm afraid it's standard operating procedure in these matters."

With that the head nurse left the room making sure the door was wide open.

"Husband, what are we going to do? Not only am I embarrassed by what has happened now either our son or daughter-in-law will be involved."

"I know my love. Let's see what happens."

-o-o-o-

About fifteen minutes later Joseph came into the room and closed the door.

"I understand we have a bit of a problem," was how he started.

"Doctor, I assure you I had my wife's consent and since she has no infirmary in her extremities why should she precluded from enjoying relationships?"

"I'm afraid it isn't so simple Mr. Wong. There is no proof you had her permission. Nor do you have my permission. Moreover, the head nurse said that in her opinion you wife had either fallen asleep or blacked out during intercourse. Under the law, that is considered rape. You have an obligation to immediately withdraw."

"That's ridiculous!"

"No sir that is the law. And, it is quite a serious law."

"What do we do now?"

242

"Well, I'm afraid I have to take blood samples from both of you to make sure you aren't carrying any sexual diseases. Then I have to call in the police and file a rape report. Since you were interrupted and freely admitted you were having sex I won't further embarrass your wife by compiling a rape kit, although under other circumstances that would be required.

"Doctor, she is my wife. We have been married for a very long time. Why in heaven's name must we be put through this hell for something we have been enjoying since before you were born?"

"I'm terribly sorry Mr. Wong, but that is the law and I'm compelled to uphold it."

A few minutes later the lab technician arrived to draw blood and the police showed up a half hour later. They were somewhat surprised the husband and wife were still in the same room, but after some preliminary questions took Peter away in handcuffs.

Peter hired a lawyer and was out on his own recognizance the next day. However, he was slapped with a restraining order that required any visits to his wife needed to be court supervised. Under the circumstances his lawyer was able to get an agreement from the court that he could hire one of the hospital approved caregivers to be an in-room witness during his visits. The only requirement was this caregiver needed to note the time of the visits and forward the schedule weekly to the judge. This curtailed any further sexual contact, but they prevailed on the woman who attended whenever Peter was present, to at least let them hold hands.

-o-o-o-

243

Marilyn was unaware of what had happened and Peter had stopped sitting in the outside common area when he was in the hospital. She noticed the strange woman in the room when she passed by, and over time realized the door was never shut. But, she never made the connection and the sexual relationships she had with Milt continued unabated.

Over time Milt too started to drift off while they were having sex. Since his erection remained intact, it was only his breathing becoming more labored that alerted Marilyn. However, since he usually ejaculated, she figured there was nothing really wrong.

However, it was only a matter of time before the head nurse took notice of their closed door and made it a point to intrude. When she did, her suspicions were confirmed and this time Dr. Juliette Chen attended. Again, blood tests were ordered and the police were called.

The main difference was the police left without Marilyn in handcuffs, meaning she was never limited to supervised visits.

They claimed it would be much harder for them to prove rape with a wife engaging in sex with her husband than the other way around. Although Marilyn was unaware of what happened to the Wongs, it wasn't long before Peter heard about her and Milt. He was naturally incensed and brought up this unfair application of the law to his lawyer.

His lawyer was sympathetic but said "This is one case where a double-standard in the law definitely exists."

-o-o-o-

Marilyn faced a personal dilemma. It wasn't long after her scrape with the law that she heard about the Wong's situation.

244

She was well aware she'd dodged a bullet. But, that didn't satisfy her sex cravings that had been awoken with the relationships she'd carried on with her husband in the hospital. The problem was, even though now she knew that any further contact of this nature could see her winding up in prison, it didn't assuage her physical yearnings.

She was devoted and loved Milt with all her being. But, the combination of knowing Milt was terminal combined with her sexual needs, eventually drove her to seek what she was missing.

After leaving Milt when he finally dozed off for the night Marilyn drove home to her condo. Fortunately for her, there were dozens of bars, pubs, and wonderful restaurants within walking distance. She had every type of libation at her disposal and with this level of opportunity, it didn't take long to discover which establishment best served her purpose.

Over a few nights she checked out the various ones within a two-block radius and ultimately settled on dimly lit bar where most of the women seemed close to her age and the men quite a bit younger. She didn't want to be considered a cougar, but figured for her purposes, technically any relationship was out of the question.

She had no doubt that she was still quite attractive and her second night at the bar was when she was hit on by at least three men. After her second appletini she softly said "yes" to the advances of a very good looking guy. Her only stipulation was she would not take him back to her place. As long as Milt was alive, she felt it was his home too and she didn't want to sully where she slept as a happy wife with a one night stand.

The sex was more a release than anything else and Marilyn was glad the man's condo was only a few blocks from her own. Although they took a cab from the bar, when she left just before sunrise, it was a short walk home. Once there she showered and changed into something less conspicuous for her day at Milt's side.

In his condition, he didn't suspect anything. However, her daughter arrived for her visit a few days later and had an acute eye.

"For someone whose husband is on the brink of death you look surprisingly bright," was how she greeted her mother at the curb outside US arrivals.

"I see you haven't lost your sharp tongue," Marilyn replied. "Let's get into the car and see your step father."

"Please mother, don't call him that. He's Milt to me and always will be."

"OK, it's a truce. I'm really glad you're here and appreciate that you made the effort to come. It's more important to me to have your support and companionship."

"That's fine with me too. I know you've loved him and I can never understand the feeling of loss you must be going through, even now. What I now appreciate by being married to a wonderful man is how different it must be losing a husband than losing a father. Dad's death was devastating to me, but I could never fathom the depth of pain you must have felt. Now with Milt, it is inconceivable to me. And, yes this is an apology."

"Thank you, Lindsay."

For the next couple of days their routine was spending time with Milt and when he drifted off in the evening, they would have supper at various nice restaurants, then turn in. On the third evening, Marilyn said she wanted to go out for drinks and convinced Lindsay to go with her. However, she made it a point to go to a different local pub rather than her normal pick-up spot. The trouble was, it was still too close to her capture site.

"I thought it was you!" was said over her shoulder by a tall gentleman in a cashmere coat.

"Do I know you?" replied Marilyn.

"How could you forget me so quickly? We hooked up only a week ago and who is this charming beauty?"

"I'm sorry you must be mistaken."

"No, I'm not. In fact, you have that cute mole under your left breast. It is unmistakable!"

"Now you are embarrassing me. Please go."

"If that's how you treat your 'big bone man' then you're damn right I'll go."

Throughout this exchange, Lindsay's jaw was almost on the table.

"Mother, what the hell are you doing?"

"Whatever do you mean, dear?"

"You're having an affair. Or, maybe not an affair but a bunch of one night stands."

"You don't understand."

"Oh, but I do. I do not condemn you, but Milt isn't dead yet. In fact, you still have to bury him, sit shiva, and then wait the thirty days before you're free to cavort."

"Honey, what I do with my life is my business. Please keep this to yourself."

"Sure."

247

"No, I mean it. You're a grown woman with your own desires. Just because I'm older doesn't mean mine have diminished. In fact, up until the hospital intervened, Milt and I were having relationships in his room. The trouble is if we continue to have sex in the hospital, I can go to jail."

"You've gotta be kidding."

"Sadly, I am not. It happened to the wonderful Asian couple in the room next to me. The husband has been charged with rape and is going through hell. Think of it, the hospital reported him and now he's got to go through a terrible criminal court case. Likely he will be convicted, and even if they give him parole, he'll be branded a sex offender for the rest of his life."

"That's unbelievable!"

"No, it is reality. And, it is precisely why we had to suspend the only closeness Milt and I could have in his condition."

-o-o-o-

Lindsay didn't say a word the next day, but on the last day of her visit she and Marilyn had their typical mother and daughter blow-up. Unfortunately, it took place in Milt's room and he was awake through all of it.

"You're a good one to talk," hissed Lindsay.

"Keep your voice down," shot back her mother.

"I am keeping it down. But, you have to believe I was about to shout it at the top of my lungs."

"Don't even think of it!"

"I will think what I want. Who are you to tell me? I am a wife, mother, and fully independent."

"You are all of those and a bitch to boot."

248

"Look who's talking. You the hypocrite, something you've been all your life. Do as I say not as I do is your motto. Why should I listen to you now?"

"Because I'm your mother and, in this case, I do know best."

"No, you're a philandering soon-to-be widow who can't keep her legs closed!"

"Now, you've gone too far!"

"Far, far? I haven't started to say my piece."

At that point Milt perked up and croaked out, "What the hell are you two talking about?"

"Honey, it's nothing. This is our typical fight before Lindsay heads home to Florida."

"Are you going to lie to a dying man?"

"Shut up!"

"I will not shut up!"

"Lindsay, please go. I'm glad to have seen you, but enough already," gasped Milt.

With this Lindsay left in a huff and slammed the door behind her.

"I better go too," said Marilyn who was clearly upset.

"No."

"What do you mean, no?"

"Please stay, we need to talk. I don't know how much strength I have to say what I must."

"What do you mean?"

"I want a divorce."

"What?"

"You...heard...me...a...divorce."

"Why?"

"Cause, I thought you were having an affair and Lindsay confirmed it. But, that's not why."

"Again why?" with tears streaming down her cheeks.

"Because, I don't want that bitch to get a penny of my money when I'm gone!" After that he collapsed into his pillow and fell into a deep sleep.

Chapter 26

2010

Peter waited for the other shoe to drop.

His fear was that before too long, Joseph would discover that he and Margaret were his parents. He'd made comments in the past about them looking familiar. But, because of their appearing well beyond their real ages and further backed up by the birth date embedded in Margaret's insurance card, so far he hadn't made the connection. Peter knew it was only a matter of time the blood work would somehow reveal their true identities.

However, that wasn't the more immediate problem.

In 1994 he was arrested for a trumped-up drug charge resulting in both his mug shots and fingerprints being on file. At that time they were still not committing everything to computers, unless the conviction held. But since the charges were dropped the same day, it was a question whether the unsubstantiated charges were likewise loaded into some remote database. Should that be the case, who knew how long it would take before someone made the connection.

With all that had happened in his life since then, Peter had completely forgotten about the episode and was shocked when one morning as he was preparing to leave for his supervised visit with Margaret there was a pounding at the front door.

"Paul Chen, open up, it is the police!"

He was chilled to the bone.

"I'm coming."

As he opened the door with a shaking hand he stammered, "Officers, I think you have the wrong house. What seems to be the problem?"

One held up a piece of paper with the sixteen year old image of Paul Chen in full face and profile in front of the old man at the door. It was obvious he was confused when he said to his partner, "Smith, I think it's the guy. What do you think?"

"I'm not sure. Let's take him in."

"Sir, do you have any identification?"

"Yes, of course. Here is my driver's license and if you want I can get my passport."

"No, this is fine, but I'm still not sure.

"Sir, I'm afraid you need to come with us to the station. There we should be able to clear this matter up."

With that they escorted Peter to their car and carefully helped him into the back seat. What they couldn't see was how he was shaking.

On arrival at the station they took him into an interrogation room and asked him politely to wait there. In the meantime, Smith stayed outside while her partner went to get the fingerprint tech. The two of them arrived about five minutes later.

Carrying a device the size of a laptop computer, the tech approached Peter. "Sir, I need you to open your right hand and place it on the screen. This is painless and should only take a couple of minutes."

Accordingly, Peter did as instructed while averting his eyes. Two minutes later there was a soft ping and his mug shot appeared on the screen along with two copies of the fingerprints of his right hand. The top set were the ones on file, while on the bottom were the ones just imaged by the technician.

"Mr. Paul Chen you are under arrest for illegal entry into the country, possession of forged documents, and fraudulent use of medical services. These charges are in addition to the current ones for sexual abuse, which will be reissued in your correct name.

"We are going to have to hold you until arraignment and revoke your current O.R. status. Do you understand me?"

"Yes, I do," he said without a trace of his normally affected Chinese accent.

"Could you please call my lawyer and let him know that I am here?"

"Certainly, do you have his name and number?"

After providing the necessary contact information, he was taken to a holding cell. His main concern was Margaret who was going to worry and wonder why he had not arrived for today's visit.

The next morning he was hauled in front of a magistrate where the charges were read. His lawyer answered "not guilty."

This time there was a one hundred thousand dollar bond required and after the two of them conferred for a minute the lawyer said his client has agreed to the terms and would post the bond immediately. Within the hour Peter, now officially known by his real name of Paul, was released. Since the wheels of justice move extremely slowly, he knew Margaret, now again Mei Ling Chen, may also be charged although she would never stand trial. He on the other hand would.

-o-o-o-

As soon as Paul was released his lawyer drove him home to shower, shave, and change his clothes.

"Are you alright?"

"How can I ever be alright? I didn't choose to live under an assumed name. I was forced to. And, now my dying wife has to endure further humiliation because of matters beyond her control, compounded by a stupid interpretation of the law. Yeah, I looked up the cases and I'm well aware of the fact the application of that abomination of a decision against two elderly consenting adults is totally beyond belief."

Paul's true self, which had been repressed for over twelve years, was starting to emerge. He was used to being in control and was now chaffing at the bit to re-establish his dominance. However, he was being more restrained than ever, and on the point of exploding.

"As I said in the courtroom, I have the money to pay you and now that you know my true identity, you can definitely believe me. It may take a couple of days to amass the cash, so please be patient. I will bring a cashier's check to your office and no, it is not from illegal gains."

"Peter or I mean Paul, that's fine with me. Make it three days since I will be in court until then."

-o-o-o-

Paul cleaned himself up and drove like a maniac to get to the hospital. His minder was waiting outside his wife's room with a scowl on her face.

"Where the hell have you been?" she barked.

"Back in jail and I'm in no mood to discuss it."

"Well, your wife is a basket case and I can't calm her down. Maybe now that you're here, you can do something."

"What happened?"

"I honestly don't know. All that I can say is she was fine yesterday even with you not showing up. But, this morning Dr.

254

Joseph was in with her with the door closed and she's been inconsolable since then."

"What did he say to make her so upset?"

"How should I know? I wasn't allowed in the room and why should I be in there if you weren't here when you were supposed to be? Anyhow, maybe you can get through to her."

"I'll try."

Paul opened the door and went in. As he tried to close it the visit supervisor stuck her foot in to block him. "I still need to be in the room."

From behind she heard Dr. Joseph's voice saying with authority, "No, you don't. I'll handle this," while gently pushing past her and firmly closing the door.

"Well, I guess we have a lot to talk about mother and father," said Joseph to his shocked parents. "And, I've asked Juliette to join me when she arrives in about fifteen minutes from now. I'll return when she gets here."

Almost to the second, the younger Chen couple walked into the stony silence of Joseph's mother's room. It was clear she had stopped her earlier wailing, but they were both obviously distraught.

Paul started, "Joseph we're so sorry. I know that sounds unbelievably trite, but you have to understand the circumstances. Had we indicated at any time we were alive, not only were our lives at risk, but so was yours. Also, the punishment we endured for ten years was clearly designed to make sure we died in China right up to our last day in that hell hole."

"Father, may I call you father?"

"Of course, you are my son."

"Then what makes it different now?"

"Because your mother and I have nothing left to lose since it wasn't me that made my whereabouts known, but the police. Should anything happen to me now, the perpetrators would be sought by the very people from whom they are hiding. They live in the shadows and wish to remain there. Attacking me or my family would bring them into the open.

"My question is that until yesterday, you were unaware of our real identities. They have still not been publicly declared, yet here I arrive this morning, and you know who we are. How?"

"Father, it is a bit of a complicated story so I'll make it as simple as I can.

"One of the electives I took for my MD involved some advanced DNA work. For that I used a sample of my own blood and compared it to specimens from a number of other participants in that study. One outcome was the discovery of an asymptomatic condition called Gilbert's Syndrome or GS for short, which I have.

"It may sound scary, but it is just a build up of bilirubin in my blood. Since I'm of Asian extraction, the small amount of jaundice it causes isn't even noticeable. However, for me and the other five percent of the population that is affected by this syndrome, this means both parents have to be carrying the recessive gene.

"When I drew blood from the two of you because of the sexual incident, the fact is our lab also did a basic DNA work-up and issued a hard copy report. Those were in your file.

"Normally, I wouldn't have even noticed them. However, yesterday morning I tripped over a mop that was angled against the doorframe just outside my office and dropped a number of files. Mother, yours was one of them and the DNA reports for you and father slid onto the floor. When I picked them up they were overlaid, and enough light shone through that the pattern looked familiar. Moreover they both had the GS recessive gene.

"Last night, when I got home I went into the garage and grabbed the storage box with the roughs for my published papers. I had to dig down to find the work I did at UCLA, but there it was. An acetate print-out of my own DNA was clipped to the documents. With this it was easy to put my profile over the two of yours and not only see the recessive gene, but that the two of you had each contributed half of my personal DNA make-up.

"Now, I had inconvertible proof the two of you are my parents."

When Paul could catch his breath he said, "Again, we're sorry."

"No father, I'm sorry. I'm the one who put you in this terrible legal bind and let's not lose sight that mother's time is limited at best.

"How do you two get to know Juliette? How do we make up all those lost years? You are facing criminal charges on a number of matters that will just not go away. And, I definitely want to know what happened to you. And, don't you want to know about my life?"

"Son," said Mei Ling, "more than you could ever believe. I have watched the two of you with tears in my eyes since we arrived in this hospital. Some of that was sheer pride, but the rest was pure pain. So many times we wanted to reach out and touch you. Not as a doctor, but as our son. And Juliette, you are our

257

daughter-in-law carrying our grandchild. You are so precious to us and we have been locked in this cocoon of silence that prevented us from even the slightest bit of interaction."

Juliette replied, "As of now that has to end."

Paul countered, "If only it was that easy. Joseph is right. I have a literal ball and chain attached to me and my mere presence here taints all of you. I'm not talking about the past; I'm referring to the present. Until my legal battles are settled, everything remains in flux.

"I am still restricted with respect to visiting my wife and even if you two wanted to allow it, the court has already ruled. As well, I need to respect the conditions of my bond until the case is heard. Now the question is whether everything will be lumped together, or will I have to stand trial for the so-called rape before the impersonation and illegal entry charges, versus the other way around. Any way you look at it, this is a mess."

"That may be so," said Joseph. "But from this point onward, I will do everything in my power to make sure mother and you are able to spend as much time together as you can. I'll personally guarantee a hospital worker is available for you twenty-four/seven so you don't have to rely on the court appointed minder until the time of your trial. As for that, we'll deal with the outcome at that time.

Chapter 27

2010

The quandary facing the police was what trumped what. On one hand they believed they had a slam-dunk rape case while on the other the illegal documents, illegal entry, and impersonation charges could not be ignored. Plus the latter ones also affect their primary rape case since the person they had initially charged didn't really exist, at least not legally. And if the latter charges were deemed more pressing than the rape, then the whole matter could move out of their jurisdiction.

Under no circumstances did they want that to happen. A collar is still a collar unless the "perp" goes free. In this situation, their fear was that uncovering this man's real identity would not improve their case. In most instances, discovering that a criminal had used a number of aliases was a prosecution bonus. This time it made the situation worse, much worse.

Yes, Paul Chen had one arrest on record from over a decade ago but the charges were dropped within twenty-four hours. Yes, Paul Chen was often a person of interest in a number of ancient unsolved crimes, many of which were extremely violent. Yes, Paul Chen dropped off the radar a long time ago, and was presumed dead. But, for once they had him on something substantial: a rape charge.

Arresting officers for the rape, Raj Singh and Alicia Hood, had enough experience to know that recidivism, even for criminals who had made it to advanced age, was rampant. And, they had no doubt Chen probably was hiding serious crimes in his missing years. But, they also knew that the law on which the rape was based was itself questionable.

"So what if he was having sex was with his wife?" asked Raj. "Courts throughout the world have ruled that the rape of a wife is still a rape. And, the fact they're both seniors is now debatable based on their actual birth dates, as opposed to what their bogus documents said. But even that isn't a defense, based on the Supreme Court reversal that upheld that once a partner was no longer conscious of the sex act, the sex must end or the conscious partner is guilty.

"There was no doubt the wife drifted in and out of consciousness while her husband was on top of her. According to witnesses, he didn't stop. So he is guilty...end of story!"

Now, all that was at risk because they had done their job by running down the fingerprints taken at his booking.

Officer Hood continued, "Sure the law they want to hang him on is a crock, at least when it pertains to a husband and wife."

"Yeah," he said, "It all started with that stupid bitch who wanted to get back at her ex-husband a few years ago. Why she was having sex with him in the first place is weird."

"You've never been divorced," said his partner. "There's something to be said about making it with someone who knows you and what you like, even if you don't love them anymore. I know that for a year after my divorce, I had more sex with my ex at that time than probably in the last few years of our marriage.

"Anyhow, the Supreme Court judges in their infinite wisdom chose to ignore the fact she liked auto-asphyxiation, and even disregarded the whole revenge angle about her being afraid her ex would use that kinkiness against her in a custody battle for her son. It boggles the mind that the poor bastard was still

260

charged with rape weeks after the event, and somehow lost his initial court case."

Her partner said, "That is beyond belief, and I admit I was glad he won on appeal. But, they couldn't leave it at that, which would have been reasonable. Somehow, the Supreme justices overturned the appeal verdict, and reinstated the original rape decision.

"Now any dumb fuck who plays rough is putting himself at risk. And, even if the sex was fully consensual at the time they started screwing, the woman can cry rape years after the fact and the idiot could wind up in the slammer."

She replied, "The problem is the court is casting a wide net and no matter what this guy Chen's real age is, his wife is definitely dying and nobody has asked her if she gave consent. Did she like what he was doing?

"Now she is going to lose out spending time with her husband in her waning days, since according to the law none of that matters. The man continued to jump her bones when she was supposedly mentally incapacitated."

"I gotta ask you, even if she lives until the case comes up in court, how could she honestly even defend him? How would she be able to know if she was awake throughout or not? Bottom line, based on the case law, guilty as charged, your honor!

"What a crock!"

Hood answered, "True, but all that could go away if the other charges eclipse this rape."

"Actually, the rape wouldn't really go away. It would only be a secondary charge and if the wife dies, yet reveals their true story beforehand as to why they resorted to living a lie, then there could still be leniency for the husband."

In spite of the officers venting their own opinions, there was no question that they would be the losers if their case was considered less pressing than the federal charges.

-o-o-o-

The Feds definitely wanted to talk to the Chens. They were also in a quandary. Do they come down hard on Paul while his wife is dying? Do they interview Mei Ling while she is still around and how clear would her mind be at this point? Or, do they let nature take its course and go after Paul while holding up the rape charge?

After the events of 9/11, certain types of illegal entry were treated very seriously. One may take issue with this when considering the southern US/Mexico border and the number of illegals that flood across it on a nightly basis. However, those that slip through the immigration process with phony documents, including what appear to be a valid birth certificates, drivers' licenses and social security cards, are definitely more troublesome. These are the tools commonly used by spies and terrorists.

Nobody thought Paul Chen and his wife were terrorists. On preliminary investigation they had already discovered he had initially immigrated to Canada as an infant and grew up in Toronto. Mei Ling was born here and was a citizen by birth. There was no known reason for either of them to re-enter the country illegally with bogus documents. Obviously, there was much more to this story than met the eye.

On checking news sources going back to 1995, it appeared the couple had been reported killed on an extended trip to China during one of that country's worst flood seasons. One of their most trusted friends had organized a memorial service, probably on behalf of their single child, a son.

Speaking of the son, what about him?

He not only went on to become a doctor, but in fact was the specialist in charge of their care. How could anyone believe he couldn't recognize his parents even if he hadn't seen them in more than a dozen years?

Is he part of their lies?

Too much doesn't fit. Whether that's just because life isn't neat and tied up with a bow, or because a conspiracy much greater than meets the eye is behind all of this? Nobody wants to admit to conspiracy theories, but, as they say, being paranoid isn't wrong if they're actually out to get you.

The federal team assigned to this matter wanted to get to the bottom of it. This may have been a solid objective for them, but what they didn't realize, was just how convoluted the past really was and the effort it would take to unravel it.

What they also didn't appreciate was how far beyond the two generations of Chens this extended, the continents involved, the amount of money that was at stake, and that the resources at the protagonists' disposal (should they choose to use them), were significantly greater than those of law enforcement.

It was amazing that the Chens' identities were uncovered in the first place. Still unknown was how the triads would react should they discover the elaborate ruse they'd created to effectively eliminate the Chens had been stymied. Moreover, if they thought Paul had caused it to become public, all surviving family members were at risk. What the thugs in China would not realize is that Mei Ling's terminal illness had rendered her irrelevant in their plans, thereby releasing Paul from their hold over him. Also, Paul ceased to care about himself anymore. His only fear was for Joseph and Juliette.

All of this was a mystery to the federal agents investigating the senior Chens. What they did know was that the clock was ticking on how much time they had before they needed to step in front of the rape charge. If they didn't, it would proceed and everything else would be in the background.

Chapter 28

2010

Milt ordered Marilyn out of the room.

Since she left in such a tearful fit, the head nurse stormed in to see what had so upset her. On entering she saw Milt too was extremely agitated and thought she would order a sedative for him. However, up to this point nothing had been listed in his chart and she was loath to contact the doctors.

Within a few minutes he had calmed down enough to talk in his labored manner. Leaning over she heard, "I love her, but I can't remain married to her. I don't want to hurt her. But, that bitch of a daughter has driven a wedge between us. And, so has this hospital."

"Whatever do you mean?" asked the nurse.

"I mean her daughter is one thing, but your taking away the only physical enjoyment we were able to provide to each other in my condition meant she has become an adulterer."

"Milt, that wasn't our choice. Do you realize that if you were a woman like the lady next door, Marilyn would have been charged with rape?"

Becoming extremely upset again, he choked out, "No ffuhhhcccking wwwaaay!"

"Yes, way. Sadly, there is a double standard in these matters. If we find a man having sex with an incapacitated woman we must call the police, even if they are married. However, it doesn't apply the other way around. If it did, I wasn't kidding when I said you would have been charged. That's why once we were aware of your having relations with Marilyn, and the fact is in your chart that you often black out, we were mandated to put a stop to them."

In a calmer voice he said, "You mean that poor bastard married to that Chinese lady in the next room that Marilyn has talked so fondly of, is now charged with rape?"

"Yes, and that isn't his only problem."

"What do you mean?"

"I mean that privacy laws mean I've said too much already. What I need to do is calm you down, and find out what I can do to help you and Marilyn."

"You can call my lawyer for me."

"Now let's not get into that."

"I'm sorry, but if you want to help me, please call my lawyer. His name is already on record as my executor, which I provided on admission. He also practices family law and I need him sooner rather than later."

"Milt, normally we don't list that information on your intake form."

"For some reason Marilyn insisted when I was admitted, so I know it is there."

Dutifully, the nurse went to the desk and extracted the necessary contact from the desk copy of the form. She placed the call and on reaching the lawyer, directly gave him an overview of what had happened. What she said was circumspect, so the man agreed to come that afternoon and meet with Milt.

On arrival Milt said, "Bob, I'm so glad you're here," with obvious difficulty.

"Milt, I understand this is some type of an emergency and I cleared some time so we could talk about it."

266

He then stammered through, "In my condition, everything I do is sort of an emergency. I don't know how much time I have left, but it won't be long. And, there are things that have to be attended to beyond the will you have on-hand."

"I know this is an effort for you both physically and definitely emotionally. Please tell me as much as you can, but most importantly, what you want me to do?"

"I want to divorce Marilyn and change my will."

"That's pretty sudden, isn't it?"

"Marilyn is an adulterer, so I have grounds. But, I still love her and I don't want to hurt her any more than absolutely necessary. I know that sounds contradictory and stupid, but it is what it is."

"OK, I get it. She cheated on you. And since you can't have sex with her you're retaliating."

"Who said we can't have sex?"

"You can?"

"Yes, but we're prohibited from it as long as I'm here. So that means for the rest of my life."

"You gotta be kidding!"

"I wish I was. But, that's the law, or the rule, or something. And, what is even more ridiculous is that if I was a woman and my husband had sex with me in here, he could be charged with rape."

"You're wrong. I have other clients in here who I know are still physical."

"If she was incapacitated, as opposed to just being old, apparently the law is quite clear. Just talk to the lady next door.

Her husband apparently has been charged with rape according to the head nurse.

"Anyhow, that isn't why you're here and I don't know how much longer I will be able to talk."

"OK, what do you want me to do and please be as specific as possible?"

"As I said, I want to divorce Marilyn. I also want a codicil to my will that except for the provisions I've already made for funds that go to the listed charities, all the rest of the money is earmarked for Marilyn and must be placed in a trust that will be paid out to her as a monthly allowance. In addition, she can keep the cars, the condo, the art collection, and all our possessions. But, on her death any balance in the trust must go proportionately to the same list of charities."

"How much is her allowance?"

"I want it set at three hundred and sixty thousand per year, adjusted for inflation, until her death or should she re-marry. Naturally, she has her own money and this only pertains to what comes from me. Also, if her health deteriorates and she remains unmarried, but has to go into a long term care facility, I want it to also be paid out of the trust. Plus, any private in-home care should likewise be covered by the trust."

"So, basically you're cutting out her daughter."

"You're damned right I am. That bitch is dead to me and has done everything she can to poison my final days."

"This won't take long. I should have it ready by tomorrow and will bring it in for signing then. I'm sure you can get one of the staff to witness your signature, and it will be done."

"Thank you, Bob."

268

Chapter 29

2011

"Please state your name for the record."

"Marilyn Morgenstern."

"And how do you know the defendant?"

"My late husband was in the next private room in the long term care facility at Lakebeach Hospital."

"Now Mrs. Morgenstern I know this is difficult for you and that you befriended the defendant. But I need to ask you some questions that you probably will make you uncomfortable, but you are under oath. Do you understand?"

"Yes."

"Alright, do you know if the defendant was having sexual relations with his wife while in the hospital?"

"Objection, calls for hearsay!"

"Sit down Mr. Rogers," said the judge who followed with, "overruled, the witness may answer."

"Judge, I still object since it is definitely hearsay."

"I already ruled on this."

"Your honor, I will rephrase."

"Go ahead."

"Mrs. Morgenstern, let me ask you this. Did you ever tell the defendant how he could have sexual relations with his wife while in the hospital?"

"Yes."

"Exactly what did you tell him?"

"That is a little personal, sir."

"No, in a court of law no matter how personal you may feel, unless the judge finds the question improper, you must answer."

"I told him that unless a woman is dead she still has needs. I told him as her husband he has a responsibility to fulfill those needs. Then I told him he could do it manually or if she was up to it, there was no reason they couldn't have full sexual relations."

"After you told the defendant that you were having relations with your husband even though he was infirm, in your opinion did he follow your suggestion?"

"Objection, relevance?"

"Overruled, you may answer."

"I noticed the door to the room was closed more often than it had been in the past, but I can't honestly say that I knew."

"Let me put it another way. Did you see the defendant being arrested?"

"Yes."

"Did anyone tell you why he was arrested?"

"Not a first. A couple of days later when he didn't show up, I went into his wife's room. She was crying miserably and I asked what was wrong. She said the police had arrested her husband. When I asked why, she said she was too embarrassed to tell me. I then asked the head nurse."

"So it was the head nurse who told you?"

"Yes."

"What did you do about it?"

"What do you mean?"

"Did you and your husband stop your relations?"

"Objection!"

"Sustained! Counselor, you know better than that."

"Yes, your honor."

"Mrs. Morgenstern, did you hear about the defendant's other charges?

"Again, not at first. He showed up a few days later and there was another woman in the room every time Mr. Wong visited and I was told he needed supervised visits as part of his bail agreement. Then the next day the police arrived again, and this time he disappeared in hand cuffs. At first nobody seemed to know what had happened. But, a hospital is like any other institution and the grape vine carried the information within a day."

"How did it make you feel to find out the man you befriended was a fraud?"

"Objection, we don't need character assassination and opposing counsel knows this isn't a financially motivated trial."

"Sustained."

"Let me put it this way. You found out that Mr. Wong was really Mr. Chen. You also discovered he wasn't a Chinese national but a Canadian citizen leading a secret life. Did that subterfuge, irrespective of why it occurred, bother you?"

"No, I figured that..."

"No, will do."

"You asked me a question and I want to answer," she said looking imploringly to the judge.

Seeing how much she wanted to answer, the judge said, "You may continue."

"Under those circumstances you get to know people really well in the worst possible setting. We understood that our loved ones have limited time, and we cling to others in the same predicament for comfort.

271

"Whether it's Peter, or Paul I don't care. The man was decent and dedicated to his wife. What they did to him was unconscionable in the first place. If they hadn't arrested him for rape, they would never have known about the rest of it and he would be a free man today."

"Mrs. Morgenstern, that's enough!"

"No sir, it isn't. This is wrong. All of it is just plain wrong!"

"Your honor, please advise the witness to restrain her answers to my questions."

"Counselor, you opened the door and she definitely shut it," said the judge. Continuing, he then said "Unless you have any further questions of Mrs. Morgenstern, she may leave."

"No further questions."

As she started to rise from the witness stand, the lead defense attorney said, "If I may, I have just a couple of questions."

"Go ahead," said the judge.

"Mrs. Morgenstern, did you also tell my client you were having relations with your late husband?"

"Yes."

"Did the hospital staff find out about your relations?"

"Yes."

"And what did you do about that?"

"Milt and I stopped. But, that didn't satisfy me."

"Objection, relevance."

"Quite simple your honor. My client is charged with one of the most heinous crimes, that of rape. However, he was having relations with his infirm wife. In the meantime the couple right next door..."

"Your honor, my colleague is giving evidence."

"Quite right, objection is overruled so we can get the witness' testimony into the record."

"Thank you, your honor. As I was saying, Mrs. Morgenstern you were saying about your late husband?"

"We stopped all relations but I still had needs. I believe Milt did too, but I didn't want to be charged with rape. So, I went on the prowl and had a series of one night stands."

"Then what happened?"

"My daughter let her stepfather know about them, and he demanded a divorce."

"Were you divorced?"

"Yes."

"No further questions."

It became obvious, right from the opening comments that the trial of Paul Chen, aka Peter Wong, was going to focus on the rape charge, with the balance of his alleged crimes being treated as secondary in nature.

The prosecution hammered the fact that in the 2011 Supreme Court decision in *R v J.A.*, the basic tenet in law clearly states that consent is revoked should one participant no longer be conscious.

With respect to Mei Ling, or Margaret as she was known in the hospital, there was no way to know when she was conscious during the act, although by the time of Paul's arrest, it was believed she passed in and out of consciousness quite often. This was based on medical observations that were made throughout the day and clearly noted in her chart.

What was unknown, and the only basis of a defense, was on the specific date the couple was interrupted, at that precise time the nurse entered the room, had she in fact passed into unconsciousness? Moreover, there was nothing to prove during the sex act that particular day, as compared to any previous occasion, that she was any less than fully aware.

The defense planned to use experts who would maintain that the heightened emotional and physical state during sex, except when erotic asphyxiation is used, would preclude her withdrawing consent by passing out.

On the other side of the court, their experts would attest to the medical chart data that showed the woman typically passing in and out of consciousness throughout the day. Thus it had nothing to do with sex but her level of fatigue, meaning the head nurse's testimony that she thought Margaret had been unconscious would be enough to convict.

However, the other charges weren't entirely ignored. Paul's defense counsel believed addressing these in light of the rape charge actually showed how dedicated to his wife he was. The issue was how to side-step the fact that to survive Paul had murdered someone instead of letting his wife die, should it somehow come up. Murder was the one crime he'd never been suspected of committing in his past, in spite of the fact he clearly had numerous times.

Thus, the question was whether to put their client on the stand or not. This is always a dicey situation and there is no legal compulsion to do so. However, they had little defense to mount against the charges relating to his illegally entering the country or assuming a false identity.

Next to rape, these seemed somewhat minor in comparison, although they were definitely serious crimes in the post-9/11 era.

Following what their jury experts were saying, it was clear they were hung up by the letter of the law with respect to rape. They didn't seem as moved as the defense team had hoped with Marilyn Morgenstern's testimony. And, the fact there was a double standard, hadn't registered on them either. So, the lawyers decided to roll the dice and put Paul on the stand.

"Mr. Chen, do you understand the nature of your charges?"

"Yes, I do."

"All of them?"

"I realize that I was charged with rape, and find it unbelievable that a husband can be charged when it is clear his wife never said no. As well, I'm charged with a number of crimes relating to illegally entering Canada and using a false identity. This meant the documents I was using were fraudulent."

"That is true sir. However please let the court know why you entered the country in this manner."

"I had no choice."

"Everyone has a choice. Why did you choose to do it this way?"

"Because, as far as the authorities were concerned I had died over ten years before and if I tried to return under my own name not only would that raise untold questions, it would result in the death of my wife and probably the rest of my family."

"How can you be so sure?"

"Because I saw the people responsible for faking my death kill too many others to name."

"Is this some fantasy you're telling the court?"

"No, it's the unvarnished truth!"

"So, exactly what is the story? What happened over those ten-plus years that prevented you, a Canadian citizen who grew up here, from returning to your homeland legally?"

"My wife and I were kidnapped at gunpoint. We were flown on a private plane to China. There we were given an ultimatum. Manage and grow their precious metal recapturing plant over a ten year period. If the two of us survived for the full term then we would be given our freedom. However, once we made it through their tortuous imprisonment, it turned out our freedom, even here, was restricted. They made it clear that we had to live under our assumed names when we went back home. Otherwise, they would not only kill us, but our son too."

"You mean you came back here and for over two years you didn't make an attempt to track down your own flesh and blood?"

"We had no choice. If we did, they would kill us all. If we didn't, we could perhaps one day see him from afar. Once we were back here we agreed that knowing the reach of these people anything, we did of this nature could be terminal."

"But, you did discover your son?"

"Yes, quite by accident."

"Please tell us."

"He wound up becoming the department head of the hospital where my wife has been living out her last days. We discovered this on her admission, but we realized that we had aged so much during our absence, plus the birth date on her identification was bogus making her ten years older than her actual age, so we figured he would never recognize us."

"Did he?"

"No, but he was the one who the nurse who walked in on us when we were having intercourse, summoned to process us.

"That in itself was beyond embarrassing. Here we were in the throes of passion and our son, who didn't realize it was his own parents, winds up do a rape processing of us. And as if that wasn't bad enough, once he demanded blood tests we knew we were doomed."

"What happened next?"

"The police came to arrest me and a few days later, by the time I was released on bail, he had discovered our true identities. He was devastated, and said he would keep it quiet. But, I knew that the police would also find out who I was."

"Why was that?"

"Because a number of years ago I was arrested for a crime I did not commit. However, they booked me. That meant my fingerprints were in the system, and even though that was long before everything was computerized, I knew that at some point a match would be made. I just didn't expect it to be so soon."

"Now that you have filled in some background, why were you so afraid of these people? They may have kidnapped you, but in the end they kept their word and brought you back home."

"Many years ago I lost a lot of their money. That is why we were captured in the first place. When we got to China and saw the hell we had to live through for the next ten years, we couldn't believe it. But, to make their point they killed a man right in front of us. Then with his blood dripping on us they refused to let us clean ourselves up for more than a day. It was beyond degrading and their promise was based on both of us surviving."

"Why was that so frightening?"

"Because of what they did to my wife."

"What did they do?"

"I was assigned to head up their business dealings. Don't get me wrong, it was little more than a rudimentary office in a concentration camp. My darling wife, however, was charged with working on-site with the children they used to do the actual metal extraction. That meant she had to work in the fire pits right next to those doomed kids."

"Sounds terrible."

"Beyond terrible. It is unquestionably how she contracted throat cancer. But as if that wasn't bad enough, approximately ten percent of her charges died each month. The monster who owned this operation made sure the bodies were kept in what he called a "morgue," but it was little more than a concrete block hut. Then once each month, after he first checked the books and how well the physical operation was going, he had a couple of people cart the dead bodies out to the end of a pier. May I please stop now?"

"I'm sorry Paul, but the jury has a right to hear this and understand your plight."

"OK, let me catch my breath."

After a few moments he continued, "When we got to the end of the pier, and please understand Mei Ling and I were there at gunpoint, he had the bodies dumped into the water. And, if we had just received a shipment of used electronics to be dismantled

278

meaning staff couldn't be spared for this gruesome task, he had Mei Ling and me tip the bodies.

"Within minutes, the first fin would appear and it rarely took more than five or ten more minutes for not only the severed body parts to disappear, but the blood too. He, though, wouldn't leave because he liked to watch the fins head back out to deeper water."

"Then what happened."

"He would laugh and tell us that was our fate, if we died."

"Alright, so we now understand the hell you survived. It still doesn't explain why, once you were back here, you didn't go to the authorities."

"With what? As far as they were concerned we were dead. I understand they took our filthy clothing that they wouldn't let us clean up after that first killing on the day we arrived, along with some of our other personal effects. These were shipped back to my business associate as proof of our deaths."

"I get the feeling you're leaving something out."

"Objection, testifying."

"Sustained."

"Let me rephrase, what else happened to secure your silence?"

"It was our last day being incarcerated. Actually, it would be clearer to say it was our last day in that hell, since I've been incarcerated almost the whole time from when I was charged with rape."

"Please carry on. What happened that last day."

"My captor came with a big smile on his face. He made light of the fact we had survived and that he was a man of his word. There wasn't much to gather for our release but he had us call up our two best workers to come and help us.

"What I neglected to mention was one of the most heroic things my wife did was find a way to reduce the death count to almost zero each month. She insisted the children eat right and that we use the produce from local farms to ensure a supply of healthy food. As well, together we developed a work program that increased the output while improving the overall safety of that despicable site."

"Why is that important?"

"Because of what I'm now about to say. It isn't something I'm proud of and ironically, my wife only will have lived a couple more years, much of it in pain, as a result of the cancer. However, the two young men arrived and unquestionably agreed to help us. They owed us their lives and they would do anything for us."

"Yes, go on."

"Well, one agent of death our so-called host liked to use was a samurai sword. He was quite adept and about mid-way through our time there he gave me a set. That may seem crazy considering I could have theoretically escaped. But, to where? There was jungle, farms, and water all around us. We were hundreds of miles from real civilization and we already knew what lurked below the waves.

"Anyhow, one of the things he insisted we take with us was as a gift was that sword set he'd given me. I was holding it and he asked me to hand it to him.

"When the men arrived he took the longer sword called a *katana* out of its scabbard and handed it back to me. He then

280

gave me an ultimatum: choose which of these two wonderful people we'd come to really love and respect, would now die.

"Naturally, I balked and he then reminded me that for us to leave that hell, both my wife and I had to survive. If I did not choose he would use the smaller of the two swords, which he had unsheathed, to kill my wife. Not only would I lose her at the eleventh hour, I would be doomed to live in that hell forever."

Tears started to roll down freely down his cheeks and he said, "I can't go on."

"You must."

"Please give me a moment to compose myself."

The judge said, "Of course, we'll take a ten minute recess."

On returning Paul picked up where he left off and said, "I made my decision and swung the sword. Without feeling the slightest hesitation in my hands, one man's head immediately hit the earth with his body following a moment later."

The courtroom was absolutely silent.

"Mr. Chen, I think you have as clearly as possible described why you came into the country with illegal documents and led a clandestine life" said the attorney. "However, in spite of admitting to murder under duress in a foreign country, the rape charge is by far the most disturbing currently under consideration. Did your wife at any point say no when you were having relations?"

"She did not."

"Did she pass out?"

"No, she did not."

"Did she give any indication she wanted to stop?"

"No."

"Was she fully able to speak or at any time, was her speech impaired?"

"There were times her voice was weak. But during sex it was like she became a tigress, even the last time we were making love. In answer to your question, no, she was able to speak and there was no impairment."

"Your honor, I have no further questions."

"Considering the lateness of the hour I will adjourn until ten o'clock tomorrow morning, when the prosecution will be able to cross-examine the witness," he concluded.

With that Paul slowly left the witness stand and shuffled his way to the defense table. Visibly shaking he reached for a glass of water, which dribbled down his chin as he tried to swallow. His pain was obvious.

-o-o-o-

At ten o'clock the next morning, Paul was back in the witness stand to face the prosecution.

"Mr. Chen, or should I say Wong, I am sorry about your wife's condition."

"Thank you, sir for your kind words. However, I'm sure that is the last considerate word you will utter this morning."

"Mr. Chen we don't have to get off on the wrong foot do we?"

"Well, since you put it in the form of a question, what is the right foot? I had consensual sexual relations with my wife. It happened to be in a hospital room. We were interrupted and as a result of that the façade that was created to give me a modicum of safety shattered, and now not only do I have to answer for a ludicrous rape charge but my life, my son's, his family and

282

although she may only have a small amount of time left, my wife too, may not die of natural causes. So please tell me what is the right foot?"

"Your honor, please strike all that. The defendant has testified without being properly questioned."

"Counselor, you opened the door so your objection is overruled."

"I still want it on the record that the testimony was offered without proper questioning and its relevance should be diminished."

"No sir, it stands as stated. Please move along."

"OK, Mr. Chen since you've already rendered your opinion on these hearings, and have freely admitted you had relations with your wife, was she conscious throughout?"

"Yes."

"How do you know?"

"Because we had been together for over thirty years and I know when she's faking, sleeping, or fully engaged. Since we'd had so little contact for so long, it was hard for her not to show her encouragement."

"But, how in fact can you prove she did not, even for a moment, pass out or fall asleep?"

"Sir, it is the same as me asking how recently did you last beat your wife? It is a nonsensical question."

"Sir, you are on trial for one of the most heinous crimes in the criminal code. As well you have a series of follow-on charges. Please don't take this trial lightly."

"Believe me. I am not."

"Do you have a criminal record?"

"You know the answer to that. I do not!"

"Then how do you account for your fingerprints being on file?"

"As you know, I was once many, many years ago charged with a crime. The charges were dropped by the time I left the police station that very same day. However, in their zeal, they photographed and fingerprinted me as soon as I was brought in, even before my lawyer arrived."

"Why were you arrested?"

"Frankly, I don't remember. It was some trumped-up charge. Look, I admit that when I was younger I did things I'm not proud of. But, I also did lots that, now everyone knows my real name, I am definitely proud of doing.

"I built the second largest video distribution and rental company in the world. I employed tens of thousands of people with well-paying jobs. I got directly involved in the entertainment industry and was responsible for millions of dollars in film production taking place. As well, I built a legitimate operation for qualified investors from Hong Kong to immigrate to Canada. For them I provided housing, driving instruction, their first car, investment opportunities, and various other services. This brought thousands of new Canadians into the country to in-turn provide jobs and opportunities for countless others.

"These are all good things that I did. My big mistake was using financing from the wrong people. These weren't your typical venture capitalists. In fact, they were true vulture capitalists and when they thought the billion dollars they had invested in my ventures was at risk, they kidnapped me. The rest is on the record."

284

"Did you say billion dollars?"

"Yes, I had negotiated that amount to be invested into my entertainment conglomerate."

"So you're saying you are a modern day Robin Hood?"

"No sir. That is what you are saying. All I claim is that I was a legitimate businessman who was kidnapped and kept in unbelievable conditions for a period of ten years. Then, when I fulfilled my so-called punishment, I was told that to remain alive and not put my family at risk, I needed to live under an assumed identity. When my wife got sick, it was serendipitous that she wound up under the care of our own son. A son we hadn't seen for over twelve years."

"So are you claiming you are innocent?"

"Of course!"

"Of all charges?"

"Of the charge of rape, without doubt. With respect to the other ones I ask for the mercy of the court. I didn't have a choice. I had already lived through all the hell these people are able to create and I believed them."

"No further questions."

"Mr. Chen, you can step down."

"The defense calls Dr. Joseph Chen."

After being sworn in the questioning began.

"Dr. Chen, did you have any idea you were treating your mother and that this was your father who is on trial?"

"No, I did not."

"Not even an inkling?"

"Well, when I first saw my mother, I felt there was something familiar. However, I was introduced to Margaret Wong and her chart listed a birthdate that was over ten years older than my mother's."

"So how did you discover these were your parents?"

"After their sexual encounter was interrupted, it is hospital policy both participants be tested for sexually transmitted diseases, or STDs, and that requires a blood test. We also do a standard DNA work-up on patient's blood. Prior to this event we only had the information for my mother. But, now that we had my father's results, so I could easily match them if I wanted and thus discover they were my parents."

"Why, if you didn't believe there was any familial relationship would you even try to do the matching?"

"It's a bit of a story. I actually dropped a stack of files which included my parent's results. As it turns out, I have a very rare condition called Gilbert's Syndrome, which requires a double recessive gene. When I picked up the scattered pages I noticed that two of them actually had that gene.

"Back in medical school I took an advanced genetics course and one assignment included mapping my own DNA, so I knew what to look for. However, at first I didn't realize these two maps were from my parents. But, I thought it strange that in such a small sample as one hospital, I would find two recessive carriers.

At this point my curiosity got the better of me, so as soon as I got home I dug out an acetate overlay of my own results from my years at UCLA. I placed the two hard copies from the dropped files on top of each other then I placed the acetate over these. When I held the stack up to the light any doubts were eliminated. I was looking at DNA print-outs for my two parents.

"So as you can see, I didn't set out to prove these two people were my parents. I was as shocked as anyone to discover the Wongs were in fact the Chens."

"I see, so if you had to do this all over again, would you do anything differently?"

"As a matter of fact, this incident has already had a far-reaching impact on our hospital."

"And what is that?"

"We now have included a new document as part of the induction package that all married patients must sign. This document is a waiver acknowledging the couple understands that if they choose to have sexual relations in the hospital, although they are not legally prohibited, that the law clearly states should the infirm patient lose consciousness, that party has de facto rescinded consent, and all activity must immediately cease. Failing that the partner who continues the sex act could be charged with rape.

"In addition, even though relations are permitted, it clearly states that the hospital is a public place and it is the couple's responsibility to ensure a level of privacy is maintained. However, that does not preclude staff, or even visitors, entering a closed door and thus interrupting the couple.

"In future, not only are admission staff responsible for ensuring the form is signed and included in the patient's record, but the chief, or in other words my wife and me, must confirm the presence of the document when a new patient arrives on the floor. Furthermore, if the staff interrupts an unmarried couple, all the current restrictions apply."

"So, does that mean if this policy had been in force when your mother was admitted, then none of this would have happened?"

"Absolutely. Although personally, I would have lost the chance to reunite with my parents, even under these terrible circumstances."

"Understood, and no further questions of this witness."

"The prosecution has no questions of this witness."

"Doctor, you are excused," said the judge.

The trial moved quickly from this point with the respective summations covering all the high points contained in the testimony, juxtaposed against the rigors of the expanded legal definition for rape. Virtually nothing was forthcoming from either side with respect to the follow-on charges, since these were pretty much negated through the explanations offered by the defendant. By the time Paul finished testifying about their ordeal in China, there was hardly a dry eye in the jury box.

This trial was going to come down to whether the jury upheld the rape law and believed that at some point during her confinement within the hospital, Paul continued to have sex with his wife after she had possibly passed out or fallen asleep. If that was the case, he was guilty. If there was any doubt that she had remained conscious throughout the period in question, the judge admonished the jury they had little choice. Otherwise, they could find him not guilty.

The chances were effectively slim to none since there was no direct testimony from Mei Ling. And, had they found some way to examine her at this point, the fact was she could rarely stay awake for more than ten minutes at a time. The defence's fear was that that would only compound the jury's perception of the possible state of the woman at the time of the sexual encounter. And, they were against doing video testimony since it was clear her memory had deteriorated, and she had few recollections of any prior events.

Twelve citizens would decide Paul's fate and the odds were against him. The judge was as fair as possible in his charge to the jury and it all came down to how sincere they believed his testimony.

Deliberations went on for almost eighteen hours and when the jury returned, the verdict was pretty much as Paul expected. On all the lead-up charges, the jury declared not guilty. Then, for the rape charge, their decision was pained yet unanimous...guilty.

"Mr. Chen, you have been found guilty by a jury of your peers," intoned the judge. "However, as much as I agree with them under the law, I don't personally agree with how this law has been applied. With that in mind, and the fact I can show some leniency, I hereby sentence you to four years.

"Court is adjourned."

The bailiffs came and carted Paul away to again be incarcerated for events that were beyond his control.

"Dad, we'll appeal," Joseph shouted through tears as his father was taken back to prison.

Chapter 30

2011

With credit for time served, along with some further leniency from the court, Paul was only in jail for less than a week.

Joseph picked up his dad from the Mimico Correction Centre in his new Lexus. The man was a shrunken visage of how he last looked in the hospital when the police barged in. They hardly exchanged a word as he made his way to his father's home in Markham. This was to be Joseph's first visit to the abode his parents had occupied since their re-immigration from China over six years ago. So much time had been lost, and for what?

As they approached the house his father asked if he wanted to come in. It was impossible to refuse and with a reluctant step, the son passed through the doorway. This was nothing like the home where he'd grown up in Richmond Hill.

Unlike the lakeside mansion with the huge porch, monstrous rooms, gourmet kitchen, fabulous art on the walls, and a side office where his father conducted his billion dollar empire, this was a modest three-bedroom home with discount furniture and little art other than cheaply framed Ikea posters. It was spotlessly clean and smelled of comfort food prepared with care.

"Son, I am sorry," were the first words since leaving the car.

"Father, nobody is as sorry as I am. I should have looked for you over the years. I should never have become so comfortable in my life that I ignored my parents."

"You were purposely convinced we were dead. And, we were instructed that if we ever revealed our true identities we would then truly be killed. Neither of us is to blame for what later transpired, but I am definitely at fault for letting all this happen in the first place."

They had some green tea and talked for over an hour before Joseph said he had to leave. He was on-call that night and needed to get back to the facility.

At that point his father asked him to take him along to the hospital. He said to give him a minute to freshen up, and he would be ready to leave. Joseph could hardly refuse the man, and took him to see his mother. He knew a nurse would have to be present the whole time his dad was in the room, since he was now branded a sex offender and by law couldn't be left alone with the woman he loved.

On arrival, it was easy to see that in the intervening days Mei Ling had deteriorated. According to the staff she had hardly eaten and spent most of her time either asleep or in conversation with relatives who had already died. The literature distributed throughout the palliative care unit clearly explained this phenomenon as one of "letting go."

No matter how well it was expressed, the toll on the relatives was taxing, and Joseph wanted to comfort his father, but frankly didn't know how. He left to cover his medical responsibilities and only asked that Paul say goodbye to him before he left the hospital.

After an hour of sitting across the room and being denied the right to hold his wife's hand he got up, walked over to the bed and gently kissed her forehead. The nurse immediately made a lunge towards the man, but quickly backed off. At that point he said, "Please take care of her. I doubt I will see her alive again."

Turning back to his wife, he smiled and followed with, "I have always loved you and always will. Rest comfortably."

A single tear escaped the side of each of his eyes as he then shuffled out of the room towards the elevators. Ignoring his son's request he made his way to the ground floor and took the first cab in the line to go home.

-o-o-o-

The old man made himself a bowl of tomato soup for dinner. He was glad the milk in the fridge hadn't spoiled and that there was an unopened box of crackers in the pantry.

His sleep was fitful at the jail and with the emotional turmoil he was going through, it wasn't surprising he turned in after watching only less than an hour of television. The good news was he fell into a deep sleep.

Around two that morning the phone rang.

It roused him almost immediately and with trepidation he picked up the hand-held next to the bed.

"Hello?"

"Dad, I'm sorry but she's gone. I'll be there in about twenty minutes to pick you up."

"OK"

Paul was numb and sat unmoving on the side of the bed for a few moments. He then got up, washed his face and put back on the clothes he had warn earlier to go to the hospital with Joseph. Next, he went downstairs to the dining room hutch.

Hidden at the back of the widest section were the two samurai swords his erstwhile uncle had given him so many years ago. Although he had talked about them at the trial, he was never asked if he still had them, nor had the police ever searched his home.

Taking the velvet covered package out of the hiding place he unwrapped it and extracted the smaller sword in its unadorned scabbard. This he took to the kitchen and from his odds-and-ends drawer pulled out a roll of duct tape.

Sitting at the kitchen table he withdrew the short killing implement from the scabbard and examined its cold beauty in the waning light. Looking carefully he could see the work the master had put into it centuries ago. When placed beside its longer sibling the two were identical. Both had ripples looking like waves rushing to the sandy beach of some lonesome Pacific island. Only instead of sand it was a murderous edge, honed to a level of perfection hard to match with all of today's manufacturing technology.

Chen then tore off a strip of tape and carefully attached the sword to his lower leg. Standing he made sure that his pants covered the concealed weapon and he had free movement. Satisfied, he put away the roll and went into the living room to await his son.

Lights flashed across the front window and Paul rose from the sofa. He walked out of the front door not bothering to lock it and made his way to the car.

"Dad, I'm truly sorry. I know how much you loved her."

There was no reply.

It didn't take long to reach the hospital. Normally, highway 401 was a solid mass of sixteen lanes of stop-and-go traffic. But, at the wee hours of the morning, there was virtually nobody else on the road. Joseph parked in his assigned spot and the two of them made their way to the entrance. At this hour visitors normally had to buzz through to the security guard on duty to be admitted, but Joseph just waived his fob over the pad and the sliding door hissed to the left.

They made their way up to Mei Ling's room where the door had been closed to permit privacy. Softly opening it, Paul let out a sob. His son wrapped his arms around Paul's shoulders and in the shadows they saw Juliette silently sitting a vigil for her nearly unknown mother-in-law. In the muted light her swollen belly looked huge, like the baby was about to imminently burst out.

All three spent some time together trying to commiserate and then Paul said, "Why don't the two of you leave me here alone and Joseph, please call the funeral home?"

The two younger Chens left Paul and quietly shut the door.

A few minutes later there was a breathless, guttural, moan that escaped loud enough to be heard at the nurses' station. Not knowing what it was they first checked their status board but there were no red lights illuminated. Then, the head nurse suddenly realized it had come from Mei Ling's room and dashed in to a horrific sight.

Paul was draped over his dead wife with his bloody entrails spilling onto the floor. He was still alive but barely and she screamed "Get Doctors Chen back in here stat!"

The two of them came charging through the door and stopped in horror. Juliette told the nurse to go and call 9-1-1. Once she was out of the room, Joseph went forward to stroke his father's head and said one word, "Why?"

At this, his dad painfully, beyond belief, pulled out a single piece of paper from his back right pants pocket. He then gasped and was gone.

With shaking hands Joseph opened it and read:

I couldn't go on without her.

I am sorry.

I am sorry for so much, but mostly not getting to know the son of which I am so proud, the daughter I never knew I had, and the unborn grandchild I will never know.

But, most of all I am sad that although I was a criminal, I more than paid my debt to society. Just look at the countless lives we saved and the histories they will write.

Though after all of that, when my love of so many years laid in pain and was only comforted by the actions we had enjoyed all our lives that were now prohibited, and I was branded a sex offender...this is wrong.

Take care of yourselves and my grandchild.

All my love your father,

Paul Chen.

Joseph then said, "My love, this is going to be evidence. Could you please pull a photocopy for me?"

Epilog

Joseph and Juliette slowly opened the door to Paul's house. It was the first time Juliette had stepped into her father-in-law's home and only the second for Joseph. It was a revelation to both of them.

Emptying the home of a loved one after they've passed away is always difficult. But, in this case it was almost bizarre as they moved from room to room, closet to closet, discovering for the first time how Joseph's parents lived their latter years.

It was even more modest than Joseph thought after his first visit the previous day. Although it felt like ages, it was less than twenty-four hours ago that he came to pick up his father.

Both parents had small wardrobes based on the limited amount of clothing hanging in their closets. They appeared to be typical older retirees and bore no relationship to the high-flying jet-setters they once were.

Sorting through the drawers in the family room wall unit Juliette came across a DVD that in bold letters on the cover said, "CONFIDENTIAL - if found please deliver to Joseph Chen, MD at Lakebeach Hospital, Toronto."

"Joseph, you better get in here," she shouted.

Silently, with a drawn face he entered the room saying, "What do you have there?"

"A DVD addressed to you. Obviously, they knew you had graduated medical school and worked at Lakebeach."

He took the disk from her and looked around to find the DVD player in his father's entertainment center. It seemed he never consolidated the controls into a single unit since there were five remotes of various sizes sitting on the coffee table. Looking at the brand names, Joseph was able to narrow it down to two and by pressing the on-button on one, he was able to turn on the machine. He next found the control for the flat screen and sorted through the input screen until he found the right option to engage the DVD.

Once the disk was spinning and the player engaged the data flow, the two of them sat enwrapped gazing at the opening sequence on the screen. Before them were Paul and Mei Ling sitting in this very room. They must have set up a recording device of some sort to capture the image which was then transferred to the DVD.

Both looked drawn and haggard, plus it was clear that Mei Ling's cancer had advanced.

Paul started speaking, "If you are watching this, your mother and I are now dead. Our hope is you will find it in your heart to forgive us for both hiding our identities and not contacting you since we returned to Canada. This subterfuge has been beyond difficult for the two of us, but it was necessary. The thugs who kidnapped us and forced us into ten years of penury made it abundantly clear they not only knew where you were but would kill you if our true identities were revealed.

"We had seen them kill before and there was no doubt they would carry out their threat. Moreover, they had eyes everywhere, so there was no chance of even surreptitiously trying to contact you.

"However, as much as they knew, there were some things they did not know.

"What I want you to do is to pause this video and get two things. One is the small samurai sword, called a *tanto*, from the display on the hutch in the dining room. Next, please go into my closet. There you will see seven pair of Tony Lamas cowboy boots. Bring one pair along with the *tanto* to the coffee table and then re-start the video."

At the time Paul made the video he wouldn't have foreseen his own death and that the sword he asked Joseph to get was now in police custody as evidence. Nor would he have realized the deadly pair had been hidden and no longer sitting on the hutch.

Joseph did as his father said, but grabbed the large chef's knife from the wooden block in the kitchen. He also saw the seven pair of boots lined up neatly at the bottom as his father said they would be. Grabbing the closest he took these back to the table and reengaged the player.

"Now, I want you to take the *tanto* and scrape off the inner leather sole that covers the heel of one of the boots."

Joseph took the knife and carefully ran the tip along the bottom of the inner boot and before long the leather started to separate and lift. He stuck his hand inside and pulled gently until the small piece covering the heel came out. He held it up to the lamp on the table and immediately saw there was some sort of shiny powder covering the exposed surface.

"Honey, please see if you can find a flashlight."

Juliette slowly rose, since her center of gravity was off-balance as her pregnancy was advancing. Rooting around in the kitchen, she found a small MagLite and brought it to her husband. He immediately shone it into the bottom of the boot and saw the whole inside of the heel was filled with the same shiny powder.

On the TV his father continued, "By now you will have discovered my big secret. What you are holding is one of fourteen boots each filled with exactly one pound, or 454 grams of pure platinum dust. At the current price, which has recently skyrocketed even faster than gold, you are now in possession of almost one million dollars worth of the precious metal.

"This is your legacy from us. Please do not let anyone know about it since each grain represents a tear shed by your mother and me for not only you, but for the waifs who died under our care. This is in part why we could not contact you. Having seen how these people treated mere children in such hellish conditions, only reinforced just what they could do to our precious son.

"So in our memory, please live your life to the fullest. Be healthy, be happy, and remember us fondly even if we missed so many of your accomplishments."

Mei Ling croaked in obvious pain, "Son we love you with all our hearts and miss you beyond belief."

With that the video ended.

Joseph and Juliette sat there in stunned silence. Neither felt confident enough to speak.

Afterword

Most of us are pawns in the legal system. We all agree that it's better than the alternative, but what happens when you're ensnared in something totally beyond your control?

Even when it comes to fighting cancer, we're encouraged to take an active role in our treatment and rehabilitation process. However, with legal matters, we're at the mercy of our advocate. And, even when things appear simple, they often are not!

Precedent may come from cases totally unrelated to the situation at hand. Moreover, the clock continues to tick like a taxi meter counting off hundreds of dollars at each click. Or, when incarcerated, it reflects the time lost until our liberties are restored. However, is there any leniency when the defendant is aged, infirm, or facing a terminal illness?

Plus, what if the whole matter arises when both partners are seniors? We shun from thinking about sex for the aged, even though experts have said time and again that a healthy sex life can last until the last breath, even when the partners are in their nineties and beyond.

As the population ages and more spouses wind up in care facilities, at what point is sexual consent between two long term partners no longer assumable?

That is, if one party is physically infirm, but not mentally, and still enjoys sexual contact from their significant other, OR the healthy partner expects favors from the infirm one, when can medical staff intervene?

For example, consider the spouse who is bedridden yet enjoys stimulation but is unable to talk. The cause of their vocal impairment isn't a mental deficit, but something physical like throat cancer, ALS commonly known as Lou Gehrig's disease or, even a wired jaw as part of the recovery from a motor vehicle accident. That doesn't mean the rest of the body is immune to positive stimuli and there's enough evidence confirming that releasing sexual tension aids in recovery. Moreover, it is the most intimate way to express one's feelings to another.

The United States, in this instance, the law defaults to the statutes of the individual states with the exception for age of consent. That has been set at eighteen years by the federal government. The British statute states *"Whether a belief is reasonable is to be determined having regard to all the circumstances, including any steps A has taken to ascertain whether B consents."* A typical example of legalese so broad it defies definition by the lay person.

Ironically, the Canadian Supreme Court is considered to be the only one that has definitively ruled on this matter, but under an extremely broad umbrella. Sadly their finding had nothing to do with senior citizens, nor a defined medical condition. In fact their involvement was spurred by an angry wife who feared her husband was about to seek a divorce and claim sole custody of their only child. She filed a sexual assault charge against him two months after the fact, in which she claimed he continued to perform various sexual acts after she fell unconscious. However, she freely admits both had repeatedly practiced erotic asphyxiation! Go figure.

A further dilemma arises with married couples where the healthy spouse may believe they're prohibited from sexual contact with their ill partner and then seeks it from somebody else. Is that grounds for divorce?

Would a "Mutual Consent Form," which if signed and filed on admission to a long term care facility prohibit staff from interfering as long as any contact is done on the premises, but in privacy?

Two cultures are about to collide in the very place where our loved ones are destined to spend the so-called "golden years" of their lives.

Young professional medical practitioners dedicated to extending life, while ensuring an expectation of happiness, are about to clash with their patients' generation. Add to this the compounding factors of the opinions of interfering younger family members, most of whom find it impossible to come to grips with their aging parents having sex in the first place.

ACKNOWLEDGEMENTS

An author writes and then his support team comments, criticizes, edits, and encourages. As they say, there is no "I" in "Team."

With this in mind I want to thank those who took the time to be part of my team. Specifically, Brenda Conway with her eagle eye, Dr. Marty Gelfand who loved both of my books so much, he said he almost forgot to comment on the typos, and Bob Otto who gave freely of his sharp legal observations.

I also want to thank Bernie Schwartz, Beneta Silberstern, Dave Gersuk, and my greatest fan – Arlene Ludwig.

Naturally, my wife and soul mate Anne was indispensible in her comments on the snippets I forced on her while writing and then the critical observations while reading the drafts. I love you!

I also want to thank the good people at CreateSpace.com and KDP who have made it so easy to self-publish. I learned so much about the various Amazon products and appreciate how they have expanded the options for both authors and readers.

Finally, I want to thank Goodreads.com, one of the best tools a budding author can have. They were extremely helpful in the marketing of "Hong Kong Hollywood," and suspect will be the same for this book.

Toronto, Canada, October 9, 2013

Here is a preview of *The Alien Patriot* for your enjoyment!

May 2011

FOREWORD

While driving past milepost 162, just after the first rest area on southbound Interstate-79, my cell phone rang. It was the third time it had chimed in less than an hour.

I was sitting in the front passenger seat since my wife had taken over the driving duties when we left the Pennsylvania welcome station. It is located just inside the state line on I-90, mere miles before the I-79 split near Erie, PA. Deciding to go against my better instincts, I decided to answer the call.

Normally when I see "private, anonymous, unknown," or some other similar notation on the call display I ignore it. This being the third instance in such a short period of time it should have been my cue to not to hit the green button. But, as they say hindsight is twenty-twenty.

"Is this Jon Davidson?" the caller asked. I didn't recognize the resonant deep southern drawl and replied "may I ask whose calling please?"

Silence...

Again I politely said, "May I ask who is calling?" garnering the same non-response.

This caused me to roll into my blast the unsolicited telemarketer mode and barked "is this an emergency call? Since this number is on the 'do not call list' and if you are calling for anything other than a 911 level emergency I will need your full name, company affiliation, and how you got this number so that I can report you to the FCC. The fine is $10,000."

Normally at this point I hear a loud "click." However, with a chuckle the caller retorted, "Chris James said you were prickly!"

Instantly, my blood turned to ice-water and my head started to pound.

I hadn't heard that name in over five years and could have gone through the rest of my life never hearing it again. Chris James was the bane of my existence and proved that every government "dirty trick" ever reported was probably true. And, he cost me well over three million dollars, personally.

Obviously, the caller took my non-response as his cue to continue; "My name is irrelevant but for now you can call me 'Smith.' So let me get to the reason for my call. Basically, Mr. James wanted me to deliver a message and ask for your help. There are three points to the message. One, you were right thinking the government stole your technology. Two, we now need something only you can provide. And three, although you may not believe him, he offers his sincere apologies."

Great, here we are a full administration later, which is a quantum leap either forward or back when measured in government time, and some unnamed three-letter agency goon expects me to listen to this crap!

I said, "It's all good and well that he wants to apologize but how do I get back the millions he cost me? And, you better understand that the bastard had the gall to say, as he convinced me to sign the test agreement with the so-called mutual privacy clause, 'if the government ever stole your technology people would go to jail, including me.'

It certainly sounded reasonable to a neophyte, but by the time his group sailed away unscathed while it looked like my team had nearly wound up in the pokey.

"Look, I'm just the messenger and people with much higher pay grades than mine wanted us to reach out to you," the man calling himself Smith said. "Since we already grabbed your tech it isn't that particular expertise we're looking for. What we want is your application know-how plus what you remember about what happened when you discovered the various confirmed threats against the President. And, the powers that be said to tell you, you were needed yesterday. They also thought that if you were able to help like you had in the past, this could be a way to somehow make up for what you lost financially."

"I'm going to have to think about this and get back to you. How do I reach you?"

"You don't. We'll contact you. You have forty-eight hours. At least that's what they said I could offer, but, don't count on it. These people play for keeps. Just remember what they did to you five years ago."

Yeah, I remembered. With that I clicked the phone's red button, something I should have done when it first rang.

My wife had heard my side of the conversation and kept her eyes glued to the road afraid to say anything. But, when she glanced over and saw how white my face was she started to yell.

Unfortunately, I didn't hear a word so when I finally looked towards her she had raised her voice to a near banshee scream of "what's wrong" barely keeping the car on the highway.

48 Hours before

Chapter 1

"Shit, shit, shit, I can't believe the lack of information contained in this so-called 'treasure trove' we recovered from the Bin Laden raid last weekend," said Master Sergeant Maryann Genesee, "maybe the boss can make some sense out of it."

At that point Director of Operations, Chris James, aggressively walked into the sterile room awash with the soft sound of ten hard drives. The seemingly meaningless contents were scrolling across a similar number of big screen monitors suspended from the ceiling.

Located in a nondescript office complex, nestled in the lush woodlands surrounding the Baltimore-Washington Thurgood Marshall International Airport, known simply as BWI, this state-of-the art Department of Defense operation is an amalgam of every crime lab ever seen on television whether you're talking *Bones*, all of the *CSI* locales or *NCIS*. It is also the ultimate destination for the computers and hard drives extracted from Osama Bin Laden's mansion in Abbotabad, Pakistan. And until his retirement at the end of this year, this facility remains the exclusive fiefdom of Chris James.

"OK team, what have you got?" James said.

"The square root of Benny!" responded Genesee before anyone else in the room could reply.

"Don't give me that garbage," he shot back. James was a referee for the NFL in a prior life and felt there was too much profanity in the world. So, he made it a point not to swear and encouraged his staff to do likewise.

"Let me see what you've found so far and if anyone else wants to chime in on what it all means go ahead."

A chorus of "nothing more to add" was heard from the group.

"I don't believe it. After all these years of Osama eluding capture, yet personally responsible for so much grief, you obviously have discovered some of the findings we've all talked about."

Genesee said, "Chris, you've made us critically aware not to feed you mundane stuff. So, we haven't told you the mundane. The point is we don't have anything other than that. In fact, much of what we have found is from mostly various US government run websites and local city travelogues plus a bunch of images anyone could download from the web."

"What did you just say?" James asked starting to go pale.

"Don't tell me that just because you're retiring in a handful of months you didn't hear me."

"I heard you just fine, but show me some of these mundane findings."

At that point Genesee pointed to the screen on her laptop sitting right in front of the two of them.

"Oh crap!" exclaimed James breaking his cardinal rule. He went on to say, "I haven't seen this in maybe five or six years. Genesee, I need you to go to the vault and pull out a really old desktop computer stored down there along with a file of three-and-a-quarter inch floppies. I know the name of the case is like one of the states; Carolina, no, Idaho, no, Dakota, yeah. It's filed under Dakota. Dakota Analysis or something like that, and I need it yesterday."

"Yes boss," she snapped as she made her way quickly out of the lab.

About fifteen minutes later when James' iPhone buzzed, he immediately said to Genesee, "Tell me exactly what is in that file locker especially how many floppies." A muffled response was heard and he replied, "Bring it all."

Shortly afterward she came through the door with a cart filled with a mix of old computer equipment and two file boxes.

"Let's see if this old locomotive will boot and if it does I want to do a side-by-side comparison with everything that came out of that monster's mansion in Pakistan."

Plugging in the power cord, a faint wisp of smoke wafted out of the back of the machine followed by the tang of dust burning on electrical components. It brought back childhood memories of James' Lionel train set, but that only lasted a couple of seconds until the monitor flickered to life. The Microsoft logo for Windows NT appeared and James loaded the hand-labeled floppy named "Disk 1."

The team watched in rapt attention as a series of Web-sourced images started to appear. He then opened the old *Word for Windows* program on the antique and called up a file named "watchlist," which immediately scrolled across a second window on the overhead flat-screen. After a few moments James went to the disk menu and located an executable file then clicked on it. This caused a third window to open.

"Give me an ethernet cable so I can transfer all this to the active computer."

Once that was done, he executed a few keystrokes and not only did the images merge but a new list of red ASCII codes, including the 128 extended character set, started to scroll across the bottom of the monitor. This time James said "fuck!"

"Who's the ASAC heading up the JTTF in DC these days?" he said (translated; who is the Assistant Special Agent in Charge heading up the Joint Terrorism Task Force in Washington, DC).

One of the other team members replied, "I think it's McDonald."

"Get him on the phone right now. I need him to contact somebody who probably won't want to get involved in this. But he's the only one who can help us through this mess" said James.

"Who is that?" Genesee asked.

"Jon Davidson."

March 2002

Chapter 2

Turning onto the northbound George Washington Parkway, having crossed the Potomac on route 50 leaving Washington, DC, I popped in my Tina Turner CD and cranked up the volume.

Now you have to understand, I don't sing. Not in the shower or heaven forbid at a karaoke bar. In fact, I didn't even sing "happy birthday" to my kids as they were growing up. But today, when *Simply the Best* rolled into the chorus I sang the lyrics with gusto!

It was a beautiful warm spring day. The trees were in bloom with the cherry blossoms reaching their mellow pink peaks. And, little Jon Davidson from Toronto, Canada had just wrapped up a one-on-one with the man who signs-off on the President's daily brief before it's delivered by the Director of the CIA to the man himself.

What was even more impressive is the Director – National Security Council not only believed what I said, but told me to contact the heads of three major defense contractors working on projects that could definitely use this technology. And, he said to make sure I told them he personally referred me.

In Washington contacts equal money, and specific references mean big money.

You have to realize, this was a mere six months since the tragedy of September 11. In New York they were still hauling rubble from Ground Zero and nerves were frayed in every government department with a security mandate. Add to this, no matter how closed the community was to outsiders before the attacks, it was growing tighter by the day.

The fact I was even involved in something like this was a surprise. I moved to Virginia after a successful career as an advertising maven. Career two was building a market research company, which ultimately led to becoming a business development consultant for information technology companies. Yet when the economy softened in the late ninety's and one of my clients, an early Internet success story, made me the "godfather's offer," how could I refuse?

Unfortunately, few saw the dot-com bust on the horizon and when it hit I segued into a dead-end position with a government services supplier who thought they could easily add a commercial business component to their roster.

Wrong!

However, during the six months I spent with that company I was a sponge. I proactively made it my business to absorb everything going on around me especially anything related to how the U.S. government contracted for any type of procurement. So, when we agreed to mutually part ways, I transferred this knowledge to a venture run by a couple of Long Islanders who had been hounding me for months to join them.

Little did anyone realize that these two misfits had stumbled upon the key to identifying where the bad guys responsible for the events of 9/11 were hiding their Internet-based communiqués.

Peter Curry, Director NSC started the meeting by apologizing for being late. He had just returned from Great Falls, VA where he'd met with a major defense contractor.

312

"David, I must say our few brief telephone conversations were extremely interesting and I have to know can you identify steg?"

Naturally, he was talking about "steganography," a technique that goes back to the days of the ancients where one army would apparently shave the head of a slave, tattoo a message on his scalp, wait for the hair to grow back and then send the hidden missive to the intended recipient while hiding it from prying eyes. Modern methods are much more subtle and take place in seconds versus the weeks or more it took in the past. In fact, there were ways to hide such things as complex as the blueprints for the Pentagon or Twin Towers within mere moments in seemingly everyday images like online copies of the Mona Lisa.

Bottom line, if you didn't know where to look, you would entirely miss their presence.

I said, "A number of years ago I led a company, which I moved from Toronto to Hollywood. We had developed a process based on this technique. Its mission was to help movie, television and music producers protect what they created from piracy as the industry started to convert to digital.

"So, if you're asking if what we've found is 'steg,' the answer is 'no.' But, if you're asking 'is this a tool to find where the steg is hiding, the answer is a resounding 'yes.'"

"In that case, I definitely want you to meet with three people. Let's start with Dr. John Robertson. He heads up a new division of Great Falls Tech that we're in the process of engaging. In fact, he was who I was meeting with that delayed me this morning. Next, I want you to get hold of Dr. Elliott Schwartz at Synthesis Labs. Did you know they invented a series of radar devices including the hated gun the cops all use in speed traps? And, lastly I think you should speak with Dr. Tom Bacon at Thrust Avionics. He's in their imaging division. My assistant will provide you with the necessary coordinates for all three of these folks."

"How do you suggest I start the dialog?"

"Be straight-up. Tell them we've met and I've provided their contact information. They are incredibly busy at the best of times and now even more so, so you'll probably need to leave a message with their EA's and if possible on their voice mail. But, I think using my name will get you a fast call-back. At that point try to set up a face to face meeting and talk about what you've already found. They'll also appreciate the history of the development since these are all lateral thinkers."

At this point he looked at his watch and went "holy crap! I probably have two or three people stacked up outside my door anxiously waiting for follow-on meetings. But first I need to understand how you got to me?"

Realizing I had probably over-stayed my welcome and the limited amount of time he would give me I said, "One of my initial hires at the company that brought me to the States is married to Senator Dobransky's senior aide. My wife and I had dinner with them a couple of months ago when I was first asked to join this company. Once I explained the technology and what we think are its benefits to the government, they laid out a plan to get me to the 'right' people. Over the past few weeks I've met with the lead staff for virtually everyone who sits on either the House or Senate Intelligence Committees along with a number of infrastructure people. This has led to meetings with many of the actual elected officials and subsequent referrals to people like you. However, it was the chief of staff for the new Director of Homeland Security who recommended the two of us meet.

"And, I guess a referral letter from the White House Chief Scientist didn't hurt either" I concluded.

At this point he wished me luck as I retreated from his office. Once outside, four impatient type-A personalities glared at me.

December 2001

Chapter 3

Climbing over the Verrazano Narrows Bridge, looking north toward Manhattan, there was still a hazy pall over the city.

It was ages since I was last in New York, which seemed odd since only a couple of years earlier I led weekly meetings in the city with my Madison Avenue sales team.

Like so many others, I too knew people who had perished in the World Trade Center and thought the skyline looked naked with the Towers missing. However, there was a big difference between seeing an online image, or even a live television feed, versus gazing from the highest bridge of the Big Apple.

Even before September 11, 2001 the two crazy Dakota brothers wanted me to join their small organization.

So, here I was driving to meet them to discuss both what they thought they discovered and to see if there really was a role for me to play.

Benny Dakota, the younger brother was my conduit and had set up the meeting with his sibling. Since he was out at a prior engagement, we had plans to all get together that night for dinner. Even though I had met Hugh a few times in the past, other than knowing he was some sort of scientist, I couldn't say I really 'knew' him.

Hugh greeted me as I arrived at his office in a small town near the geographical center of Long Island with a hearty "Welcome and it's about time you agreed to join Dakota Analysis!"

Whoa, not so fast. I'd just exited a company that had unrealistic expectations with sales projections for a new division that they pulled entirely out of thin air. The principals thought it would be a "no brainer," but boy were they wrong. The only good thing that came out of that experience was I inadvertently learned about marketing to the US government and immediately understood how that tied into what the Dakotas' wanted to do.

Seeing the confused look on my face Hugh said, "Let me show you what we have before you make a commitment, but I'm sure you'll be impressed."

He went on to say "you already understand the core concept of our technology that I originally built for NASA. It's based on both a predictive and comparison engine. You've also seen a bit of how it works when applied to Internet distributed files that we track for clients who want to know what their competition are saying about them, how much advertising they're placing and the types of promotions, coupons or contests they're running through their websites.

"What you haven't seen is the material we found that pertains to 9/11, and which keeps me awake at night."

He then proceeded to call up a series of image files on his computer starting with one of the Twin Towers. Each had a time/date stamp and they all looked the same. However, there was an additional number showing how many kilobytes made up each file. Although in many cases the number was the same, there were differences.

"You obviously see there are groups of similarly appearing files where the numbers are exactly the same, while others have subtle differences. By checking the photo credit information in what is normally found in the 'metafile' attached to each of these we were able to actually cluster them together. But, what you may not realize is that there are instances where the same shot

317

taken on the same day by the same photographer has definitely been altered and that's registered in the byte counts. We don't know what has been inserted. Yet we do know something, other than additional metafile data, has been added."

"Let me get this straight, you have common images that over time have had their digital makeup changed? So what! Artifacts can be inserted through packet transfer via the Web and captions revised by whoever posts or re-posts the image on subsequent sites."

Hugh shot back, "Yeah, that's true and we knew it right from the get-go. But, once we started looking at where this was happening and drew a timeline, things started to jump out at us. For instance look at this series of images from the six-week period of August 1 to September 10, 2001."

I examined the new file groupings he brought up and noticed that the innocuous images were taken from the online general information sites for Logan, Dulles, and Newark airports. And, they appeared to be increasing in byte size over time. Suddenly I realized these were the three airports the hijackers used to board the flights they ultimately commandeered. That begged the now obvious question - what clandestine data is possibly buried in these images?

"You see what I mean, these are scary and once we started to switch from emphasizing our comparison engine and set the predictive one loose, it brought back a ton of images from what are effectively US government sites. Moreover, when we looked at the time/date stamps these not only both preceded the events of 9/11 but in many cases continue to this day. In fact, some of the early ones tie directly to what FBI agent Robert Wright Jr. red-flagged in his now infamous memo from last May when he warned about what was going to happen in September."

I was dumbfounded.

"To be clear, what we have is true serendipity. It wasn't my intent to find hidden messages that may pertain to September 11 and could possibly be an ongoing clandestine communication channel. However, my dad is good friends with the town's chief of police and at our Sunday family dinner a few weeks ago Chief Mack and his wife were there as guests. Naturally, the discussion turned to all the people we knew who didn't survive the attacks and the chief said he'd heard rumors about the FBI memo, long before it became public. Then, he went on to say 'I bet they used the Internet to plan this out and I somehow doubt they were dumb enough to send open e-mails to each other.' That got me thinking and first thing Monday morning I re-ran all the raw data we had on file from the period of May 2001 to the present. What you've seen is the fruit of that labor."

"So what exactly do you think you have here?"

"We have the best fish finder or treasure hunter available for the Internet."

"What?"

"All kidding aside, I think we have developed a tool that may not know exactly what the messages are but, increases the likelihood of finding exactly where they're buried. Hell, once you know that you can turn the files over to virtually any three-letter agency and they should have the wherewithal to decipher them. And if they don't, they certainly know how to create it.

"Having approached some people who know about this stuff, we've been told that finding where the information is buried

319

is the hard part. There are thousands of people working for the government tasked with figuring out what it all means."

I was impressed and a little overwhelmed. "OK, where do I fit in?"

"You're based in DC, you have smarts, spent the past six months in a firm that sells to the government and really know how to market data. Make no mistake, this is data and what we need you to do is get the U.S. government to realize exactly what we've developed, then negotiate a fair deal for its use."

Hugh knew that data management and the ability to generate millions of dollars in syndicated sales from the final output was exactly how I built my first company. It was sold to International Research Limited over a decade ago where his brother Benny had been specifically hired to be the day-to-day liaison between my operation and their head office in New York.

But he then hit me with a kicker, "We don't have much cash to pay you, though being a public company we can cover your expenses and a small monthly stipend. The rest will be accrued and paid in restricted shares until there is sufficient cash flow from this initiative.

At the time, I figured with savings from past deals, and with the sensitive nature of what they seemed to have discovered, it should make selling it a relatively easy sale. The hard part was convincing my wife. However, she too felt deeply about what had happened back in September and had come to love her new country.

The next day I called Hugh first thing in the morning and said, "Count me in!"

www.ingramcontent.com/pod-product-compliance
Lightning Source LLC
Chambersburg PA
CBHW070308280626
47159CB00017B/573